Praise for
Second Hand

"An uncommon sweetness and charity toward the castoffs of the world animate this book, which is both funny and moving, especially as it moves toward its surprisingly beautiful ending. Michael Zadoorian has written a fine and wonderful novel about one of the most unusual subjects: junk, and those who care for valuable objects, living and dead, that others have thrown away."

—Charles Baxter, author of *The Feast of Love*

"How can one capture the spirit of this wondrous book in so few words?...Contains marvelous observations about secondhand items and life in general...readers will thoroughly enjoy this book and will be sorry when it ends."

—*Library Journal*

"Wonderful...even readers who can't stand the idea of used clothes or old dishes will find *Second Hand* cheering and satisfying, a novel about finding value in the most unlikely places."

—*Tampa Tribune Times*

"If you have ever taken a date to a garage sale or thrift store, this book is for you. Charming, sweet, funny—Zadoorian conveys the oft-overlooked beauty of castoffs, be it the vinyl records, photographs, mismatched dinette chairs, or even people."

—Al Hoff, author of *Thrift Score*

"A charming comic novel."
—*Marie Claire*

"A wonderful book."
—Chris Jussel, host,
Chubb's Antiques Roadshow

"All my life I have been searching for Satori Junk, the illuminated junk store of *Second Hand*. When Richard, the junk knight of *Second Hand*, stands in line at an early morning estate sale, I am standing over his shoulder salivating. Michael Zadoorian speaks to the heart and soul of the junker, but when he writes 'Junkers know that we don't have to want the things we're told to want, that it's important to love that which seems to have no worth,' he speaks to all of us searching for worth in our lives."

—Mary Randolph Carter, author of *American Junk*

Second Hand

a novel

Michael Zadoorian

DTP
Trade Paperbacks

Dell Trade Paperback
Published by
Dell Publishing
a division of
Random House, Inc.
1540 Broadway
New York, New York 10036

DTP, is a registered trademark of Random House, Inc., and
the colophon is a trademark of Random House, Inc.

Library of Congress Catalog Card Number:
99-046418

ISBN: 0-385-33570-9

Reprinted by arrangement with W.W. Norton & Company, Inc.

Printed in the United States of America

Published simultaneously in Canada

May 2001

10 9 8 7 6 5 4 3 2 1
FFG

For Rita

Acknowledgments

Enormous thanks to my parents, Norman and Rosemary Zadoorian, for all their love and support and for knowing I could do this;
Tim Teegarden and James Potter for their friendship and stories;
Andrew Brown for his unerring eye and unwavering encourage-
ment; Keith McLenon, sharer of junking secrets; David Spala for
immeasurable enthusiasm; DeAnn Forbes for spreading the news;
the amazing people at the Michigan Anti-Cruelty Society for their
boundless compassion; writer/teacher/friend Christopher Towne
Leland for always taking the time; Charles Baxter and Samuel
Astrachan, for giving me the good word; Lori Pope of the Faith
Childs Literary Agency for her kindness and for making this so
much easier; Faith Childs for remembering me; my editor, Alane
Mason, for getting it, then for making it better; the Salvation
Army for furnishing our house and this book; and to junkers
everywhere. Live long and leave wondrous estate sales.

Now that my ladder's gone,
I must lie down where all the ladders start,
In the foul rag-and-bone shop of the heart.

—*W. B. Yeats*

Could be what you throw away is all that really counts;
could be that's the whole point of things,
wouldn't that be something?

—*Anne Tyler*

I drink my tea from a broken cup.

—*Bobby "Blue" Bland*

Part 1

Junk

When I die, I will leave nothing but junk. If I went to my house, to my estate sale, after I died, I would buy everything. Of course, since I bought it all in the first place, that shouldn't be much of a surprise. Yet even if I wasn't me, I would buy it all. There are others that would do the same. People come to my house and are amazed by my junk, covet my junk. But those people are junkers. When people who aren't junkers come to my house, they laugh at my things. Or they say my house is creepy because everything in it was owned by people who are now dead. I tell them, "They're not all dead. Some are in nursing homes."

They just don't get it. If they walk into a house and don't see a plaid couch beneath a color-coordinated "Starving Artists" painting (the big, big sale in the parking lot of the Southfield Ramada Inn—for all your art needs!), they become confused, disoriented, even hostile. I make a note of it: They will not be invited to my estate sale. The ad for it would probably go something like this, if I died today:

Estate Sale
Friday & Saturday, 10-5
15318 Vera

Thirty years' accumulation. Lots of items! 1940s Chinese-red armchair, 1960s genuine cowboy davenport with ten-gallon hat sewn into cushions, 1950s department-store mannequin (male), 1930s dining-room set, 1970s lamp and artificial potted plant, 1940s red/white kitchen table, 1950s cherry-wood Olympic Deluxe console hi-fi. Hundreds of LPs and eight-track tapes, large selection of lurid paperbacks, extensive black velvet art collection: crying clowns, matadors, naked ladies, thin Elvis and fat Elvis! Other collections include: kitchen clocks, ugly lamps, ashtrays, pitchers, cocktail shakers, bongos, souvenir buildings, souvenir spoons, salt & pepper shakers, and more! Full garage. Full basement. Spend the day! No early birds.

Occasionally, I am forced to deal with plaid-couch types in my house. E.g., those now-frequent occasions when my sister Linda comes by, for some reason connected with my mother's health.

Linda believes everything has to be new. She drives a new car, lives in a new house in a new subdivision with her new husband. After a few minutes in my living room, Linda is in a dither. (Or would it be a snit? I'm never sure about those two.) Linda simply doesn't know what to do around objects from garage sales and Salvation Armies and thrift shops and secondhand stores. She looks at my stuff and I can tell she can't wait to get home and sit on her beige plaid couch next to her beige plaid armchair across from the beige plaid love seat (parlor-tanned hand on the beige plaid antimacassar), under the hotel painting done in tones of tan, bone, beige, sienna, and sepia. If Linda sits at my place at all, she perches on the edge of my cowboy couch, like a small white bird trapped in a smudgy, unclean cage. This is sad to me.

Personally, I find new things boring. They have no history, no resonance. I feel at home with junk. Secondhand. The word says it all—other hands have touched that object. Think of all the things we touch every day, the million tiny linchpins that hold our lives together—the coffee mugs, the tie clasps, the alarm clocks, the sunglasses, the key fobs, the beanbag ashtrays. What if they absorbed some scintilla of you, as if the oil from your fingers carried the essence of your soul? Then think of all the stuff you've ever owned, that's ever passed through your hands, where it all might be right now. Think of the million other lives you've touched through those things that you've owned, that carry the essence of you. Amazing, huh?

Oh shit. You're right. Most of it is probably in a landfill in New Jersey. But I do think that when you own something that once belonged to someone else, it's like some secret contact with them, with their past. A way to touch people without having things get all messy and emotional.

That's what secondhand is. But then there are always people who worry about whether those hands were properly washed.

My Store

My store is located in a small dingy town on the fringe of Detroit, Michigan (a large dingy town), on what was once a lovely little Main Street. I assume things went to seed in the late Sixties, when a lot of things in and around Detroit went to seed—what with the '67 riot, white flight, urban sprawl, and then the malls. In my town, the only businesses to really survive the deadly onslaught of the malls are the repair shops—shoe, shaver, vacuum, etc. Each run by one unkillable old guy just toiling away, fixing things. Judging from what's in the thrift stores, I wouldn't have thought anyone got anything repaired these days, but apparently people do. There's also a used-book store on my street, a Thai joint, a record store started by some young punks (bless their LP-loving hearts), and a few sistah businesses (hair salons, nail joints, wig shops). And lots of empty storefronts.

I opened my place about five years ago with a little money my father left me when he died, three thousand dollars to be used "for artistic endeavors." Which seemed a bit strange, frankly. The money didn't mean much to me, compared to having my father around, but I wasn't going to argue. At that time, I was going to art school downtown, living in a roachtrap apartment on the Cass Corridor, working two jobs, one waiting tables, the other sorting at the distribution center for the Salvation Army. I was still finding my junk roots then (art with "found objects"), and working there allowed me to see stuff as soon as it came in. It was a piss-poor job, but I picked up a lot of great things, filling my already too-small apartment with much more junk than I needed for my little "projects." I didn't realize it then, but I was stocking up for the store.

I still don't know exactly where Dad got the three grand, but he had it somewhere. After I got the money, I blew some of it on junk, but I saved most of it. (Okay, so I save money. It's very Midwestern of me, I know.) Shortly afterward, I got fed up with pretentious art school rebop. I realized I liked the objects I was finding better than the art I was making. I started thinking about a store.

My Idea of Junk

I stock a hodgepodge of items ranging from the Thirties (not much) all the way to the Eighties (even less). I can't say I specialize in any particular era (though I do profess a weakness for the junk of the Fifties). The criteria for merchandise is simple: If I like it, I sell it. A few items I have out right now: chrome kitchen canister set, old bar glasses (Harry & Alma's Show Bar for dancing and good food!), a wall of bowling trophies and majorette trophies, disco shirts, cobalt seltzer bottle, Boy Scout knife and canteen, Reddy Kilowatt playing cards, strings of glass grapes, Niagara Falls napkin holder, framed paint-by-number paintings of horse heads.

As you can see, I've got some quality junk. And at very reasonable prices. (But not ridiculously so. I learned that lesson when I opened up the place. I had all sorts of great stuff, dirt-cheap. A few people came in and bought it up. The next week I saw it at some vintage stores uptown at three times the price. Bastards.) My clientele is mixed—tattooed black-leather types, hipsters, alterna-teens, design victims, weekend beatniks, psychobillies, people that just dig old stuff. If you had to use one word to describe them, it would have to be "cool." Which also seems to be the highest accolade one of them can bestow upon a person or object.

"Very *cool*."

"Extremely *cool*."

"That is just so *cool*."

"Fuck-king *cool*."

And so on. I hear this word in my store quite a bit, except in regards to my person. I get other folks, too: bargain-hunting locals, black and white, blue-collar and white-collar, who just come in looking around, not necessarily for *cool* junk, but because my place is in their neighborhood and it's actually still in business.

Have I mentioned the name of my store? It's called Satori Junk. I painted the sign for it myself, then encrusted it with all sorts of stuff—pieces of broken plates, buttons, old doll parts, marbles. When the sun is just right, it looks really great. The rest of the time, it just looks like a sign with a lot of crap hot-glued to it. As for Satori, I realize the Zen thing is a smidge on the egghead side, but I do believe that we can gain a kind of illumination from junk. We just have to be open to it. Unfortunately, most people live their lives without the wisdom junk can give them.

Bowling Shirts and Poodle Planters

Today, I open up and a few people straggle in. About one-thirty, one hipster buys an old bowling shirt that I picked up at a Value Village. I must say, it is an extremely *cool* shirt, white with turquoise sleeves, an original King Richard, Sanforized for your protection. The best part is the back of the shirt. Embroidered in red script it says:

Bowlero Lanes

According to the name over the breast pocket, the previous owner of the shirt was Pete. Strange thing, but hipsters will really pay for a shirt with a name embroidered on it. The older and goofier the name, the better—Herb, Sid, Marvin. Better yet, a kooky nickname—"Bud," "Dot," "Buzz." Man, nothing sells like quotation marks.

The only other thing that happens is a gone chick in Forties glamour shades looks in my front window. Definitely a potential customer and, well, kind of attractive in a wan, beat girl way. I wave for her to come in. This sort of extroversion is against my character, but as a merchant, when someone looks in your store window, you're under an obligation to get them to come in. Still, this hardly ever works for me. I think I wave wrong or something. People usually just kind of wave back, then clear out. But this time the woman actually heads for the door. As she walks in, she props her glasses up on her head and looks at me.

"Hi. Cool store," she says.

I want to look over at her and smile, say hi, but I'm suddenly very embarrassed about the waving. Yet, for some reason, I wave again. She gives me an odd look, then starts to browse. From my place behind the cash register, I sort of check her out. She's dressed in a short Seventies leather over a Fifties frock with pearls and a black sling mom purse. I must say, this girl has something, and it could be style. She has that wraith kind of look, pale skin with bobbed, dyed-black hair. There are dark circles around her eyes, but somehow she manages to pull it off, like she meant to do it, as if they were daubed with kohl. I notice that her pearls are not pearls at all, but small skulls. This makes me a bit jumpy.

She skirts around the side of the store, behind my rack of dime novels. She picks up a copy of Henry Gregor Felsen's *Hot Rod*. She might be avoiding eye contact with me. I don't blame her. She's probably afraid I'm going to wave at her again. I try to shake off this cloak of weirdness. I am about to say something, then I change my mind. A sound is emitted unfortunately, a sort of monosyllabic grunt.

She looks up from the book, looks back down quickly, in a way that tells me that she doesn't really want to talk to me. When customers respond this way, I leave them alone. But for some reason, I start babbling.

"Can I help you with anything?" I say. "I could help you with something if you needed it." I laugh loudly. (The laugh echoes through the store, then just falls on the floor, dead.) She keeps looking at *Hot Rod*, then picks up a copy of *Street Rod*. (Perhaps she is interested in the whole Gregor Felsen oeuvre, I think.)

Then she looks up and smiles at me. This is a very good smile. I like this smile. "Do you have any, like, dog stuff?" she says, nipping at a cuticle.

Finally, something to concentrate on. "Hmm. Anything in particular?"

"No. I don't know. Just some sort of knickknack thing. It's for a friend."

"I may have a little poodle planter somewhere," I say, walking over to one of my tables of bric-a-brac. She starts to follow.

"Shit," she says, looking at her watch. "You know, I've got to go. I shouldn't have come in here. I don't really have time—"

At that point, the door rings open and in walks big hipster stud: black-on-black-on-black leather, goatee, tatts, pierced ears, nose, etc.

"You ready?" he says to her. He doesn't even look my way, at the doofus standing next to her.

"Yeah," she says. When the Prince of Darkness turns around, she follows him, but looks over at me, three crooked fingers in the air, hint of broken smile, shade of concern in her eyes. "Sorry. We gotta go."

Slam of door. No reason to apologize. It was all in my mind anyway.

Same Old, Same Old

The rest of the day is pretty normal. Quiet, yet full of small events that I can control: mail, a few more customers, polishing an old chrome penguin ice bucket, sweeping the sidewalk. I like it that way. I can't get enough of the rut, the blur, the grind, the same old. Every evening, when I sit down to eat at my boomerang Formica kitchen table, I say a little prayer to the god of repetition. He is a god of my own creation, a lowercase "g" god, but I am fond of him all the same. I don't really say my prayer out loud, just sort of in my head—I thank him for the sameness of this day, for the bounty of today's junk. I thank him for one more day like so many other days. . . .

How to put this. I need routine, I need stability, I need repetition, in order to be the best junker I can be. There is a precise place a junker needs to reside psychologically to keep his chops, to manipulate the fates, to maintain the search.

The Search

My merchandise comes from estate sales, thrift shops, garage sales, Salvation Armies, church rummage sales, block sales, tag sales, moving sales, you name it. I score the most salable items for the store at estate sales, even though that's where competition with other store owners is the toughest. It's much harder to find good stuff at all the garage sales and thrift stores and such, but I have to go to them. *I have to go.* Junking is much more than just obtaining merchandise, or even finding the things I want, though it started out that way. It's a way of life, a manner of thinking. Junking is my own grubby metaphor for everything; life portrayed as the long trudge through smelly, clotted aisles on the way to what might seem like the big score, but is simply more junk.

When you're a junker, you surrender yourself to the search. The problem is, you never know exactly what you're looking for, until you see it. Even then, you're not always sure. Sometimes you see something, but ignore it, or decide against it, or maybe you're just not in the mood to buy. Then later, when you think about it at home, or worse, when you notice it in someone else's hand, you realize that was the thing you had wanted all along. I suppose I am looking for something of value, some unattainable piece, but who knows what that is? Not necessarily something that will let me retire and live out the rest of my days in luxury, like that guy who found the Dalí at the Salvation Army. I mean, what would I do with myself then? You have to keep looking.

The looking is something you are born with and die with. I see it in the eyes of the chunky old women who haunt the Goodwill and the Council for the Blind. There they are, well into their seventies, with their limited incomes, still shopping like maniacs, although one of the ineluctable prerequisites of ownership is time enough to possess. They get around that by gift-giving. I see them every day, Pall Malls dangling from rumpled mouths, holding themselves up with shopping carts filled with soiled toys and other articles that almost always look like offerings for loved ones.

When I see them, I go out of my way to be nice to them, show them more than the usual courtesies, even more than I would extend to a fellow junker. They break my heart, these women.

They are the swollen-ankle foot soldiers, living the junk life. No matter what I do or what I find, I am merely visiting. Understand that there is an unnavigable gulf of difference between those who choose to shop at thrift shops and garage sales and those who have no choice, who would much prefer to be out chasing the dragon of newness along with the rest of the world.

My Secret Shame

After dinner, I give Mom a quick call at the hospital. ("Are you coming tomorrow?" "Yes, Mom." "Don't bring me anything. I've already got too much garbage here as it is." "I won't, Mom.") After I hang up, I check the papers for estate sales. There's not much going on in the classifieds of the *Free Press*, but when I get to the *Observer*, I grab my red pen. Right there under "Estate Sales," between all the three- and four-column-inch sale ads run by auction houses and professional liquidators advertising items like "French hand-painted marble-top commode," is one tiny ad. I wipe the old horn-rims before I read:

Estate Sale
Hamtramck
Sat only, 9–4.
40+ yrs accumulation.
Furniture; household; basement; garage.
Many unusual items! Don't miss.
Sale by Betty L. & Co.

These are the kind of ads I live for.

Hamtramck: ancient factory town, adjunct of Detroit, home of the now-defunct Dodge Main, one of the city's toughest plants; birthplace of Kowalski Sausage (note twenty-foot-tall neon kielbasa); labyrinth of cramped streets of prewar bungalows and two-flats (covered in *trompe l'oeil* brick asphalt sheet) with welcome-mat lawns and porches so whopping big you could park a '57 Chrysler 300C on them; populated by factory rats who did their forty years at the plant, then keeled over in their first year of retirement, leaving black-clad peasant-stock wives to live another thirty years, hobbling to church every day, clutching their rosaries, cursing the invading blacks and Chaldeans and Bangladeshi, then returning home to clean their forty-year-old ovens. Junking demographics don't get much better than in Hamtramck. Not only is it filled with older folks who take care of their things (things that were built to last in the first place), but also there are more Eastern Europeans than practically anywhere outside Warsaw—meaty people with a low center of gravity, so they don't move around much. That's what you need for good junking. People who stay in one place forever.

At an estate sale, a person's life is laid in front of you. A man's Bakelite Donald Duck pencil sharpener from his Twenties childhood can be found in the same room as his walker and oxygen tank. (I snagged that pencil sharpener, by the way.) It's strange to see someone's life collapsed in this manner. Strange, but exhilarating. Like it or not, the blood rush of the estate sale is that you have won; you have outlived one of your villagers, you were born later, luckier—now you are entitled to what was theirs. When I buy this fondue dish, I have eaten the heart of my enemy. Maybe this is what makes people so nuts. (They scowl and push, toss elbows, body checks. A shame, really: People can't be pleasant while plundering.) It isn't just greed or competition or the thrill of the hunt that drives them—something else is going on: elemental, scary, addictive. When they call your number and let you in that house and you start running around with all the rest of the junk-crazed lunatics, something happens. A door has been opened and you are suddenly privy to the secrets. Not just the deceased's secrets, but to *the* secrets: fears, joys, angers, despairs, boredoms. Life and death were acted out, but you missed the show and now you're backstage, going through the props, trying to figure out if the production was *Hamlet* or *Under the Yum-Yum Tree*.

My Public Shame

The problem with estate sales is that I can't seem to get to them on time. You need to get at the houses very early in the morning when they hand out the numbers. That's how you get the good stuff. The problem is, that's when all the dealers and other people who own stores show up. They come at six and seven in the morning, sometimes earlier. They hand out their own numbers on the street. I get there at eight and there are already twenty people ahead of me. By the time I get in, a lot of the good stuff is long gone.

However, this is not what happens to me on Friday. I am the first person at this sale. This has never happened before. It's at an old house down a tree-lined street with no vehicles parked in front except for my truck ('69 avocado-green GMC Suburban) and Betty L.'s Toyota (license plate: SALE GAL). I can't believe it. There is no line of kibitzing store owners, no hipster chick handing out street numbers at the door, no whiny estate operator fending off the crowd. There's not even an "Estate Sale Today" sign. I'm a little afraid to even go up to the door, but I do.

I peek inside and even though the place is dimly lit, I can see someone in the living room applying price tags at a table of tchotchkes, very precious, a lot of porcelain figurines and salt cellars and crystal, definitely not my cup of tea, but still not a bad sign. I look around. The walls of the vestibule are brown with years of nicotine, but beneath the haze I see stenciled designs on the walls, arabesques of red and blue lining the walls. I see them in the dining room as well. Decades ago, someone actually came in and hand-stenciled this person's walls. Probably some craftsman they knew from the old country. Amazing. I never cease to be astonished at how much care some people put in their houses.

I tap at the door hesitantly. The person at the table, a middle-aged black woman with towering hair and a pair of silver sneakers, whom I recognize as one of Betty L.'s freelance assistants, looks up, then comes to the door.

"You handing out numbers, Dorothea?" I say to her through the screen.

"Not today, skinny," she says. "Just line up. We open at nine."

This is Dorothea's thing. She calls everyone by their most noticeable physical attribute. Every time I see her, I'm glad I don't have a big nose. "Any chance of getting in early?" I say.

"Nine o'clock."

"Come on, don't I get a reward for being here before everyone else?"

Dorothea tips one of her jeweled claws at me. "I'll tell you what. When we open up, I'll let you in first."

"You're killing me here, Dot," I say, trying to keep from laughing.

Dorothea smiles and heads back into the house. I park it on the porch and pull out my book. I look around and think about how much I love this job. This is all I need, I say to myself. Eight-thirty on a beautiful summer morning, first in line at a great old house in Hamtown that could be glutted with treasures. How many people's lives have this sort of excitement? I can feel the possibilities in the fillings of my teeth. There's something here for me, I know it.

The Art of Plunder

At nine o'clock, Dorothea lets in the first five people with her usual declaration: "The estate sale has begun. I would like to welcome the first five lovely people."

We all charge in. I scan the front room, which could only be described as a parlor. The items scattered on tables and even on the tattered maroon couch are as precious as the objects I saw on the table. I pass it by and head into the dining room—more crystal, and porcelain and crinoline. There is an old red vinyl kidney-shaped ottoman that I snag.

"Can I start a pile?" I ask Dorothea as I drag the thing over by the dining-room table where she has set up shop.

"At your own risk," she says, but I know she'll keep an eye on it for me.

The kitchen: a great old turquoise kitchen clock, in the standard place above the stove. A little cleaning, and that bad boy will sell. Salt and pepper shakers shaped like Squirt pop bottles, chrome wax paper and foil dispenser, cool old Mister Thrifty tin bank—mine, mine, mine. I pull out the nylon duffel from my back pocket and carefully place the items in it, then head downstairs. It is a narrow staircase, made more narrow by the pots and pans hanging from the walls. This is something I've seen a few times before in the homes of very, very old people who thought of their basement as some sort of cellar, instead of, say, a rumpus room. By the time I reach the bottom of the stairs, I don't expect to find much. And I don't. It is strictly laundry, rusty tools, and canning supplies. A misstep. I've wasted valuable time.

On my way back upstairs, I run into Betty L., say hey to her. She acts like she hardly knows me. This is her way. Don't get too close to the junkers or they'll turn on you, start accusing you of preferential treatment.

"Hey, Betty, where's the upstairs bedrooms?" I say.

"The bedrooms are all down here. There's just a big attic."

Even better. "Really?"

"Uh-huh. It's that door off the kitchen. It goes right upstairs." I didn't even see the door. That's bad. I can't afford to miss things like that. I hear Dorothea letting in the next five lovely people.

"There's an Eames chair up there you might be interested in," Betty yells to me as I fly into the kitchen. "I'll give you a good deal."

Swanky junk. I hate to admit it, but I like some of that stuff. Of course, it's all way too expensive. Still, I make a mental note as I zoom upstairs. There are already two or three people up there, but they are looking at the clothes, collected on two long metal poles hung along either side of the narrow coved ceiling. I should take a look myself, but I like to check out the goods first. There's not a lot else really—books, which I can leave for last, pieces of an old Lionel train set, lots of drapes, which are beauties—wonderful old Fifties fabric, great gaping tongued pink-red orchids and spiky greenery—I grab the whole batch, with the hooks still attached, and stuff them into my bag. I figure if they're in the attic they can't be too expensive.

I find the chair Betty was talking about. It's not an Eames chair at all, but a Thonet upholstered in funky green vinyl. It's cool-looking, and in decent shape, but there's something about this designer junk that grinds me. You start dealing with a whole different market, the cognoscenti, people who collect "Deco Futura Moderne." Still, I can turn it over uptown for a quick few bucks. It doesn't have to get near my store.

Back downstairs, I pay for all the stuff. It's a good haul for one sale. There are plenty of times when I don't find squat. Luckily, I brought enough cash with me.

"They just opened the garage, skinny," Dorothea says to me.

"Really? Okay, thanks," I say, snatching up my receipt.

Garages are one of my favorite places for snooping. Way back when, the garage was strictly male territory. The woman took care of the home—decor, cleaning, social obligations, cooking, washing, ironing, canning, etc. But the man took care of the garage. It never fails to amaze me what men will store in their garages, squirreled away in cigar boxes. I have found the strangest things—medieval-looking tools, Rube Goldberg gadgets, stockpiles of oddities like rubber washers or car keys or heel cleats. Why did they save this stuff? What sparked all that manly hoarding?

In this garage, there are sawhorses with plywood sheets set on them, covered with his tools, pretty standard stuff. There are knobs and Molly anchors, nestled in jars hanging from their lids, nailed to wall-mounted two-by-fours (the traditional Midwestern garage storage system). There are shelves filled with more cans and jars and plastic tubs, useful refuse from her territory—Maxwell House, Cool Whip, Crisco, Velvet Peanut Butter. I peek, but I know what they contain—nails, screws, tacks, clamps, staples—things that hold other things together. I check the tools again and realize everything metal is covered with a mist of rust. The man of this garage has been gone quite a while. The woman of the house never got around to cleaning up his territory. Now it's time for us to do it.

Crackpot Theory #1: The Junk Principle

Have you noticed that the older someone gets, the bigger his car gets? It's like number of years on earth is directly proportional to square footage of sheet metal. This is related to a theory of mine. The older you get, the more stuff you own. Why? Because stuff protects you. It acts as ballast, a sort of passive restraint system to mortality. Think of the feeling you get when you buy something. That little rush. It's like a flash of forever. You're telling yourself, at that moment when you lay down those hard-earned shekels, that you know you'll be around to enjoy that purchase. You're giving yourself something more to carry on your journey, because you know it's going to be a long one.

I've noticed that when people hit their thirties they start seriously acquiring things. Once they have the big things—cars, houses, spouses, children—they keep at it—acquire, acquire,

acquire—fancy second cars, pool tables, boats, recreational vehicles—really big things. But they're not making their lives fuller, just heavier. What they don't know is that they are trying to protect themselves. The thirties are the end of feeling that you're going to live forever.

Even the thirtyish hipsters who dig my kind of junk, beneath the requisite nonconformist's black leather jacket and jackboots, most of them are living fairly conventional lives, working in ad agencies, hair salons, bars, art studios, restaurants, etc., and loading up on junk just like everyone else (including me). It doesn't matter whether you surround yourself with metal and fiberglass or Bakelite and gabardine, it's all the same. Our possessions comfort us, protect us from the bad things we know are going to happen. As witness to a thousand estate sales, I know this to be an illusion, but at that moment of purchase, it is as real as the object in your hand. Fact: I just found out that my mother, right after she was told that she was sick, went on a shopping spree. Maxed out her credit card. Figure that one out.

I Brake for Garage Sales

This time of year (early summer), Fridays are also a great day for garage sales. Today, every other telephone pole, it seems, has a homemade sign appended to it, some with a few stray balloons. (Although that's often not a good sign. Balloons are busy work for children. That means toys and children's clothes for sale, instead of real stuff.) Still, I cruise around, hitting one after another, parking, making that walk from truck to garage, garage to truck. This walk often consumes more time than the sale itself. Yet, I find a few things—chocolate-colored leisure suit (I actually know someone who collects them. He hangs them all around his apartment when he has a party), Seventies board games, an old "Uncola" glass, and a great pair of big-headed, bug-eyed Keane children paintings. They would be perfect for my bad art hallway that features all my black velvets and paint-by-numbers.

At eleven, I head to the hospital to visit my mother. When I get there, I meet up with Linda by the elevators. We just say hi to each other and head on up. She has some daffodils for my mother. I bring her a little snow globe of Milwaukee that I picked up yesterday at a garage sale. I've been averaging one a week on my junk rounds, so I bring them for Mom. She has quite a collection on her windowsill—Niagara Falls, New York City, Detroit, Tallahassee (glitter), New Jersey, Sault St. Marie, Cleveland, Chicago, Toledo. I think they're kind of cheery. Still, I'm not sure she appreciates the effort.

When we walk into her room, our mother is sleeping. I sense she is not having a good day. Linda and I are just standing there, not knowing what to do, when suddenly Mom opens her eyes from what seemed like a deep sleep and starts talking to us. This is the kind of stuff I can't get used to.

"Thank you, kids," she says to us, completely awake now.

My mother does not look good today. Her bones are starting to show through her skin. I swear I can see not just the shape of them, but the color. She has her Hedy Lamarr pink satin skullcap on. She gave up on the wig this last time they put her in the hospital.

"How do you feel today, Ma?" I say, putting on my best smiley face.

"Like I'm dying," she says. "How do you think I feel?"

My mother does not believe in letting her family live in denial. I glance longingly at her morphine drip.

"But it's nothing like they keep saying," she continues. "No pleasant walk toward the light, relatives beckoning me. It's just pain, excruciating pain."

"I'm sorry, Mom," I say. Behind me, Linda emits a few preliminary sniffles. Any minute now she will start crying, like she does every time we come to visit Mom together. I agreed to Linda and me coming together once a week, just so Mom doesn't give me too much grief about the two of us hating each other's guts. Actually, for quite some time, Mom and I didn't get along too well either. (Then she started dying. Now we get along swell.)

"What have you kids been up to?" says Mom, trying to forestall the inevitable scene.

Linda doesn't say anything, so I speak. "I just came back from a great estate sale," I say, knowing that neither of them could care less. "I picked up all sorts of neat stuff for the store."

A long wheeze as my mother lifts her head up. "I wish you'd get a real job, Richard, so I could stop worrying about you."

"Mom, this is my job. I'm—"

"I know, dear, you're a junker. You've made this royal proclamation in the past."

I sit down next to the bed. I'd like to take her hand, but she doesn't like being touched much these days. "Mom, I'm doing fine. I've got enough to eat and a place to live. I'm better off than three-quarters of the world."

"It's just that I would feel much better with this situation if I knew you were going to be all right."

I notice that she judiciously avoids the "d" word here, for

greater effect, no doubt. I love my mother, but even on her deathbed, she drives me crazy.

"Mom, I'll be fine."

"I just don't see how you can make a living—"

Behind me, Linda starts bawling, then latches on to Mom in bed. Mom puts her arms around Linda. I sit in the chair next to the bed, waiting out this part of our ritual. After a few minutes, Mom gives me the eye signal, slightly annoyed at this blubbering, convulsing mass that is practically ripping out her IV, seemingly amazed that they share genetic information.

"Richard, get your sister a tissue, would you, dear? Then get her off me."

I do what my mother says. After Linda calms down, we talk about nothing: Linda's new drapes, how I am wasting my life. When I try to swing the conversation over to news from the doctor, Linda and my mother swing it back to insignificant matters. After a while, I assume there is no new news.

Soon, after I announce that I have to leave to go open my store, my mother calls us over to the bed for the final part of our ritual. Just then one of the nurses walks in to tend to my mother.

"Could you give us a moment, Sheila?" she says to the nurse. "I want to tell my children something." Sheila steps back to the doorway.

"Both of you," she whispers to us intently, as if she were about to impart the secrets themselves. "I want you to go into that bathroom and wash your hands before you leave. And don't touch anything on your way out."

Linda nods her head, like she always does. I try to keep from laughing, like I always do. My mother cracks me up. She's lying there with tubes hanging out of her and she's worried about us washing our hands after being at the hospital. As if dying is contagious. I suppose it is, but will a squirt of pink soap really help? It doesn't matter. We both go in and wash our hands like good kids.

On our way out, Linda is very quiet. I think she is even more upset than usual. In the parking lot, she breaks down again.

"Come on," I say, trying to give her a little hug, but not quite sure where exactly to put my arms. "Let's go over to my house for a cup of tea."

Linda is so distraught she actually accepts my offer. My house is only a few minutes away. I know that I'm supposed to open the store around noon, but that's the good thing about owning a small business in a dumpy area. It's not that big a deal if you're late. When we get to the house, I sit Linda down on my cowboy couch with the wagon-wheel arms. She hardly flinches. I head for the kitchen to make tea, feeling proud of her.

"I'm sorry, Richard. I didn't mean to get so worked up," she says, voice raspy and congested.

I hand her a smiley-face mug of Sleepytime. I'm hoping it will calm her down a bit.

"Doesn't any of this make you upset?" she says.

"Yeah, I guess."

I sit down on the couch next to my sister. Except for her red nose and her running eyeliner, she is the perfect human Barbie doll, all made up, hair fluffed and coiffed and frosted, a little wing of blond jutting back aerodynamically from her forehead. She probably spent an hour on her hair alone this morning. I can't understand how anyone can do that. Even still, she is my sister and I'm sorry that she can't seem to stop crying.

"Come on, drink your tea," I say. "You'll feel better."

"It's too hot."

"That's okay. A mouthful of seared flesh will get your mind off things."

Linda squints and manages to squeeze out a faint smile between sobs. Then, as if that half-chuckle activates some sort of awareness, I notice her looking around at my stuff. First, her eyes light on Tom the mannequin (in dashiki, kilt, and fez), whom I brought home from the store after I stopped selling sharkskin suits. But Linda has expressed her feelings regarding Tom on a previous visit. ("That thing gives me the creeps, Richard. How can you stand it staring at you?) Finally, her artificial baby blues settle on one of my prize possessions, the liqueur dispenser on the mantel, a swirled tan-and-brown sphere, identical to a bowling ball, only with a little gold bowling man mounted on the top. When you pick him up, the ball opens in half to expose a pump and eight shot glasses. I can tell Linda is intrigued by it, enough to pause from her sobbing.

"What *is* that, Richard?" she says, stuffed-up, but still managing a twang of irritation in her voice. She is turning back into her old self. She'll be wanting to leave soon, I can tell.

"Bowling-ball liqueur dispenser. For the connoisseur with rented shoes."

"God, Richard. Some of the things that you own, I swear. Who would want to drink out of something like that?"

"There's blackberry brandy in it. Care for a snort?"

Linda blows her nose, looks at her watch. "I really should get going. Stewart is waiting for me to get home." My sister has officially stopped crying. She gives me a pained look and then sniffs loudly. Then she sniffs again. I know what's coming.

"What is that smell?" she says.

There is no smell. I may like secondhand things, but I clean it all before I use or sell it. I'm a very good housekeeper. It is one of the many conventional, bourgeois things about me. The smell is simply Linda, needing to justify her squeaky-clean, unbrave new world. When I was little, I knew a kid who would always hold his nose whenever he passed a funeral home. I liken Linda's sniffing to this. Suddenly, the inclination to comfort my sister disappears and I give myself over to tormenting her.

"It could be anything," I say. "It's probably the couch, though. Probably dried semen from one of the previous owners."

She emits a tiny huff of fear. The expression on her face is priceless. She can't tell if I'm kidding or not. "Richard!"

I stand up. "You should go, if Stu is waiting for you."

She nods her head, then stands up to leave.

Darkness at Lunch

In the truck, driving to the store, I notice the sky start to change. It's a bright blue, but objects look thinner, as if the light that illuminates them is evaporating. I think a storm is coming, but no one is seeking shelter. Everyone's out walking around. Not the typical summer tornado-weather behavior in Michigan. The sky keeps changing, taking on an eerie, hollow kind of darkness. Finally it occurs to me. It's the day of the eclipse.

People are milling on the sidewalks, in front of stores, on porches, in the parking lots of office buildings, everywhere—watching. What's bringing them all out at the same time? Novelty or some universal sense of our own irrelevance? I vote for the former. I've found that people don't like dwelling on their own irrelevance. Me, I wallow in it. I have it pointed out to me every day in about a thousand different ways. Every time I see an old pair of white shoes or a copy of *Rusty Warren's Knockers Up!* or a Presto FryDaddy I am reminded of it. I traffic in irrelevance. I can safely say it's not all that popular.

As I pull up into the alley behind the store, these things happen: a sudden drop in temperature; the shadows from the trees thin out and mottle the ground; the birds start screaming, creating this confused, shuddering shroud of noise. I feel a headache coming on.

Junk + Junk

Despite my throbbing lobes and the general weirdness of the eclipse (or perhaps because of it), today is good at work. I sell the penguin ice bucket, a Sears crank ice crusher, and a sportsman's cocktail shaker painted with drink recipes and sporting equipment (including a shotgun and shells. Alcohol and firearms—the perfect combination!), with swizzle sticks, all to some square-looking cat who must be an accountant by day, booze-swilling playboy by night. I'm very big on junk combos. I like to put things together, then sell the whole shebang. (Sometimes this kind of kit also helps the uninspired to realize the beauty of good junk.) I sell a jade-green bouclé chair in decent shape, some neat old Exotica records (Phase 4 Stereo, Command, RCA Victor Living Stereo), and a Pez dispenser. (I know I shouldn't mess around with cheap junk like that, but I have a thing for Pez.)

Right before closing, I watch some ska-punk rip off an old porkpie hat, practically right in front of me. He is young and wispy-thin and smaller than me, but I still don't do anything. I don't confront him at the door. I don't chase him down the street. I don't do anything.

After I close, I go visit Mom again. She is sleeping.

Big Evening

When I get home, I think about calling Linda to apologize for today, but I decide that I just can't deal with her right now. I toss a Salisbury steak TV dinner into the oven, watch a little television, then read in bed. (*The Connoisseur* by Evan S. Connell, about a man that becomes obsessed with an object he finds in a curio shop. Imagine.) Eventually, I fall asleep.

Mom on Saturday

Six-thirty in the morning, I get the call from the hospital. The voice on the line tells me that my mother has developed pneumonia. We are now on a sort of constant red alert. The voice recommends that I get there as soon as possible. A Saturday. This is like my mother. *It's all right. I'll die on the weekend. I don't want to be any trouble for anyone.*

I throw on some clothes and head straight for the hospital. Linda is already there. She has talked to the doctor and he has told her that they have done everything they can. It's only a matter of time now, blah, blah, blah.

When I walk into my mother's room, she is sleeping, if you can call it that. She has an oxygen mask over her mouth and nose, but still her breathing is loud and labored. Each breath is a gasp. I sit down on one side of the bed and Linda sits on the other. The morning nurse tells us that if there are any changes to just buzz her. She leaves. We sit there and watch my mother breathe. After a while, a new nurse comes in to check.

At around noon, Linda wants to turn the television on, but I will not let her. I keep thinking about this story I read once about AIDS victims at a hospital, their faces irradiated by the blue light from the television. One of the characters says that the one thing she couldn't bear thinking about is someone dying with the TV on. I agree, though I think this is probably how I will die. It's a junk death—Charlie Parker laughing at the Dorsey Brothers' show, Kerouac watching the Galloping Gourmet. As a child, whenever I was afraid or anxious for something to happen, I would turn the television on. I would probably do that same thing if I knew I was going to die soon. I would just lie there, watching television, killing time before time killed me.

At around four in the afternoon, my mother's condition worsens. Her breathing is more strained, almost mechanical at this point. The sound of air entering and leaving her body becomes painful to hear. I tell Linda that I have to go downstairs for something to eat. I suppose I shouldn't be feeling hunger, but I haven't eaten anything since yesterday. I tell her that I will be right back. She says get something for me, too. That makes me feel better.

Downstairs, in the hospital cafeteria, there is a Wendy's hamburger stand. I get a single burger and an extra-large Coke, and the same for Linda, even though I know she will consider it all way too fattening for her to actually consume. I rush back up to the room. A nurse is in the room now, Leslie from the afternoon shift, who has been very nice to my mother. My Aunt Tina is there now as well, the perfect sister, the perfect hostess, the one that secretly can't figure out what went wrong with me. She is impeccably attired in a little outfit from, oh, let's say Neiman-Marcus. She has timed things well, as usual. Tina has a shrewd social talent for showing up at the exact time when the important things are just going to happen.

I have a few tiny bites of my hamburger. I can't help it, I am so hungry.

Thi∧ I∧ How Your Mother Die∧

My mother's breathing has gotten more erratic by this time. The breaths are coming farther and farther apart. I am having a hard time looking at her. I don't know what to do with myself or my hamburger. But I feel as though I cannot move or something will happen. So I just sit in the chair next to the bed, paralyzed, clutching the hamburger in one hand, my mother's shrunken left hand in the other.

A few minutes go by and my aunt says, "Has she breathed?" Immediately after Tina says that, there is one more breath, then Leslie the nurse informs us that she is gone.

I take a bite of my hamburger.

Leslie's condolences; Linda's hysterics; untimely entrance by my mother's doctor; promises by cool-headed Tina to make the calls to the right people—all these things happen. I get up, step out into the hall. An orderly passes, pushing a cart loaded with dishes of green Jell-O covered with plastic wrap. There is laughter coming from the nurses' station. An old man is moaning a few doors down. I step back into my mother's room, grab the first snow dome I see, then get out of there.

In the parking lot of the hospital, I take the snow dome from my pocket. It is the one from Niagara Falls, where my parents went on their honeymoon. But this is not what affects me. It happens in the truck, as I drive home, a phrase keeps running through my head. I keep thinking: *If you eat hamburgers, your mother will die.*

Funeral Home Hijinks

Sunday morning, before meeting Linda and Tina at the funeral home, I hit an estate sale. It is just for a few minutes and I know that I might be a smidge late, but I also know that I won't miss much. I do a quick round of the housewares and right away pick up a pristine Sixties Erlenmeyer-style coffee carafe, still in its original four-color carton. The couple on the box are enjoying an intimate dinner in their modern suburban dining room. The woman, hair in a French twist, is pouring her husband, successful junior executive, clad in a suit and tie, a relaxing cup of coffee. They're both smiling and really enjoying themselves. I decide that this is where I'd like to be right now, in this box, in that room, living that life. Not in Detroit, in the Nineties, on my way to a funeral home to pick out coffin-lining fabrics for my dead mother.

When I arrive at the funeral home, late, I get the evil eye from Tina, but it's no different from the evil eye I have been getting from her most of my life, so it doesn't make much of an effect. Behind the cherry-wood desk, there's some middle-aged, lantern-jawed, Christian-looking Michigan State graduate all official and concerned and sympathetic, probably deciding which stiffs he's going to hump at lunch. Linda is crying, of course. I am silent, still coping with this horrible sense of relief I'm feeling. By this time they have already picked out a casket and most of the other stuff, which is fine with me. But they show me what they've chosen, out of some twisted sense of obligation. I remain silent until I hear the price.

I pipe up. "You know, John Donne used to keep his coffin in his house and he would lie down in it every day just to remind himself of, you know, where he was headed."

"Really?" says Mr. Compassionate Funeral Director. "That's fascinating."

"Yep. Now there's a guy who got a lot of use out of his coffin. And I bet he didn't spend anywhere near this much money on his."

Silence. I decide to take the direct approach. I stand and turn to Tina and Linda. "Look, are you guys out of your mind?"

"I assure you that this is a very good price for all that you're getting," says Clutch Cargo, from behind the desk.

Linda starts sobbing even louder. "Don't do this, Richard."

"Richard," Tina hisses.

"Is it just me, or has everyone forgotten that we're going to put this into the ground?" I say.

Tina looks at me. "This thing, may I remind you, is going to contain my sister. Your mother."

"My mother is dead, Tina. And you know what she would say if she were here. *It's okay. A simple pine box will suffice.*"

"She'd say that, but she'd expect what we're giving her."

I have to give Tina that one. But I can't seem to bring myself to say it. "This is stupid," I mumble instead.

Stu and Casseroles

Afterward, we all go over to Linda's absurdly tidy, enormous new house in the exurbs. A few of Linda's neighbors are there and have brought casseroles, pans of lasagna, plates of cookies. What manner of Midwestern lunacy is this, I ask you? It's not like Linda even eats much of anything. She is worried about being thin and beautiful, so Stewart will love her. Ultimately, I don't think percentage of body fat will matter. Stewart will stray. It is bred in the bone. He is the archetypal man-dog. Every time I talk to him, he tries to relate to me on some sort of Cro-Magnon level. He talks only about sports or the Windsor Ballet (totally nude strip joints across the bridge in Canada), where he takes his gearhead clients. This is the only way he knows how to talk to another man. I'm sure he thinks I'm an effeminate wimp and just generally a weirdo. Yet it doesn't even occur to him that I might tell Linda that her husband huffs Canuck muff twice weekly. He trusts me simply because we have an appendage in common. The weird thing is, I don't tell her. Who knows? Maybe he understands male bonding on some deeper, unconscious level. Or maybe he just assumes I know that he would beat me senseless if I told her. Guys like Stewart can spot a coward like me from a mile away.

Stewart is there when we all show up at the house. He is blond and clean-cut, but a bloated kind of clean-cut, frat-boy muscles gone to fat. We nod our greetings at each other.

"Richard," he says to me, crushing my hand within his massive ruddy ham. "How you holding up, man?" Stewart frowns caringly, that special brand of fake male concern. I think he's pleased that I'm not blubbering like a girl.

"Okay, I guess. I'm glad Tina's here for Linda. I'm not being much help."

Stewart's eyes dart over at the two of them jabbering away across the room, and I detect a certain disdain. "Yeah, well, I think that's what Tina gets off on, being there for people."

I nod. This is more perceptive a comment than I would expect from Stewart. This is one thing he and I have in common. Neither of us cares much for Tina. She is, put plainly, a misery junkie. She feeds off others' pain. I have noticed that she is always best friends in the family with whoever is having the most problems. (As soon as someone develops cancer, she becomes their best friend. If she ever starts getting palsy-walsy with me, I'll know I'm a goner.)

Stewart may be the one in trouble, though, for I suspect it won't be long before Linda becomes Tina. I recognize the signs: the perfect hostess, everything always in place, the quest for status, the dislike of all that is not conventional.

"See the Tigers game last night? What a blowout."

"No, I missed it," I say. Apparently Stu has not quite figured out yet that I miss all sporting events.

I excuse myself from Stewart, go to the bathroom, then sneak out the back door. On the way here, I noticed a yard sale on the next street. I'm not going to be able to open the store for the next couple of days, so I might as well see if I can pick up something. Besides, I need to.

I find a perfect turquoise Harlequin dish. I also pick up a Tonette, a lumpy little black plastic musical instrument (obviously what they gave the kids in elementary school with absolutely no musical talent). It comes with an instruction book called *Melody Fun! How to Play the Tonette!* It's just crazy enough for someone to buy.

Have a Nice Day

They have plaid couches at the Meldrum Funeral Home. And lots of coordinated paintings—eerie, serene, surreal landscapes hanging up there like picture windows overlooking Planet Mauve. That stuff always gives me the heebie-jeebies, but especially this morning. (Give me dogs playing poker or a crying clown anytime. It's at least a *good* kind of bad.) Then there's all my relatives loping around, sniveling, laughing, yelling, going out to eat, saying things like "It's so nice to see you, sorry it couldn't be under better circumstances!" or "Isn't this a nice funeral home?" or "Ellen looks so nice, like she was sleeping." (No, she does not. She looks horrible and sallow and shrunken beneath her massive wig.) I don't know what it is with my family, perhaps some genetic toxic event, but they are all programmed to say the word "nice" every fifteen seconds. Everything is so fucking *nice* that it makes me want to neuter myself with a rusty church key, simply as my gift to humanity, so not to perpetuate this mutant strain of *nice*-niks that is my extended family.

Everyone, of course, is being very *nice* to me. My mother's friends and cousins and neighbors come up to me with their sad, big Keane Kid eyes, offer me their supportive hugs and reassuring back pats and sincere condolences, and though I know that they mean well, they make me uncomfortable. They keep telling me that I'm holding up well. What do they mean by that? Even Tina is being pleasant to me, but then she always is when she's in front of other people. Later, she catches me alone and makes a crack about my classic vintage tweed suit. ("How appropriate for the occasion, Richard. Clothing from a corpse.")

That night, I am so tired I don't even hang up my clothes. I just throw my suit coat on Tom the mannequin in the living room, drape my pants over his outstretched arm, ready for tomorrow, then I head for bed.

I do not feel very *nice*.

My Dream of Hands

This night, I have very specific dreams. My mother appears in all the ones I can remember. There are no dream plots—no chases, no flying over water, no conversations even—it's more of a series of mini-dreams, a montage of my mother doing weird stuff, like the kind that appears at the end of a movie as one of the characters reminisces. Things like this: her moistening a handkerchief at her lips and wiping something from my cheek; lighting a cigarette; brushing crumbs off the kitchen table; drinking a cup of coffee; slapping me across the mouth; holding my hand on the way to school; mixing a drink; filing her nails to points; shredding a tissue; wiping widow's tears; straightening out my father's tie; showing my sister how to apply foundation; reading a book; covering her face, palms sunk over migraine eyes; pinning a diaper; dying, hands withered and useless, tops punctured purple, veins collapsed, telling me to wash my hands. That's when I realize something. In the dreams, her face and body are slightly darker, but her hands are highlighted, as if they are the only part of the photograph that has not been underexposed.

When I twitch myself awake at three-thirty, I am certain that I have just felt my mother's hands straightening my hair. I touch my head, looking and looking for the area where I know my hair is smooth, where I know my mother has just smoothed it out the way she did when I was little. I suddenly remember something she told me when she was in the hospital, a rare moment when she wasn't hounding me. "I would go into your room before I went to bed, just to check on you," she said. "You would be sleeping and I would push your hair back and give you the lightest kiss on the forehead and sometimes the corners of your mouth would raise just a bit and you would smile in your sleep. It was so cute. Your father never believed that you did this. When I'd try to show him, you'd never do it, you little brat."

I can't seem to stop touching my hair. But all I feel with my hands is my own sweaty snarls, twisted and protruding painfully from my head. Finally, I give up and go back to sleep.

Tina Puts the Fun in Funeral

My mother's memorial service: no need to really get into it. All the standard things occur. The pastor, or whatever the hell he is over at Linda's church, makes some vague generic comments about my mother, what a wonderful person she was, how much she loved her children, her godliness, the personal fortitude she showed in facing her disease. Then he calls her Elaine instead of Ellen. The usual crapola.

Aunt Tina, who has been fairly reserved up till now, tucked between Linda and me, has saved all her grief for right in the middle of the service, where it will make the most impact, show the maximum number of people how loving a sister she was. I notice that although there is lots of uncontrollable wailing and sobbing, there are no tears. After all, that sort of thing could ruin one's makeup.

After the cemetery, everyone heads to Linda's house, where there are more supportive hugs and reassuring back pats and sincere condolences, more comments on how *nice* the service was, and more food. Yep, everyone ties on the old feed bag. They eat all the stuff Linda's neighbors have brought, plus the things that my mother's other relatives and friends have brought—corned beef, baked beans, ham, potato salad, vegetable trays, and Jell-O salads. Lots of Jell-O salads—orange Jell-O with suspended bananas, green Jell-O mixed with Cool Whip and mini-marshmallows, red Jell-O with pineapple and nuts, and a bunch of others. A whole herd of cattle must have been melted down just for the Jell-O for my mother's memorial dinner.

It's like a bacchanalian feast. All that is needed is for everyone to go out to the deck to vomit, then return to gorge themselves again. There is some subdued behavior, but before long it's a big shindig, lots of laughing, especially after they break out the hooch. I don't know how I expect everyone to act after my mother dies, but boozing it up and eating themselves sick isn't exactly it. Yet it was the same thing after my father died: *He's in the ground. Let's chow!*

The Day After

What can I say? I resume my life.

I sleep in until about ten-thirty, which is unusual for me. It's a little late to go junking, but I definitely want to open up the store. I feel surprisingly okay. I'm looking forward to work. I shave, shower, get dressed, grab a Pop-Tart, and head out the door to work.

At work, nothing happens. No one comes in. I just sit there.

Finally, at about three o'clock, this guy walks in, not the kind of guy I usually get in here, with an expensive-looking overcoat and a tie.

"How much is that old Emerson radio up there?" he says, pointing to one of the ancient radios that line the ceiling of my shop.

"Those aren't for sale," I say. "None of the radios are for sale." This is not for any big reason, it's just because radios from the Fifties and Sixties are something I still like to collect. It's not like they're worth that much. We're not talking old Catalin radios. These just look kind of neat up there.

He looks disappointed, then he says, "I'll give you a hundred for it."

My heart rises, then I remember its history. Half the tubes are missing, the others toasted. I just like looking at the things, I'm not really much for fixing them up. "It's really not in working condition," I say.

"I don't care. I just want it. One twenty-five?"

The guy's practically pleading with me. Now maybe I'm a dope who doesn't know his radios (which I am), but I start to think I am looking at someone who just really wants this object. I can see it in him. Serious collectors always maintain their distance, like they couldn't care less if you sell them something. They always need to have the upper hand. That's why I always do my best to bust their chops when they come in here.

"Okay," I say to the guy. "But it doesn't work. Just so you know that."

He's smiling like a maniac by this time. "It's okay, really."

This is a rare occurrence. No one ever comes in here and offers me a lot of money for anything. There are plenty of weeks when I don't make one hundred and twenty-five dollars. Despite the cash, it makes me feel good to see someone really want something just for the beauty of it.

"Do you collect old radios?" I say, after I box up the Emerson and collect the cash. I'm hoping that he doesn't tell me that I just sold him a rare prototype worth thousands.

"No. My mom and dad had one just like it when I was a kid. I've never seen another one like it until today."

This makes me even gladder that I sold it to him. This is something I have experienced myself, wanting something because it reminded me of my childhood. This is a strange thing about people. We own something as children, then as adults we are willing to buy it again for about a hundred times the original cost. We think we're buying back our youth or our innocence or something like that, but what we're really buying back is our ignorance. We want to remember a time when we didn't know so much.

The Power of Junk

There's a guy in California who runs a junk museum. That's not what he calls it, but that's what it is. The purpose of the museum is to have people see things that spark intense memories of their lives. I experience this sort of thing often in my travels. I see it at my store. Here's what happens: You're strolling around, taking in everything, then suddenly—pow!—you see a juice glass just like the one you had when you were six years old. There is no doubt. You know just as you know your name that it is just like your favorite juice glass.

It is a slap in the cerebrum. This object that was so important to you at one time of your life had so completely disappeared from conscious thought, been so thoroughly buried, you hadn't even thought about it in decades. Memories, feelings, ideas, fears from that time return to you. And it doesn't have to be a juice glass, it can be anything—a radio, a Strawberry Shortcake lunch box, an old Ferrante & Teicher LP, spaceship bedroom curtains, a Harlequin gravy boat, anything.

These epiphanies, these occasions of shattering remembrance, are the junk moments of our lives, memory detritus that we have scattered and stashed in the musty, bent-corner cardboard folds of our brains, wrapped in psychic newspaper, Magic Markered with the appropriate memory centers, then left to molder. It's quite a mess there in our attics. Things get chipped, they fade and shrink, crumble and yellow. But these things that seem insignificant are what compose our personal histories. That's why we need junk stores. As time passes, we realize those things we ignored have become valuable. We must revisit them, give them life again. That's what my store is about.

I remember something from college, Wordsworth or one of those old buggers, talking about "spots of time," moments of experience when something ordinary becomes significant. That's what junk is for me, finding these little spots of time, only they're things that you can hold in your hand, things that you can find everywhere. You just need to know where to look.

A Chat with Sis

Early Saturday morning, four days after the funeral, Linda and I meet over at our parents' house. We are at the kitchen table. I am having tea, she a mug of instant Maxim.

"What makes you think that you should get to go through the whole house by yourself?" says Linda to me. "Are you some sort of expert just because of your little shop? More than the people who do the estate sales?"

"No," I say. "But I do know what's probably worth something and what isn't. And maybe some places where things can get a good home. And the people who run those sales are only in it for a quick buck themselves."

"Richard dear," Linda says, in her mock-sincere voice, touching my hand, not in a warm way, but a way calculated to make me feel some sibling obligation, "I don't really care if things get a good home. I would just like to be done with all this. I'd like to get rid of this stuff, sell the house and get on with my life."

We are trying hard to get along. I know she's trying, because she did not bring Stewart along, who does not care about anything except the dough. He would happily try to intimidate me. And as much as I hate to admit it, she does have a point. I could probably spend a year going through every room, categorizing everything, sorting it, etc.

"I know what you're saying," I say. "But I would like to be able to take a first look at the stuff. Besides, I can probably end up getting a lot more money for the things that are really valuable."

My sister looks at me and exhales, no patience. But I can tell that I have struck a nerve. All you have to do is say "more money" to my lovely sister and she will listen to what you have to say.

"Oh God. I'll give you a couple of weeks, but that's it. And you have to tell me everything that you take out, and what you do with it. You promise?"

I smile at Linda. "Scout's honor."

"You were never a Scout, Richard. You went to one meeting and got beat up. Besides, you didn't like the uniforms, remember?"

My sister can be tough when she wants to be.

One Mannequin's Story

This done, I clear out quickly. I decide to stop at Fred's Unique, a small shop not too far from my parents' house. It's a good cheap place, like my store, though Fred doesn't really specialize in the same merchandise that I do. Fred's junk is, well, of a different caliber. His is sweeter, more appealing to elderly ladies and antique lovers, than mine. Sometimes Fred lays his groovier junk, the kind he can't sell, on me.

Fred used to live near me and we would run into each other at estate sales. We even go on the occasional junking expedition together. Once, we found ourselves in a small town north of Flint, where the local department store was going out of business. (This is something a junker develops after a while—the intuition, the ability to know when there's something there for you. I can't explain, it just happens.) Fred and I walked through this big old department store and you could just feel the history, all the time that had passed, all the life that had occurred there. I could tell there were a lot of people walking around, having junk moments. I had never been to this place before in my life and it felt familiar to me. It reminded me of the old Hudson's store in downtown Detroit before it closed years ago.

I forgot all that when I spotted a very cool old mannequin for fifteen dollars. I had always wanted one and here it was, cheap. Don't ask me why, but mannequins are something junkers like. I grabbed the upper torso, Fred grabbed the lower, and we headed off to find the cashier.

As we were stuffing the mannequin into the truck, trying to figure out whether he should sit up with us or just lie in the back, a woman walked up and started watching us. After we got the mannequin set up (backseat, sitting, seat belt fastened), I asked the woman if there was anything wrong. "No," she said. "I just came down to say goodbye to Tom."

The woman told us that she'd been dressing this mannequin for the last nineteen years and had grown quite attached. She was still standing there when we started to drive off, so I had Fred lift the mannequin's arm up to the window to wave goodbye. It seemed to help. Then she ran up to the window and yelled, "I forgot to tell you. He's a sixteen-and-a-half neck and he wears a size-ten shoe!" That's basically how Tom came to be my mannequin.

As I enter Fred's store, the bells strung to the top of the door jangle against the glass. He appears from behind a thin cotton curtain of a faded orange-and-yellow Sixties design. He's in his mid-fifties with Mondrian glasses and a long white goatee with a rubber band around the end of it.

"Richard," he says to me, smiling. "How goes it, Junker?" We shake hands warmly. We are both part of the junk community.

"Fred, my man."

"Cup of tea? Water just boiled."

"Just a quick one," I say. He leaves for about a minute and returns with an old mug that has a picture of a factory on the side and says "KenCo Spline Gage" beneath it. I accept the cup. It is Earl Grey, one of my faves. "So you got anything for me today?"

"Not much," he says, going into the back again, carrying out a box of items. He places them on his counter one by one. "Standard black dial telephone—Fifties is my guess—beat-up Easy-Bake Oven, two Shawnee planters, ViewMaster with slides from the 1964 World's Fair, some old Donald Goines paperbacks, and a couple pairs of genuine 1960s Floyd the Barber sunglasses that I haven't been able to unload to save my life." When Fred says "genuine," he stretches it out and says "gen-u-wine." This kind of thing cracks me up about Fred. He is a peach, that Fred, a good egg.

I look through the stuff, set aside the toy oven. "Don't you want to get this to some toy geeks?" I say.

"Too much trouble. Besides, they want everything in perfect condition."

"Okay. I'll take it all. Hey," I say, hefting copies of *Eldorado Red* and *Daddy Cool*. "How did Goines pop up here in the vanilla suburbs?"

"I don't know, man," says Fred. "Probably some gangsta-rap-obsessed suburban mall rat. Not like they're worth anything. You can just have 'em."

"Thanks. How much for the other?"

Fred gives me the squint eye. "Weather's been warm. Those glasses will sell like crazy over there in hipster central."

"That's not my turf, you know that."

"Close enough. You're looking flush. I sense you're good for about twenty today for the whole lot."

"Ouch. How about ten?"

"You're killing me, Junk. Fifteen."

"Done."

I don't usually like buying stuff this way. It goes against everything I stand for, but Fred always has junk I can sell. And I need junk that will sell.

Everyone Loves Soup!

That day at the store, it is totally dead. At least I have something to do: Before Linda got to Mom's house, I filled a grocery bag with some old cookbooks. I don't know why I took them, force of junking habit most likely, but I just saw them there and needed to take them. I didn't mention it to Linda because she would have made a big fuss. Of course, this means I had broken my oath to Linda before I even made it. Frankly, this doesn't really matter, because I intend on taking anything I want. That sounds terrible, but really isn't, because I guarantee that anything I want will be nothing that Linda wants.

In the middle of the afternoon, out of boredom, I start to browse through the cookbooks. They are quite amusing. I notice that a lot of the ones from the Fifties and Sixties, the pamphlets, were put out by appliance manufacturers, or special-interest groups like the National Sauerkraut Council or the League for Gland Meats. Just from the titles, you can learn about how the world worked back then: *12 Pies Husbands Like Best, Meats for Men, Good Food for Hungry Husbands*. They are splashed inside and out with supersaturated, overprocessed four-color photography of supersaturated, overprocessed foods. The dishes were supposed to look appetizing, but have the exact opposite effect—cakes frosted with toxic waste, lava-coated meatballs, hide-scarred hams from red Martian hogs. In almost all the books there are funny, sketchy line drawings of animated foodstuffs: vegetables with legs, happy fish in the frying pan, smiling cows licking their lips over hamburgers. *Eat me, I'm delicious!*

I look through a book by Campbell's called *Cooking with Soup*, filled with "608 skillet dishes, casseroles, stews, sauces, gravies, dips, soupmates, and garnishes." Every recipe has some sort of canned soup in it, usually cream of mushroom soup. This was a staple in my mother's kitchen all through my childhood. Next to a recipe for Zesty Green Bean Casserole, I see a little notation in my mother's hand in the margin, "Add 2 tsps of butter." Then below that, "Richard's favorite."

This really gets to me. I mean, it really gets to me. I suppose this is a good example of how some small piece of junk can awaken waves of emotion in a person, or in my case, simply clutch a guy by the thorax. Anyway, I start bawling, right there behind the counter of my store. All the crying I couldn't do at the hospital, at the funeral, late at night when I meant to get to it, or anywhere else seems to pour out of me right now. I can't stop. The tears just keep coming and coming. Before long, I can't even breathe. I can't even explain why this hurts so much, it's just that it's such a sad sweet little gesture, this addition of two table-spoons of saturated fat. It is something that almost makes me feel sorry for my mother, that I was so important to her that she would not only mark my favorite dish in her cookbook, but modify it to make it even more special for me. It makes me long for the housewifely, maternal person she was back then, the person I can no longer remember. I can't even remember the person I was. I haven't liked Green Bean Casserole for decades.

I am blubbering and blubbering, to the point where my nose is starting to run on the counter, on this stupid Campbell's Soup cookbook, when, of course, the bell on my door clatters, and after three straight hours of being completely by myself, a customer walks in, some loopy hipster woman. Then I realize it's the dark-eyed one from last week looking for dog tchotchkes. Great. I don't even care. By this time, I am practically in convulsions, so there's nothing to do but move behind the curtain into my back room and finish my jag there. I don't care if she steals anything.

After a few minutes of silently weeping next to the bench where I keep my hot plate and electric kettle, I finally start to calm down. I hear the bell ring again. She's gone. I'm glad because there's too many boxes of junk back there and nowhere to sit down. Besides, I need tissues. Four of them to be exact, and I've got a box next to the cash register.

When I come back out, the hipster woman is still there. I must look surprised, because she looks up at me and smiles. "Hi. That was just someone who looked in the store and then just left," she says.

I grab a tissue, blow my nose two good times, then wipe my eyes. "I get a lot of that," I croak. "People aren't always sure what kind of store this is, then as soon as they see, they just split."

She looks at me and smiles again, a smile that says she is not the least bit embarrassed for me, or even for herself.

"Feel better?" she says.

"I feel like I can't breathe," I say, sounding like I have a dishcloth stuffed in my esophagus. I blow my nose again, or rather, I honk it. "Is there something I can help you with?"

"I always feel better after a good crying fit. I do it just about every day. A good ten-minute cry clears out the whole head."

I blow my nose again, wishing she would leave.

"Can I ask why you were crying?"

I frown at her. But if I was really annoyed, I wouldn't have done anything. "It's too stupid to talk about."

"That's okay." She bites at her thumbnail.

"My mother just died," I say, grabbing another tissue.

"I'd hardly call that stupid."

"That's not the stupid part. I was just looking at her recipe for Zesty Green Bean and Cream of Mushroom Casserole when suddenly the levee broke."

"Yeah, well. You never know what's going to do it."

I'm starting to feel pretty self-conscious by this time. This woman is kind of attractive, in a garage-sale kind of way, which is a good kind of way. She's got on her Seventies leather again, but with a faded "MC 5" T-shirt and big blousey Sixties flowered stovepipes. I want to say something else, preferably something witty and erudite, but I need to blow my nose again. I try, then try again, but my sinuses have reached critical mass. I see blood on the tissue.

"Oh man, my nose is bleeding." I squeeze my nose shut, but within seconds, the tissue is soaked.

"Here," the woman says, handing me another tissue. "You

shouldn't blow so hard." She gives me a good looking-over now, and I immediately turn bright red and lower my head. "Don't do that. You'll just make it worse."

She walks around behind the counter, puts her hands on my temples, and tilts my head back a little, knocking my glasses slightly askew. Her hands are warm and damp. "Stay like that," she says. When she pulls her hands away, I notice they're covered with scratches, her nails bitten to the pink of the quick. I glance up at her, try to smile, while I stuff tissue up my nose. I can't believe this is happening.

"I think it's stopping," I say.

"What's your name, Mr. Junk Man?" she says.

"You can call me that," I say, trying not to gag. "I answer to anything with 'Junk' in it."

"Are you afraid to tell me your name? I've just watched you cry for like ten minutes."

I lower my head. "Richard," I say. "But people do sometimes call me Junker."

"Hm."

My nose has stopped bleeding by now. I still feel blood down the back of my throat. I sneak another look at her. Large brown eyes, thin lips, mouth just a bit crooked.

"How come I've never seen you here before last week?" I say.

"I didn't know it was here."

"You still looking for dog stuff?"

"Nah."

"What's your name?"

"Theresa. Zulinski."

"I'd shake hands with you Theresa, but my hands are covered with blood."

"Yes they are."

"Well, hi."

"Hi."

Just as I am starting to relax a little, she starts to look kind of jumpy. She starts to turn around. "You know, I should probably go."

I try to think of something to keep her here a little longer. "Were you looking for anything in particular, um, Theresa?"

She is at the door. "Well, no. I thought I was. Not actually. I didn't really look. I was more interested in why you were crying back there."

"Stop by again some—"

Gone.

Sorry Seems to Be the Easiest Word

After she leaves, I find myself thinking about this Theresa. It didn't bother her at all that I had been crying. Had I walked into a store and seen some maniac blubbering his guts out, I would have been out the door like a shot. Plus, I would have felt embarrassed about it all day. But she wasn't the least bit rattled.

Another interesting thing about her: She did not apologize about my mother dying. This is something I am already tired of. You tell someone that your mother died, and they apologize. (Admittedly, I have never known what to say when someone tells me that a loved one of theirs has died. I've even apologized a few times myself, but I don't anymore. It is one of the few occasions when I don't apologize.) Hell, I'm still hearing apologies about my father. I have actually participated in this dialogue:

ME: . . . that was about five years ago, when my father died—

OTHER PERSON: Oh, I'm sorry.

ME: You're sorry? Why are you sorry? Did you force him to smoke three packs a day for thirty-five years? Did he collect the coupons from Galaxy Cigarettes to redeem for valuable gifts for you? Did you encourage him to ignore his symptoms for seven months? Did you laugh at him as he wheezed, when he tried to climb two steps? Did you sneak him cigarettes in the hospital? Did you hide his oxygen tank? Did you squeeze the last bloated breath from his lungs? You didn't? Then you have nothing to be sorry about.

I ask you, when do you stop saying "I'm sorry"? Two months? A year? Ten years? Do I have to apologize after someone mentions Lincoln's assassination? That was why I decided to quit altogether. Now I simply cast a concerned look toward the bereaved. I send them a telepathic sympathy card. Saying that you're sorry seems so empty. I should know, because I apologize for everything.

What I am truly sorry about is that I didn't do anything more about this Theresa woman, like ask her where she lived, or where she worked, or if I could give her a call. I'm sorry about that. But like I said, being sorry is no big thing for me. I reside in the state of sorry. My watch is set to Sorry Standard Time. I sit alone and read comic books in a treehouse of sorry. I have had people yell at me for being so sorry. They say that in apologizing so often, it's like I'm apologizing for my very existence. I tell them that they're right. You'll never guess what I do then. I apologize.

I close my mother's cookbook, put them all in a box, then go into the back to make myself a cup of tea.

My Not So Swingin' Bachelorhood

I should explain something here. I have never been married and I really have no need for that sort of thing. Which is handy, because there are not a lot of women in my life. I have never been very good with women. The truth is, they scare the bejeezus out of me. They always have. I can't go prowling around in search of women, the way some men do. If I meet one, it has to be accidental. I have to stumble on her, like I might an interesting lamp at the Goodwill. Even when that happens (which it rarely does), then there's the problem of my personality. Women have told me that I need to open up more, and I would, except I know that once I opened up and they found out that there was nothing there, I'd really be in trouble.

I decided a while ago that I would no longer worry about going out with women. It just became too much work somewhere along the line. (Not the going out, because I wasn't doing any of that, but the worrying about it.) I had a girlfriend once, during my twenties. We were both working at the Salvation Army. She was single, but had a kid. Things went fine for awhile. She didn't mind the junking, the crowdedness of my apartment, or even me. Then she found out that I had been to college and that changed the way she looked at me. Suddenly I became this person with potential. Someone who could be making money, someone who could help her escape a world of food stamps and tornado-magnet trailer parks and depressing, stinky Salvation Army stores. (A world that, to her, I had unrightfully installed myself.) She set about, frankly, trying to snare me into marriage. If I hadn't seen so many of those "tender trap"–type movies from the Fifties where just this sort of thing happens, I might very well have fallen for it.

Okay, it wasn't exactly like that. Let's say it was like a Doris Day movie, only instead of a virgin, Doris is a white-trash alcoholic who is very proficient at blow jobs. Now, it wasn't like I had never had sex before Doris came along. (There had been one other time.) It was just that no one had ever really indulged me sexually before. (I'm not talking anything too bizarre here: basic participation, lack of annoyance, occasional enthusiasm.) Even knowing what was going on, it was hard to resist. (All right, the truth is, I really didn't know what was going on. I was totally snared. I had completely fallen for everything. I didn't figure anything out until much, much later.) If Doris hadn't met a used-car salesman, a man who was actually making money, as opposed to having the potential of making money, I would probably be married now, in some office job with a necktie noose, supporting her and the Spawn of Satan (ex-husband now serving ten-year sentence at Jackson State Penitentiary, four counts, Armed Robbery and Assault), living from shekel to shekel, and probably suicidal. At least I'd be having sex occasionally, but maybe not. Anyway, that's how stupid I was.

In the end, the whole thing just took up too much time that I could have spent doing something more important, like junking. I like my life, I am content enough being alone, and I am completely self-sufficient. As always, junk provides for those who believe. I have a compelling collection of vintage *Argosys*, *Nuggets*, *Adams*, and *Stags*. No matter how I end up, those stanchion-breasted blonde and raven beauties will always love me—the Betty Pages, the June Wilkinsons, the Lilly Christines, the Mamie Van Dorens. I have no regrets.

What Junk Has Taught Me

Junk has been my friend, my teacher, my mentor. It has taught me what is not required. It taught me to enjoy things, but not need them. That buying new leads only to the three D's: debt, despair, and death. It has taught me that to find new use for an object discarded is an act of glistening purity. I have learned that a camera case makes a damn fine purse or that forty copies of *Herb Alpert & the Tijuana Brass's Whipped Cream and Other Delights* may be used to cover a wall of a bedroom.

Junk has taught me to find my own nature. Everyone in this country seems to want to do the same things—make money, have sex, get drunk, watch television, buy stuff. You can see this in the junk—everybody trying to live the same life, buying the same things, displaying the same sad selves to the world. Junk has taught me that we do the same things over and over, decade after decade, using basically the same equipment, with minor differences and improvements. Junk has taught me that at some point in time, people sincerely wanted to own all the stuff that I find so amusing. They coveted and saved for that pink granite bowling ball, that quadraphonic stereo with the eight-track, that wringer washer—they sacrificed other things to get these things. Now it's all junk. Of course, the other things they sacrificed would be junk by now too, so it probably evens out in the end. But most people are still happily running the junk gauntlet—saving and sacrificing for stuff, then throwing that stuff out and saving and sacrificing for more stuff.

Don't get me wrong. I love material things. I just don't understand why things have to cost so much, why people give up so much of their time on earth earning money for things that are new, when once they own them they won't be new anyway. I am a prisoner of my own conventional materialistic nature, but junk has taught me to do what I can to counteract it, at least a little. Junk has taught me that all will come to junk eventually, and much sooner than you think.

Dinner at Mom and Dad's

It is cool outside, Monday night, the first night I go to my parents' house. There is a sudden bizarro Michigan dip in the temperature. Even though we're in the middle of June, it's fifty-five degrees outside. After shivering in my truck all the way there (broken heater, cut-off work pants, TV repairman shirt), I hustle into my parents' house. As I close the door behind me, I notice that across the street, in this tidy Fifties middle-class subdivision where my parents lived their final years on earth, one of the neighbors opens her front door to look at me, in that way people look at you in the 'burbs, *just to let you know I'm watching*. These jittery white folks are not used to seeing me or my truck in their neighborhood. You'd think they'd remember that I was Ellen's son, but I haven't been over here all that much since Dad died.

Inside my parents' house, it is incredibly quiet. It sounds like the house of dead people. Every sound I make as I walk in seems to be absorbed by the silence: door opening, keys on table, screech of rubber heel on linoleum. When I walk into the living room, I can tell that Linda has already been here. Two of the televisions are missing, along with the microwave oven, as well as a couple of floor lamps. Even though we said that things would be divided evenly, I knew it would happen like this. Linda will take all the "valuable" things and I will take the other. I feel better, since it was not me who broke the promise (except for those cookbooks, which don't really count, I say).

I did not get a chance to eat, since I came here right from the store, so my first task is to have some dinner. My mother has cupboards full of canned goods, some of them way too old to consume. I make sure to check all the dates on all cans. I'm in luck. I find a Dinty Moore Beef Stew, as well as Franco American Ravioli and Spartan Creamed Corn. I heat it all up in three different pans, then dump it all on the same plate. It all seeps together, creating a sort of TV dinner effect. But it tastes good. I haven't eaten this much food in weeks. I know Linda won't touch this stuff, so it's all mine to take home.

After dinner, I don't know where to start. So much will just have to be discarded or given away. Even I know this. That's part of respecting junk. You have to be selective or you'll wind up drowning in it. I learned that after a year at the Salvation Army. My apartment was so full I could barely move. So tonight, I will take it easy. First, I go to the hi-fi to put on a record. I choose an old Gene Krupa album from my father's collection. Then I stroll through the house (six-room bungalow, finished attic), walking in rhythm to Krupa's relentless beat, just to see what catches my eye. A good method if you're fully versed in junking technique. Here are a few of the things I spy:

—A well-preserved Danish Modern living room and dining room set. (Not surprising that it's well-preserved, considering that my mother never let any of us into the living room. Even now, walking through the living room makes me feel naughty.)

—A pair of great old Sixties lamps, not hideously ugly with sparkles and textures and pointy lights sticking out of the side, the way I like my lamps, but very tasteful, brown-and-white, notched and pear-shaped, like the inverted heads of figures in a de Chirico painting.

—Plaid couch and chair. Worthless. To replace the sleek Sixties blue-green couch that was kept in pristine condition for decades, then handed over to Linda after her first marriage, and was worn, abused, and discarded within two years, as soon as they could afford something "better."

—Toastmaster two-slice toaster. A wedding present to my parents in the Fifties. Still working and worth plenty to someone who appreciates quality workmanship and timeless design. That leaves Linda out.

—Two red-and-black shadow boxes with Fifties oriental figures in them. The figures are strangely occidental, yet exaggeratedly Japanese, in the same way that pickaninny and other Thirties mammyabilia are exaggeratedly African. (I see these items around, but am afraid to carry them in my store for fear of racial unrest.) My mother got me started collecting these oriental figures after I bought a couple of hers at a garage sale she had. (Two for a quarter, a good deal.) I have seen these shadow boxes in her hallway for quite a few years now, and have coveted them.

—A room full of wicker furniture. Actually my old room. My mother, for some reason, feeling the need to eradicate any sign of me after I left home, repainted and filled this space with the dread white wicker. (There is no problem. Linda loves this stuff. For now, though, I will close the door.)

—The Early American furniture of the "family room." Despite the fabric covered with parchment-type drawings of patriots and the Bill of Rights, despite the knobby lathed maple legs, this stuff will never seem funny or interesting or ironic to me. Perhaps to some kids born on the Bicentennial, but not to someone who grew up with it.

My Parents' Bedroom

Somehow I am not quite ready to go in there. But I head upstairs anyway. I have not been in my parents' bedroom in many years. Yet it's not all that different than it was ten years ago, just grubbier. Still the same Fifties limed-oak bedroom set that they've had for as long as I can remember. The same Seventies beige shag on the floor, now matted and discolored, gone nappy by years of neglect, the way only old people can neglect. I can almost feel the oil and dead skin under my feet, through my Felony Fliers.

Boomp, boomp, goes Gene K., in fine jungle rhythm. *Boomp de boomp de boomp.* Up here the air is thick and acrid: my mother's personal potpourri of ointment and disappointment. After my father died was when everyone said she changed, but the truth is that she had stopped liking everything, including herself, long before that. As I grew up, I watched her discontent bud and blossom with every dead parent and financial disappointment (courtesy of my father). She hated getting older and took it out on the times. It didn't really matter what was going on in the world, she didn't like it one bit. "Back in my day," she would say, "people were much better groomed and a lot less likely to shoot you." In my early twenties, she grew bitter and there was nothing my father or I could do about it.

After I moved out, it was strange when I came to visit—just her and me at that kitchen table, straining to make conversation. My father would sit a few feet away, in his Early American La-Z-Boy, in the family room. I think he was happy for the brief respite from my mother's wrath. He'd just sit there, reading the newspaper. You'd think he wasn't paying attention, but every once in a while, he would chime in with some wry comment that made you realize he'd been listening to every word. My father thought it was interesting that I loved junk. He felt I was onto something. "You like the past, Richard," he'd say to me. "You like to hold it in your hand. I think you may need to do something with that."

After he was gone, my mother and I seriously started to not get along. He had been the buffer. She became perpetually annoyed with my choice of profession, or lack of it. She would ask me where I got this *thing* about looking through other people's garbage. I would tell her time and again that there was a big difference between garbage and junk, but she never seemed to listen. Without realizing it, I began to give up on her. Before long, she got worse, not just settling for her own misery, but becoming a collector of other people's unhappiness as well. When something bad happened to someone in the family, she would compete with my Aunt Tina to get closest to that person, get the most details, feel that person's pain, experience their regret.

Two Styrofoam wig heads observe me from the dresser. One has a full head of peppery curls, the other is bald, having held the seemingly outsized wig with which we buried my mother. Both heads are battered and worn dark from being handled and probably yelled at, knowing my mother. The nose of the bald one is broken off.

On my mother's side of the bed, there is something hanging on the wall that I have never really looked at before: a small wicker shelf, sprayed white, with strange old perfume bottles on it. They all have exotic names: Evening in Paris, Aphrodisia, Jungle Gardenia, Tabu. Their shapes are very cool and it gives me new ideas about things to sell in the shop. These are obviously presents from Dad, though I can't remember Mom ever wearing anything more mysterious than what was available from Avon. I pick up the bottle of Evening in Paris and turn it to the side. Through the cobalt glass, I can see that there's a little of the perfume left. Suddenly I want to smell it, this gift from my father to my mother. But when I try to open the bottle, the top will not come free. I check the other bottles. They all seem to contain a few drops of perfume. All of them are glued shut.

On the other side of the room is my father's dresser. I walk over to it. After he died, my mother left all his things sitting on it. They are still there. I can't decide if this is eerie or touching. If it were me, I would keep expecting the dead person to come home. There are only a few items on the dresser: brushed metal lamp with fiberglass shade, stained yellow with cigarette smoke; small ceramic golfer head with detachable hat (to stash manly items); a leather-covered jewelry box with a grimy gold pawn stenciled on the top. The box is what I am drawn to. I was fascinated by it as a child. In our house, there was not much territory that was solely my father's—the garage (natch), a small workbench downstairs, and this box. It seemed to contain all the secrets involved in being a man, stuff I still haven't figured out. I open the box. Inside are all the items I remember: cufflinks, collar stays, tie tacks, lucky coins, etc. What freaks me are the lapel pins from the corporation where my father worked—logo pins that marked ten, fifteen, twenty, twenty-five years of employment.

This is a secret I can do without. My father's whole life is here in this box.

Boommp, boommp, boommp. I walk around my parents' bed. The top drawer of the nightstand on my mother's side is partially open. In that drawer there are the expected items: aspirin, Tylenol, Vicks VapoRub, Myoflex, extra pair of dime-store reading glasses ("These are fine. I don't need to go to an optometrist"), an old bottle of Valium, Danielle Steel book. When I try to open the bottom drawer, I find that it's really stuck. I shake and jiggle, try to ease the drawer back and then out, but no luck. Finally, I take all the items off the top of the night stand (how could I have missed it? My mother's perfect green Bakelite clock!) and slide the upper drawer completely out, then tip the nightstand forward and put my hand inside. In the back, I can feel a smooth hard drop of something that has cemented it shut. I press my fingers behind it and pull. The bottom drawer flies out and the corner hits me in the groin. Besides the pain, the screech I let out is so loud in the deserted house that it scares me.

At the back of the drawer, stuck to the inside of the nightstand, is an amber globule, a half-melted cough drop with a few slivers of wood attached. It has been a long time since this drawer has been opened. Inside, there are some old checks and paperwork, but beneath them what catches my eye is the package of ancient Trojans and the copy of *Everything You Ever Wanted to Know About Sex* but were afraid to ask.*

I start to understand. This is the Sex Drawer. I have run into these creatures before. As a kid, with my friends, rummaging around in their parents' bedrooms; also in estate sales, snooping where I shouldn't. I dig a little deeper in the drawer. Farther down, along the side, I find a gold-colored coin of some unknown alloy. Stamped on it is the image of a nude woman holding a cock-tail glass. One side is front view ("Heads"), the other side is the same pose, only rear view ("Tails"). I know where it's from.

A Sexy Junk Moment

I am eight years old, on a road trip with my parents and Linda in my father's green Pontiac Bonneville. We are headed out west to visit some relatives. Our second day on the road, we stop for gas at some place along Route 66 (Dad had taken this way years before and still liked it, crumbling road and all). After we fill up the car, my father and I head for the men's room.

I am through before my father. As I wash my hands, I see a chrome-plated machine mounted high up on the wall. There is a bleary picture of a topless woman on it, with the words "Sexy Souvenir" beneath it. Being eight years old, I am, of course, fascinated by it. I manage to tear my eyes from it just before my father walks out of the stall. I can tell that he notices the machine himself. He tells me to meet him out in the car. Reluctantly, I head outside.

On the road, Linda is asleep and I am thinking about the picture, feeling that weird sense of fascination and fear that only kids can feel, when my father leans over and says something to my mother. He glances in the rearview mirror, so I pick up a comic book and act as though I am reading. Then I see him slip something from his shirt pocket. Even from the backseat, peeking over a comic book, I can tell that it is a coin. I know that it's the Sexy Souvenir. When my father passes it to my mother, it catches the sun and a glint of gold flashes across the ceiling of the car, a twine of light connecting them. My father has a sly sort of grin on his face that I've never seen before. My mother's expression as she looks at the coin is almost embarrassment, perhaps mock embarrassment. After a moment, I watch her laugh and whisper something to my father while she squeezes his arm. He murmurs something back to her. I wish so much that I could hear. It is one of the last times I see them act affectionate toward each other.

A year or two later, I saw the coin again, while nosing around in my father's jewelry box. After that, I snuck in every day to look at the woman on the coin, until my mother caught me a week later. (That was probably when it wound up in the Sex Drawer.) I wanted to ask her what she had said to my father that day in the car, but knew I couldn't. Whatever it was, I could never imagine anyone talking to me like that.

I shouldn't be here now, looking through my parents' things. But there's nothing I can do about it. From the living room, I hear the Gene Krupa LP skipping, repeating the same passage of "How High the Moon" over and over. (Ah, vinyl.) I'm tired and ready to go, though it's only been an hour or so since I arrived. The whole idea of the Sex Drawer upsets me in some inexplicable way, yet I dump everything, including some old books and envelopes, in a box for further exploration at home. Then I put the box next to the front door with all the other stuff I'm taking. I shut off the hi-fi, turn out all the lights, pack up my truck, and go home.

Moose Lodge Malaise

The next morning, I'm exhausted. All night long, I kept waking up after dreaming about the old house. Finally, at around seven-thirty, I give up, drag my sorry ass out of bed, and whomp up a pot of Morning Thunder. I drink half with lots of sugar, pour the rest into my red plaid thermos. I check the newspapers. It is Tuesday, nothing much in the way of estate sales going on, but luckily there is the weekly flea market over at the Moose Lodge. I say luckily, because by now I am so juked on atomic tea that I truly need something to do.

When I get there, it's awful. Mostly *Star Wars* crap, trading cards, comic books, etc. You'd think they would have something decent at least. Some old dishes or ashtrays or something. On the way out of the place at nine-fifteen, I spot a few garage sale signs tied in with the flea market. I am saved. I pick up a few old post-cards and a set of Sixties coasters (with antique cars on them).

At work, I stumble through the afternoon, already dreading that I have to go back to the house again tonight and probably every night for the next two weeks. It is a day of no sales and stupid questions. ("Don't you have anything *new* at this place?" "Do you want your windows squeegeed?" "Do you sell monkey stuff? It doesn't matter what, just as long as it's a monkey or has a monkey on it.") It is a lunatic day. I check the calendar to see if there is a full moon tonight.

The Midwestern Heart of Darkness

When I show up at the house, I find that Linda has cleaned out everything from my mother's china cabinet. This annoys me. Not that I wanted any of that stuff, but still. It's time to be more practical. It's horrible that it has come to this so soon, but I have to start plundering my parents' house. I feel like crap about it, but I guess this has to happen, because it won't be long before Linda runs out of "valuables" and starts zeroing in on the junk. Then there will be problems.

I decide that my best plan of attack is to plunge headlong into the maelstrom. The basement. This is where my mother kept practically everything she ever owned. I expect to find untold treasures here. My mother, for quite some time, even before I became an official junk store owner, barred me from coming down here, knowing what would happen if I did. I would see all sorts of things that I would want. And she was not ready to give them up. I think she decided, You're not picking the bones of this old corpse yet.

"You just stay out of there, young man," she would say to me, when I would beg her to just let me go downstairs.

Since she died, I haven't had much desire to do it. It was different when she was alive, it was all still her stuff, stuff that she could have easily given to me to keep or to sell, no strings. Now, it's all my dead mother's stuff. Interesting how that works. It's not so bad when it's someone else's dead mother.

I open the door, turn on the light at the top of the stairs. The air is slightly dank, the walk down the steps eerily familiar—the feel of the banister against my hand, the creaks of the floorboards. At the bottom of the stairs is my parents' knotty pine basement. I see the studio chairs and lowboy coffee table from my parents' first apartment, the mosaics that used to hang upstairs in the living room. This place is amazing—Fifties paneling, Sixties furniture, Seventies shag carpeting. The whole room was a time warp by the time I was seven years old. I loved hanging out down here.

I want to examine everything, sit in those chairs, look at the magazines, but I have a job to do. I think that the place to start is in the storage room, the one my mother has had locked up for the past eight years or so. I walk through the bamboo curtain that separates the knotty pine side of the basement from the unfinished side, raise my hand to a string that connects to a light. The bulb snaps on, my parents' furnace looms in front of me, mottled rusty tentacles clutching the unvarnished floor above. As a kid, this furnace gave me the heebie-jeebies. The *whoosh* of its hot breath would wake me in the middle of the night, remind me of the presence of something awful, keep me up with an erratic scat song of pings and pocks. Even when I got to be ten, eleven years old, it bothered me to walk past that furnace. Tonight, I still feel some of the old chill. I hasten my step, not acknowledging it, toward the storage room, which is simply a big walk-in closet my father built from cheap paneling and two-by-fours he got on sale.

I undo the wooden catch and open the door. It feels as though I am entering the tomb of Tutankhamen. I pull yet another string over my head. A hundred-watt bulb splashes harsh light on a bright jumble of middle-class miscellanea. The shelves are lined with fantastic objects: a ranch-style dollhouse leaning on its side; a red plastic kitchen clock; a chrome coffeepot; a lime-green cocktail tray painted with caricatures and drink recipes. I start opening boxes: more of my mother's oriental figurines; Fifties gold-spattered hubcap-sized ashtray; derringer table lighter; portable pink hair dryer; "Mystery Date" game; yellow enameled cowboy tin plates and cups from camping; kids' books (*Go Dog Go*); my father's Polaroid Land camera; every purse my mother has ever owned since the Fifties; my eight-track player shaped like a detonator that I thought was long lost; Command records from the Sixties (my father's hi-fi kick); plus many boxes taped up and presumably filled with more of the same.

I am woozy from all this great junk. I can't believe my good fortune. My junker's instincts tell me that I have hit the mother lode and need to act rapidly. This is probably where all of the good stuff is. I trot upstairs to open up the side door, then pull the truck up. Without even bothering to see what's inside of them, I haul box after box up from the storage room. When the truck is full, I head back downstairs. There are still a few things inside, but they will keep. I close the door, set the catch, try to make it look like no one's been there.

I Discover Something About My Father

It's ten o'clock when I get home, ten-thirty by the time I get all the boxes down into my basement. It's a tight fit down there, what with all the other junk, but I manage to create a pathway so I can get to everything. The problem is, I have nowhere else to put this stuff. My store only has so much storage, so I have to keep a lot of merchandise here or in my garage. I will have to keep up on my sorting.

I know I should go to bed so I can get up early tomorrow, but I start to get excited again about what's in the boxes. I tell myself that I can open one, but that's it. I sit down on the rug, then pick out the blandest unmarked box, thinking there might be something really cool inside. When I open it, there are no treasures, just a leather shoulder bag and three or four bright yellow boxes labeled "Kodak Photographic Paper." I begin to regret my decision about blindly loading up my car with boxes. But the bag is kind of nice, a smooth brown leather, not unlike some of the old briefcases I pick up once in a while at estate sales.

I pull the case from the box—it has a real heft to it. I unsnap the clasp and inside, encased in crumbling foam rubber, are two cameras, a beautiful old Leica and a large boxy one called a Rolleiflex. There is an assortment of lenses too. I turn the bag around and stamped in gold on the front is my father's name: Terrence Stalling. This is news to me. My father took snapshots all through my childhood, but they were just that—snapshots. Mostly with his Polaroid and later with cheap popular cameras like Swingers and Instamatics. But a Leica?

I open the yellow boxes. They are filled not with photographic paper, but with photographs—8x10 black-and-whites. Judging from the cars and the signs on the buildings and the clothes on the people, they appear to be mostly from the Fifties and Sixties. They are professional-looking, but not slick at all—moody, dark-edged images of regular people performing menial tasks. Some of the photos remind me of Walker Evans's Farm Security Administration work that I saw in college. A few others, of Robert Frank's pictures from *The Americans*. Then there are more that don't remind me of anyone else, but are wonderful just the same. Here are some of the photos I see:

—Women seated behind huge machines, sewing seat covers for automobiles.

—A line of six men cutting hair at the Detroit Barber College, a place downtown where my father took me for cheap haircuts.

—Workers emerging from the old salt mines downriver, ghost faces white with salt dust, carrying lunch buckets. One man in particular, looking almost comical with squarish horn-rimmed glasses, Kabuki with astigmatism.

—A bright-faced young black man polishing a hubcap at a car wash called Paul's Wash-O-Mat.

—A photo of my father (dashing in worn trench coat), looking very happy, holding the Leica that is now next to me on the floor, taking a photo of the person taking the photo of him.

—A mechanic, head tilted downward, dark brow creased, cigarette dangling from his lip, hand far up under the fender of a large two-tone car. The patch on his grease-stained work shirt reads "Buick V-8."

This is unfathomable to me. I cannot believe that my father took these photographs. When did he do this? Why did he stop? How come he never told me? I open another one of the Kodak boxes. Beneath some manila folders, there are old spiral calendars, five of them, from a photography studio downtown, a place called Tollman Photographic. "Graduation Portraits Our Specialty," it says beneath the name and the Woodward Avenue address. Each calendar features a photo of a Detroit landmark—the Penobscot Building, the Log Cabin in Palmer Park, the Edison Memorial fountain in Grand Circus Park, the Shrine of the Little Flower, the Mariner's Church. The calendars are from the years 1960, 1962, 1963, 1964, 1965.

My father's angular handwriting can be found all over them, scratched into the tiny boxes of the days. Most of the notations are times when he was apparently scheduled to work at this place. But also, there are many notations like "Out tonight," "10:15 shoot," or "Factory." For 1960 and 1962, there are a lot of appointments and photo shoots, along with notes like "Submitted photos to LOOK," or "Three prints to LIFE," "2 to Sat. Eve. Post."

For each of those notations, there would be another that followed three or four weeks later that said "LOOK—rejected" or "Photos back from LIFE" or "Sat. Eve. Post—No."

In 1963, the notations start to change slightly. There are more personal remarks. Things like "New couch," or "Paint living room." Soon, every Sunday is marked "Look at houses." The submissions and rejections continue, though, with my father branching out into some other magazines, obviously setting his sights a little lower. "Argosy mag—Rej." "LIKE—sent three photos." "Vue mag—4." On December 23, 1963, there is a notation that overlaps into the surrounding squares, that says: "Rejection from LIFE. Almost made it. Photo back covered with initials." I start to feel bad for my father.

Yet, I open 1964, and right there on January 6, it says: "ACCEPTED—LIKE Magazine!!!" I feel a burst of elation for him, as though it just happened moments ago. I want to know more, but there are no more details. My father never mentioned any of this. I'm stuck here in the future without a clue. I look forward into the year to see if anything else is mentioned, but there is nothing else about the acceptance, nor when it will appear. On April 16, 1964, there are two words: "Baby due." A week and a half later, on the 26th, it simply says: "A girl!" Linda's birthday. The notations get scarcer and scarcer for the following months, but by midyear, he's submitting again and going on the occasional shoot.

Right there in my basement, a place he never visited, I feel the presence of my father, but it's a father I don't quite know. It's not the father who worked for American Mutual for twenty-seven years, the father who was never disappointed in me because I was bad at school and bad at sports and bad with girls, or the father who sat in his car on the Belle Isle Bridge coughing silently into a handkerchief. This is a different father, the artist, the photographer, the one who I had no idea existed, who I suppose wasn't really my father, because once he became my father he became all those things I know.

Suddenly I am very tired. There on the floor of my basement, sitting on a rag rug in the shadow of my own massive dark furnace, surrounded by the junk of my parents' life, of my life and of so many other lives, I realize just how tired I am.

Son of Crackpot Theory

The next morning, I drag myself from the basement floor at about seven-forty. Aside from my spine, I feel all right. In a daze, I pack the photographs back in their boxes and head upstairs to boil water for tea. Checking the papers, I spot an intriguing garage sale. It's within a few miles of my house, so after my Pop-Tart, I toss on some threads and head over.

At eight-thirty, they still haven't opened yet, which is fine. I sit in the truck and finish the paper. This is probably one of the best things in the world: to sit in a quiet neighborhood, sun bright and warm in your face, cup of sweet reassuring tea from your thermos, waiting for a sale to open.

When the garage sale finally opens at nine-fifteen, I am the first one in. I really shouldn't even mess with garage sales, I know. They're usually a waste of time and I often don't find anything. Most store owners don't bother with garage sales because they're too hit-or-miss. But I like that about them. You never know what you're going to find. This one, however, is all crap—baby clothes, broken toys, old video games, and bad Eighties rock records—and I am just about to leave when I spot it in the corner of the garage—a beautiful old wooden toy box with cowboys and Indians and wagon trains painted on it. In bold letters across the top it reads "THE FRONTIER." Priceless.

I stroll over toward it. I can tell that it has been out in the garage for quite awhile, because one of the rope handles has rotted away and there are a lot of scratches on the surface, but it is nothing that can't be cleaned up with Liquid Gold and a little junk love. I run my hand over a bucking bronco painted on the lid. I know this: Whoever owned this object was one happy buckaroo. Maybe I haven't mentioned this, but when I lay my hands on certain junk, I can tell if the owner enjoyed it. (Actually, most junk doesn't give off much in the way of vibes, but once in a while, I can really feel it.) I also believe that it's possible to extract that enjoyment from the junk. I have to admit, I haven't quite figured out the whole alchemical process yet. When I do, I'll have a very powerful product, a sort of concentrated memory distillate. I know it can be done. In the meantime, I'm settling for osmosis. My master plan is to surround myself with these happy people objects. The more the better. Something like a toy box is the best. It's been around kids, and kids are much better at enjoying themselves than adults.

After I see the toy box, I try to stay cool while I search frantically for a price tag. There is none. I walk up to the pregnant woman behind the card table, who has her nose in a thick Jackie Collins novel.

"How much for the toy box?" I say.

"Toy box?" she says, looking up from her book, all confusion, just too much activity before her second cup of Folger's Instant.

I point to the relic, try to keep from drooling. Have I given myself away? Does she know how much I want it?

She squints in the general direction. "Oh, that thing. I had forgotten all about that. It's my husband's from when he was a kid. I don't think he cares about it."

I believe she is seriously wrong about this, but dastardly me, I say nothing, only shrug.

"I don't know," she says. "It's pretty beat up—five dollars?"

When a price is fair, I do not dispute it. "Uh. Okay."

I pay the money, stash the box in the truck, and take off, absolutely giddy.

I Get Snippy with a Customer

Once I get to the store, I decide to open up, even though it's only ten-thirty. No sooner do I open the door than the bell rings and *she* walks in again. Theresa. What is it with her? Why won't she leave me alone?

I look over at her, no expression. I'm not really pleased to see her. I know that I have no reason to be mad at her, but am anyway. She lifts her Lana Turner shades and waves at me, a big animated wave, like I'm Johnny Stompanato before her kid kebobs me with the kitchen knife. She's pale as hell again, wearing a Seventies flowered Quiana disco shirt, cuffs unbuttoned, a pair of men's khakis, and her old, obviously thrifted Red Wing work boots. She snaps her purple gum, smiles at me.

"How you doing?" I say, noncommittal-like. I'm starting to feel stupid to think there was something there.

"Fine and dandy. And how's your bad self today, Mr. Junk?"

I try to refrain from smiling. "I'm fine."

"You're open early. You must be feeling better than the other day."

I frown at her. I frown right at that sweet round face with the lank of slightly greasy brown hair hanging down near the left eye.

"Why are you here?" I hear myself say. "This is the third time in like a week and a half. Are you stalking me or something? Or are you hoping that I'll start bawling in front of you again? Are you ever going to buy anything?"

She raises those glasses again, cocks her head, and looks at me—large liquid brown, slightly bulbous, weary eyes. These eyes melt me. Soon there will be only a pile of soggy gabardine and aloha cotton on the floor.

"You want to get some lunch? We could go over to Sammy's Thai. You like Thai?"

I am officially thrown for a loop, as my mother would say. "I, uh, it's kind of early, isn't it?"

Glasses back down. "This is more of a question of how hungry you are."

I go for the change-up. "Where's your friend today, the Prince of Darkness?"

She looks confused for a moment, then smiles with loopy clarity. "Oh, okay. You mean Roger? He's fine. Is this some sort of dating status question? Are you curious if he's my boyfriend?"

How do I get myself into these things? "No, I just . . . "

"You look freaked. Are you freaked 'cause I'm asking you out for lunch?"

I hate myself for being so transparent. "No, I—"

She goes around the counter, takes my icy hand in her warm, sweaty one, and starts to drag me to the door. "Well then, come on."

This sort of thing never happens to me. I try to keep from swooning. "Wait," I say. "Can I show you what I got today? At a garage sale?"

I can tell she is interested because she takes off her glasses. "What?" I lead her to the back room, where I have stashed the toy box. "This."

"Wow," she says. "Very cool. You going to sell it?"

"I don't know. I might keep it, clean it up, use it as a table or something."

"How much you pay?"

"Five."

"Excellent score, Junk. Congratulations. Lunch is on me."

Lunch with Theresa

We get to Sammy's just as it opens. We order Pad Thai and Pad Prik and Thai iced tea with milk. While we wait for the food to arrive, Theresa never stops talking, like she can't get it out there fast enough.

"—my friend Bettina, she works over at Reva's Salon de Beauté—don't you love that name? Here we are in this gloomy little neighborhood and somebody decides to give their hair place what they think is this sophisticated French name. It cracks me up. Riva's Salon of Beauty. Have you ever noticed that? How long have you had your store, anyway? I'm surprised

I never noticed it before. I really do like the stuff you have there. You really have a good eye for cool stuff, you know? It's not a snooty kind of resale store. Those people are starting to ruin it for everyone. How long ago did your mother die? Mine died six years ago—"

Basically, if you punctuate this with the occasional "I—" or "Well, um," you pretty much have my part in the conversation. She is full of questions about me, about the business, about everything, all punctuated with wild kinetic gesticulation. Her hands, I notice, are no better today than the first day I saw her, reddish and covered with scratches, some healing, some new, some beneath Band-Aids. When the food comes, I try to get her to slow down, talk a little about herself. But our conversation takes on this wobbly momentum. Her honesty is infectious, and I find myself saying what I'm really thinking, which is unlike me. When it comes to the art of conversation, I generally prefer to stand in the middle of a large cloud of equivocation and diplomacy and apology. I can't seem to do that with her.

"Am I talking too much?" she says, finger between teeth (not coquettish, but hungry). "I do that when I'm nervous sometimes."

"You're nervous? Why are you nervous?"

"I don't know. I want you to like me."

"Now you're making me nervous."

"You were nervous already."

"I'm always nervous."

"So do you like me?"

"You scare me. I'm going to ask you a regular question now. What do you do, like, for money?"

"I work at the Detroit Anti-Cruelty Shelter."

"Is that people or animals?"

"Animals."

"So I guess that's why you can dress the way you dress."

"What's wrong with the way I dress?"

"Nothing. It's great. I love it. I'd dress that way if I had the courage."

"You dress fine. You dress like you walked out of *Rebel Without a Cause.*"

I study a piece of ground peanut at the end of my chopstick. "But not like James Dean. More like his goofy friend that winds up getting killed in the end."

"I thought he got killed in his garage."

"What?"

"Sal Mineo."

"What are we talking about?"

"I was making a joke. Anyway, Sal Mineo was cute."

"In a goofy sort of way," I say.

Right then, Theresa runs her fingertips over the top of my hand, which is still holding the chopsticks. I feel parts of me vibrate when she touches me. I feel it behind my ears and on the tops of my thighs.

"What," I say. "Do you do with them?"

"Who?"

Three of her fingers are still touching my hand. I don't want to move it, but it seems sort of weird, me frozen, her hand just hanging there. The vibration has spread to the wings of my back and my navel.

"The animals," I say.

"I tend them, clean out cages, make calls to find them homes, check the classifieds for missing-pet ads, and a lot of times, I kill them."

"Are you kidding?"

She pulls her hand away. "No, I'm not."

"That seems sort of cruel for an anti-cruelty shelter."

She folds her hands in front of her. For the first time in our conversation, she's not looking me right in the eyes.

"It's really the only thing you can do with a lot of them. A lot that we get in are too sick or wild to be put into homes, if there were enough homes, which there aren't. So it's either put them down or leave them out on the street to get sick, or hit by cars, or killed by sickos. And either way, if they're out there, they wind up *fucking*, and making more animals, which we really don't need."

I feel a slight constriction in my throat when she says that word. "So you have to kill them?"

"I euthanize them."

"You euphemize them?"

She looks down at her hands, now twisted together, white and pink and red, and blurts a partial laugh. "No, I kill them, like I said before."

"Oh," I say, sorry that I brought the whole thing up. But now she doesn't seem to want to stop, only she has slowed down now, is more thoughtful than before.

She picks up her chopsticks, then sets them down again. "The ones that make you feel like hell are the healthy ones, the ones that no one wants because they're two or three years old, or ten years old. A lot of times, people only want puppies or kittens. The others we can keep only for so long, then we have to get rid of them to make room for more. It's pretty horrible, really."

"It must be."

"It has to be done."

"I'm sure you're right."

"On the other hand, the pay is bad and the nightmares suck."

She is laughing, but I see something in her eyes change. The energy seems to leak out of her, as if from a pinhole. I feel awful. Suddenly, I have to do something. What I do is so completely *not* me, I can't believe that I do it. I pick up some Pad Thai with my chopsticks and I feed it to her.

The light leaks back into her eyes and she looks at me.

"Yum," she says.

I Prattle On

After lunch, Theresa and I stand there on 9 Mile Road, in front of Sammy's Thai. Traffic roars past—rattling pickups, neighborhood muscle cars with open pipes, blacked-out imports with stereos bumping hip-hop music—yet we are sharing cozy conversation. I forget about the noise, the empty storefronts, the normalniks walking past us, gawking at Theresa's clothes—we are insulated from it, wrapped in a cocoon, connected by filaments of gauze and light. I am laying on her my various crackpot theories regarding junk, chance, the search, and how to get good used dining-room chairs, when I realize that I've been talking nonstop. "God, I'm sorry. I didn't mean to go on," I say.

Theresa leans over and kisses me, just like that. Her lips taste of peanut and hot oil and the purple SweetTart she has just popped. While she kisses me, she places her left hand on the side of my face, right along my chin, then with her finger runs a line down my throat.

"Mmmmmm. You have a good Adam's apple," she says, after she pulls away.

I want to tell her to feel free to snack on it, but I cannot talk right then.

"I like you, Junk. You're an odd one."

I am paralyzed for a moment. Finally, just when I move to kiss her back, she says, "I gotta go." She hands me a rumpled piece of paper, damp and ink-smeared, with her phone number on it. "Call me as soon as possible, fucker," she yells over her shoulder.

I watch her walk down the street to a municipal parking lot. Even with the big pants, I can tell she has what my father would have called a nice caboose. I, of course, being an enlightened man of the late twentieth century, would never think of such a thing. I watch her get into a beat-up silver Volare. She tools past me, a few fingers fluttering out the window, flashing sweet raffish smile.

I float back to the store, and strangely enough, have a decent day. I sell a set of old bull horns to someone, along with a pair of black velvet matadors, just like the ones I have at my house. It's a great wall installation, I tell them. And it will be. There's nothing like putting good pieces of junk together and creating something.

Night and My Father's City

When I get home, there is a message on my answering machine from Linda, hounding me about all the stuff at our parents' house. ("When will you be done, Richard? Are you making any progress? I want this all to be over soon.") I choose to ignore it. Even still, I know I have to go over there and get some things done. Maybe compile a list of things to get to dealers, take some Polaroids to show around.

But when I get to my parents' house that night, I immediately head downstairs to the tomb to look through the boxes I left there last night. The first box I open is full of old Christmas cards and address books. I slide it over by the steps to go out with the garbage. Another box has sets of cups and saucers, all different colors and styles and sizes, wrapped up in newspaper. Obviously some sort of collection of my mother's. They look like Fifties and Sixties, but I leave them alone, close up the box.

I realize what I'm looking for and inside the next carton I find it—more of the yellow Kodak boxes. When I open the top box, I notice that these photographs have a different feeling to them than the others. All taken at night, they are brash and contrasty, eerie and urgent. Looking at the photographs, I get the feeling that I am discovering my father's work during periods when he was influenced by different people. There is a kind of Weegee quality to these images, of being somewhere at the right moment to record something wrong happened. It also occurs to me that the interest I developed in photography at school was first instilled in me by my father. He would refer to Weegee or Walker Evans or Ansel Adams, but it never occurred to me that he was speaking as a fellow photographer. Here's a few of the photographs:

—A man outside a nightclub called Frank Gagen's, passed out on the gleaming hood of a Cadillac.

—The lit window of a darkened deco apartment building in Palmer Park, two figures silhouetted behind a closed shade. One of the figures' hands are in the air, gesturing violently, as if in the middle of an argument.

—Men waiting in line, at dusk, in front of the old Capitol Burlesk on Woodward, hats pulled down, looking away.

—A furtive, blurry night photo of a woman running down a street, light streaming off of her, a glow of fear.

—A white man with a gawky leer talking to a black woman in front of the old Willis Show Bar in the Cass Corridor.

—A murky downtown pawnshop, at night, with its front door open. An old black man is at the doorway, staring harshly into the darkness, at the person taking the photograph.

A couple are marked in pencil, "1960," on the backs. I wonder when my father had time to go out at night to take pictures. He had just gotten married and it surprises me that he could be part of this netherworld, roaming the streets of downtown Detroit way after dark, back when you still could.

Inside the next box, there's another calendar from Tollman Photographic, along with some pieces of mat board, an old aluminum-handle X-Acto knife, and a rubber stamp imprinted with my father's name, address, and phone number. The calendar is from 1966, the year I was born. For the first few months, the notations are like the other calendars—work schedule, errands and chores, mostly of a domestic nature, "Dentist," or "Hang drapes," or "Finish upstairs bedroom." As I page forward, I spot a few notations regarding submissions to magazines, but nowhere near as many as read "Job interview." After my birthday is noted in May ("A boy!"), there is nothing else that year, except for one note two weeks after my birth, on the 23rd. "Start new job," it says.

While I try to understand why I have never heard of my father working at Tollman Photographic, these things occur to me:

A) Right after I was born, he became an insurance salesman.

B) He did not like to talk about this period. I recall asking him once about the years when he and Mom were first married and getting vague answers about how he "worked at a lot of different places before I found my niche."

C) After I was born, there was no time for him to snoop around in the night, taking moody, unprofitable, unsalable photographs. He had to get up early in the morning, punch the time clock, go work for the establishment. After all, he had to pay the mortgage, buy the drapes, get wall-to-wall carpeting for the living room, put Malt-O-Meal in our starving, screaming, demanding little pie-holes.

D) I am the reason my father gave up photography. Sure, Linda was the first step, but obviously, I was the straw that broke my father's spirit.

I ruined my father's life. This is a hell of a thing for a person to realize. But I see now that this is what happened. Dad needed to make money, so he gave up what he loved to pay the rent. (The old story: art versus commerce, creation versus procreation.) Otherwise, what kind of man would he be? (I believe "happy" is the word we're looking for.) I sit down on some boxes and try to let this sink in. I know there was nothing I could do, that it wasn't my fault. I didn't ask to be born. I didn't ask him to take part in this tired old scenario—get married, have children, give up your dreams, become a drone in a clip-on tie, pay the bills, take care of your ingrate spawn, be miserable, embitter your spouse, keel over dead. Tired or not, apparently it's the story of my father's life.

It's all too depressing to think about. I get up, pack up the rest of the things from the treasure room, a couple of gaudy Sixties lamps, the coffee table and studio chairs (no longer caring if Linda notices). I also pack up three boxes of old books of my father's—all private eye and spy stuff—Matt Helm, Mike Hammer, James Bond. These books now make a lot of sense to me. After seeing some of my father's photographs, I see a man craving excitement, looking for intrigue as he prowls the midnight streets of the city. Then later, when he is tethered to a tract house, two yowling poop machines, and a nine-to-five gig working for the man, he finds his spice in books by Mickey Spillane and Ian Fleming, doing the Sixties spin on romance novels, only for frustrated, hyperdomesticated men, not women. After I read these books, they will sell like crazy to a couple of customers of mine who dig this pulp stuff with the lurid covers and the authors who pose packing Lugers or snub-nosed .38s.

Closing the door to the treasure room, I decide that my mother meant for me, not Linda, to find all this, especially my father's photographs. It makes me wonder if she felt guilty herself for encouraging him to give up something that he had obviously loved. For her, that must have been like giving up the man she fell in love with. She married a photographer, not The Man in the Gray Flannel Suit.

I can't think anymore. I want to go home, to my cowboy couch, to my striped Bake-Oven bowl of SpaghettiOs, to my basement rapidly filling up with my dead parents' haunted treasures. I want to go home and call up a woman, but it's getting late.

Why I Hate Answering Machines

The first place I hit in the morning is a Thursday estate sale, a house in East Dearborn filled with good stuff that is way too expensive, even on the things that I like, that aren't really worth much. It's as if they're afraid that someone will get a deal on something, so they overpriced it all. Obviously, the work of some diabolical estate sale coordinator. Even still, I walk out with gold-leaf bowling-pin-and-ball salt and pepper shakers, an Old Faithful spoon for my collection (I have measured out my life with souvenir spoons, and it ain't much), and a single kitchen table chair with a cool pink-and-yellow-and-turquoise space-age design on the vinyl. Clean it up a little, perhaps a dingle ball fringe around the bottom, and it's perfect for someone with mismatched kitchen chairs.

Even though there is another sale I could stop at, I show up at the store early again, hoping that Theresa will stop by like she did yesterday, but there is no sign of her. I head over to Delia's for a cup of tea and nonchalantly walk past Reva's Salon de Beauté, but I don't see her. This means I will have to call her. I am not very good on the telephone. In fact, as I've gotten older, I have grown to hate the telephone and all its annoying concomitants—the pager, call waiting, the cell phone, and especially the answering machine (mine included). So of course, when I get back to the store and call her place, I get her machine. I should have known, there is not a regular message, it is fucking *interesting*. The message is a fragment of an old Laurie Anderson song I recognize called "O Superman." In the song, there's a repetitive sample of Laurie Anderson's voice going "ah ah ah ah ah ah ah ah" and right about when you're ready to scream, Laurie Anderson says, in a singsongy electronic voice: "Hi, I'm not home right now, but if you'd like to leave a message, just start talking at the sound of the tone. . . ." This would be the logical place to end the message, but it keeps playing, with Laurie Anderson saying in a different voice: "Hello? This is your mother. Are you there? Are you com-

ing home? Hello . . ." Then it beeps. And the part about the
mother throws me off, so that at the tone, I am struck dumb. I
just say, "I . . . I . . . I . . ." I can't say anything else, so I just hang
up. Perhaps it will be enough for her to hear my voice and recognize me as the genius author of this minimalist message.

Afterward, I feel so stupid, I don't know if I should call back
and leave another message to explain myself or just forget the
whole thing and hope that she just comes back in the store again.

But she doesn't show up today. All through the day, every time
the bell on the door rings, I look up, hoping it's her. I find myself
thinking, *It's only a customer. Damn.* On the bright side, there are a
fair number of customers. Business has been okay lately, a few
more hipsters coming in, buying things, just goofy useless things
like paint-by-numbers or those big brass plates that you see at
every thrift store in the country. I have been picking those plates
up pretty consistently for the past year. At fifty cents each, you
really can't go wrong. When I got enough, I covered one whole
wall of the store with them and it was rather stupendous, if I say
so myself. One or two of them would simply be stupid, but a
whole wall . . . So now these plates are selling, the ones I have left,
two or three at a throw. You just never know what people are
going to buy.

At around four-thirty, I decide that I should try calling Theresa
again. I get the machine again and say, "Theresa, it's Junk, I was
wondering if you want to get together later. I'll be at the store
until six o'clock." Then I give her the number. I'm about to hang
up, but I want to say something else, like "I'd really like to see you
again." But I can't quite squeeze it out, so it sounds more like
I'm clearing my throat, I think.

I try again just before six, just to see if she's there, knowing that I'm being too pushy, but I can't seem to stop myself. And when she answers, I hate myself for doing it, because I can tell that I have called at a bad time. It sounds like Theresa, round-faced, lank-haired, polyester-clad junk goddess, my Theresa, whom I have no right to call my Theresa, has been crying. Now I really don't know what to do.

"Theresa?"

She doesn't try to hide the fact that she's been crying. I guess that's healthy.

"Hi, you."

"Look, are you all right? Would you like me to call back later?"

Sniffle, then a loud honk. "Excuse me. No. Actually, I would like you to come over here and eat dinner with me and give me a kiss and maybe some other stuff, I don't know. But you have to bring some kind of food, 'cause I'm all out. Is that okay?" Another sniffle.

"Ten-four," I say. "I'll be over in a jiffy." I am, at this point, and I know no other word for it, exultant. Although I am a little worried about the crying. But then, who am I to judge? I'm the goofus who sits in his shop and bawls, the weeping entrepreneur. She gives me her address and directions. I hang up, then quickly lock up the store, flipping the sign to "Closed" on my way out.

Her apartment building is a shabby one, by far the poorest one in a town that has just become in the past few years a center of groovyosity, a 1/25-scale, Midwestern version of Melrose Avenue. Her apartment is quite a ways off the main drag, and inhabited by people who look like they are one step from the street—welfare mothers, ex–halfway house residents, and gentlemen retirees who start their days at about nine A.M. at the few beer-and-bump dives that have not yet been converted to wine bars and cute theme bistros. I'm surprised that no real estate mogul has bought the building, turned it around, and booted out all the "undesirables."

I am standing in Theresa's tandoori-scented hallway, pizza in one hand and in the other numerous bags that contain: a falafel, large Greek salad, two coney dogs, and Pop-Tarts. I'm not really sure what she likes to eat, we did not discuss it the one time we have eaten together, so I have tried to cover all the culinary bases.

I am standing there, immobilized, from woman fear and the fact that I have no way to knock. I move closer to the door and I can still hear sobbing inside. Finally, I slam my head against the door, and for some reason this makes me feel better. I say, "It's Richard."

The voice from inside, who I can tell is Theresa, says, "Who?"

"Junk."

"Oh. Come on in," she says. Another long sharp honk. "I can't get up right now."

I balance the pizza against the door, slowly turn the knob, and am immediately overwhelmed by junk, at least as much as at my place, the glow of Christmas lights, and the acrid tang of cat piss. In front of me, sitting in an old electric-blue corduroy La-Z-Boy chair, is Theresa, less pale, with red-rimmed eyes, in an old guy's green Ban-Lon shirt and black bell-bottoms, surrounded by, blanketed by, eight to ten cats of various sizes, shapes, colors, breeds. She reminds me of Saint Francis of Assisi, only with all cats. Before I opened the door, they were all quiet, now they are all talking to me, yelling at me, squawking, *murring*, a few even hissing. A big marmalade cat jumps off the chair with a plop, strolls over to me, sniffs my pant leg, then sinks his teeth into my ankle.

I scream, almost dropping the pizza, and the cat runs into the other room. I rub my wounded ankle up against my calf, as I examine a wall with a line of hubcaps bisecting it.

"Well, you passed," says Theresa.

"Gosh, I'm so proud," I say. "Does he do that to everyone?"

"She. They're all shes. And yes."

"Does this mean she likes me? Is that her test?"

"No. It's my test. If you had tried to kick her or something, you would have had to leave."

"Oh. Well, it really doesn't do much good to hit a cat, anyways. They always win. The best you can really do is just annoy them." I look over at Theresa. A small thin black cat climbs onto her shoulder and howls at me. "Someone's jealous," I say.

Theresa smiles at me. "They're all jealous. They'll get over it. What did you bring to eat, J?"

"A bunch of stuff. Pizza, falafel, conies, salad."

"Smorgasbord. Swell. Put it all down on the table over there."

"Okeydokey."

She points to an old red-flecked Formica kitchen table with chrome tube legs. She is one of those people that I was talking about who does not need for all her chairs to match. The table is surrounded by four different chrome kitchen chairs, each with different-color upholstery—turquoise, yellow, green, and red—Fiestaware colors. I head for the table and take a look around the apartment. There in the corner of the dining room she has a female mannequin. (I told you junkers go for these things.) Hers is female, nude, but covered with little yellow Post-It notes. I only have a chance to read two—"Remember to pick up dog" and "Take food to shelter." Then I hear Theresa say, behind me, "All right, everybody. Time to let me up. Thank you."

There is the sound of thirty-two paws hitting the floor. I put the food on the table, which she has set with an assortment of plates like I have never seen. (She must have taken a break from crying to set the table. I'm touched.) There is Starburst, Poppy-cock, Color-Flyte, Jadite, American Modern, Western Tepco, and a lot of great ones that I don't even come near recognizing. I cannot find one dish that matches another. I am smiling when Theresa comes up behind me, a gray tiger cat following her. "Lovely place settings," I say, turning around.

"Yeah, I'm a hopeless dish queen."

"What were you crying about when I called earlier?"

She leans forward slightly, and her cropped hair shifts and covers her face. She runs a hand through it, pulls it behind one ear.

"Sometimes I get depressed after work. Most of the time, I just come home and sit in that chair and spend time with some live animals."

I look at her. "Well, looks like you've managed to save quite a few."

"Nowhere near as many as I've had to kill."

Long barren pause. "I can see how that could get to you after a while."

Theresa nods her head. "Two different people brought in boxes filled with kittens today. They hand them over to me like it's some sort of gift. *You'll be able to find homes for all these, right?* They want me to lie to them. I tell them, "We'll find homes for as many as we can, but most of them will probably be put to sleep." Then they look at me like I'm evil incarnate. They're throwing these animals away, but *I'm* the bad guy. These fucking people, they love to give us their guilt along with their animals." Theresa takes a long breath and looks at me.

"Sorry. Didn't mean to vent. It's just the season. People have just been bringing cats in like crazy lately. We've got way too many at the shelter."

She smiles at me, then grabs my left earlobe and tugs. "But you, Mr. Junk, you've got the best job in the world. Just going to estate sales and garage sales and thrift stores. Lucky dog." The big marmalade, back from the other room, yowls. "Hush, Sedgwick," she says.

I wince a bit at this. I really don't like any conversation that ends up with me being lucky. "Yes, going through people's refuse all day really can be quite fulfilling." I say, sitting down at the table.

"I've never really thought of it that way," she says. "I guess we both handle what other people throw out."

"I guess." I desperately need something to do. "Would you mind if we ate some food now? I'm kind of hungry."

"An excellent idea," says Theresa. She rips open the pizza box, paying no attention to where it has been neatly stapled, grabs a slice, and takes a bite. "Ummmm. This is good. Try some." She holds the slice in front of me, and I take a bite, right where her teeth marks are. Is it me? Or have I never tasted pizza this good?

"Thank you," I say.

"You are way too polite, you know that?"

"Yeah, I know. It's kind of a problem with me. I never end up with anything I want because I'm too polite to ask."

"Not good, boyo." By this time, Theresa has had a bite or two of the falafel and I am now watching her reach across the table to start digging into the Greek salad. She has a healthy appetite. As she reaches, the Ban-Lon shirt she is wearing rides upward, and exposes a pale but tender midriff, flowing slightly over her belt. Behind my right ear, I feel a bead of sweat drop off the ear-piece of my glasses onto the back of my neck.

"Tell me something you want," she says.

It must be just the direction of this conversation that embold-ens me, or just the fact that I am starting to feel that there is noth-ing I, Richard "Junker" Stalling, sad little man who picks through other people's things, could possibly say to shock this woman next to me. Even still, I cannot look at her when I stammer, "You."

Theresa Mocks Me

When I finally look up, Theresa is watching me, eyebrow cocked, with surprised but casual disbelief. "Well, well. It's always the quiet ones, my mother used to say. They're the ones you have to watch out for."

I, of course, take this as an insult. I'm not sure why. I know why. I hate being one of the quiet ones. I have been one of the quiet ones all my life and it hasn't helped me a darn bit. I didn't realize it, but I must look all sulky. I do that a lot. I get it from my father.

"There, there. Now don't look so hurt, J. Why do you think *I* kept coming into the store? For all your fabulous merchandise?"

I am about to pipe up here. You don't make fun of a man's mer-chandise.

Theresa smiles at me and all thoughts of rebuttal skirt out the window.

She pats my left hand playfully, gives it a squeeze. "Not that you don't have good stuff, J. It's just that it doesn't quite take three trips to get through it all. I came in to see you."

Me? This can't be right. I am about to try to say something here because I realize that a whole conversation is going on without me. Still, I wonder if Theresa even notices. She doesn't seem to even need me to talk, because she anticipates everything I say. The strange thing is, she's usually right. I attempt to speak.

"I, just, uh—"

But it's too late. Theresa gets up from her chair, walks around the table, pulls out my chair, with me in it, and plops herself down on my lap like one of her cats. She is not light. I like that. I like the feel of her body on mine. I like all of this, yet that doesn't make me any less terrified by her assertiveness. I haven't even gotten a chance to wipe my mouth. She smiles that smile again at me, then pulls the horn-rims from my face.

"I've never had anyone take off my glasses before," I babble, finally managing to get a sentence out. Theresa says nothing as she slides one hand inside my bowling shirt and kisses me full on the lips.

After she pulls back from me, Theresa says, "Hmmm. I feel like I'm in one of those movies where the boss takes off the secretary's glasses and discovers that he's beautiful."

At this point, I'm seriously thinking that I may lose consciousness, for no other reason than that all the blood has rushed from my brain to my nether regions. My heart is pounding, I'm perspiring heavily, I'm thinking a great many things simultaneously. (Subjects include: fear, glasses, breasts against my chest, my breath (how it smells, lack of it), warmth of her body, condoms, cats, lack of sexual experience, light-headedness, fear.) Yet, during all this, here is this woman, this junk goddess, on my lap, sliding her sweet, silken, feta-flavored tongue into my mouth.

Theresa pulls back from me again. "This would be so much nicer if you participated, J."

I try to talk, yet am unsuccessful at this attempt. "I, I, haven't— anyone in a long time. I'm really not very— Maybe I should—"

At that moment, Theresa sinks her teeth into my neck and I feel my self-consciousness disappear. I forget the fact that I'm me, which isn't easy because I have pretty much resigned myself to this fact.

I'm a little embarrassed to say what happens next. Actually, I'm rather mortified to say what happens next. Theresa and I are kissing furiously at this point and it is quite wonderful. After she opens a few more buttons on my bowling shirt, she stands up, without even disengaging herself from my lips, straddles me on her kitchen chair, and starts rocking on me.

"That's the good thing about these old chairs," she says. "They're so sturdy."

I don't think she could have said anything more arousing to me. She sheds the Ban-Lon shirt. I might have expected something wilder in the way of lingerie (or a lack of it altogether), but she is wearing a sweet little pink brassiere with a line of lace around the cups. It makes me think that this dark, pale, strange creature is someone's daughter. I notice that the pink looks dusky against her flesh, against her breasts (which are lovely and full, and that's all I'm going to say about it because you know how men can go on and on about breasts), and I can see veins beneath her chalky skin, glowing blue. The sight of this makes me want to cry, for her, for me, for all mortal humanity, but I decide that I want to put my penis in her way too much to do that.

In fact, that is the problem, I want to do it way too much. And when Theresa reaches down between her legs to down between my legs, something happens, the name for it best left in Latin. This is one dysfunction that has never happened to me before and frankly, I couldn't be any more unhappy about the whole thing. But let's face it, I haven't had sex in like four years. I'm a little worked-up.

"Uh," I say.

"Oh," says Theresa, noticing the rapidly widening stain on my now ruined gabardines. (I officially blame vintage pants for this. Unlike today's sensory-deadening synthetics, those old comfortable, loose-fitting fabrics that breathe and ride smooth against the skin can create a dangerous amount of friction.)

"Oh fuck," I say. "I'm sorry."

"It's okay," Theresa says.

I also need to say right here that there are no two words that a woman can utter to a man in a sexual situation that are more devastating than "It's okay." Truly, they are much worse than anything, except perhaps "It's just like a penis, only smaller."

"Oh fuck. Oh fuck fuck fuck fuck."

"J, it's okay."

"Please stop saying that. It is most certainly *not* okay. Okay is the last thing that it is."

All I want to do is get out of there, forever and ever. And I try to get up, but Theresa wraps her legs around the chair and traps me. I would make some comparison to the black widow spider here, but I don't think she kills her victim until he successfully completes the mating process, which I have most definitely not done. "Please," I say. "Just let me go—"

Theresa does not say anything. She just kisses me again. I

struggle a little bit, then stop. This turns out to be a good idea. She kisses me like everything *is* okay. I start to enjoy it and suddenly, I don't feel quite so horrible about everything. Finally, after a few minutes of this, I feel less lousy. I still feel wet and sticky, but less lousy.

"We were going too fast," she says. "This is my fault."

"Thank you for that lie. I do appreciate it."

"It's not a lie."

"Maybe I should go," I say weakly.

The legs tighten again. "No, please. I'm afraid you won't come back. This means nothing to me, J. I'm not going to talk about it anymore, because I know you don't want to talk about it. So now we're done talking about it and I'm going to get you a pair of jeans to put on and we're going to finish dinner, then maybe we'll watch a video, okay? In fact, don't answer that, because that *is* what we're gonna do. We'll finish this other business when the vibes are right." She smiles at me, that damned wonderful closed-mouth, thin-lipped smile of hers.

What can I do? I shut up, kiss her, and try not to think about the fact that she has a pair of men's jeans in her house that will fit me.

Getting Past the Unfortunate Occurrence

I am amazed that Theresa has an extensive collection of bootleg Seventies blaxploitation movies (ex–video store boyfriend, she tells me), including a copy of one of my stone faves, *Coffy* with Pam Grier. It is a great flick, with Coffy avenging the death of her kid sister by using her incredible sexiness to trap the dope pushers, then blowing them away. Theresa is pleased that I like this movie (is this really surprising, considering how much time Pam Grier spends topless?), and it occurs to me how important this sort of thing is to certain people, like ourselves. It is how people like us find each other. "Have you seen this strange film?" "Do you have one of these bizarre objects?" "Have you ever heard this weird music?" It's really fucking sad, in a way, how we have to communicate through esoterica and ephemera and marginalia, our little politics of cool. Usually this sort of thinking depresses the hell out of me, makes me feel like a useless member of a useless generation, probably because I have basically devoted my life to the perpetuation of all of it, but with Theresa, I don't care. It's all just fun. And I don't care what any of it means.

Even after the awful thing happened, I still have a great time. While we watch Coffy kick ass, Theresa and I sit on her striped sectional Seventies couch with five or six cats settled around. Then Theresa just scoots over and leans back against me, her head on my collarbone. I can't imagine it is very comfortable, because I am, well, a kind of bony guy, but she stays there. That's all she does, nothing else. After a while, I can just about feel the contentment ooze from my pores.

It is about ten o'clock when the movie ends. Theresa hits the rewind and turns to me.

"I got *Black Caesar*, J. You up for it or do you have to get home?"

"Maybe we could do that another time?" I say this, then wince from the irony, thinking, *What if there isn't another time? What if she's just being incredibly nice to the sad little premature ejaculator? What if this is the only night we'll be together and then I'll never see her again?* I really don't know what to do if all this is true, but I try to push it to the back of my mind. "You know what I'd really like to do?"

Theresa squints at me, trying to discern my intentions. "What?"

"I'd like to take a good look around at your stuff. Would you mind?"

She starts laughing, puts her hand on my knee. "J, you are just so, so . . ."

"Yeah, I know. It's a problem."

"Gee, I guess I should have given you the two-bit tour when you got here."

"Yes. Shame on you," I say, wagging my index finger at her. "After all, we are Midwestern, you know."

Theresa hangs her head in feigned shame. "Sorry. It won't happen again."

"So you don't mind?"

"Knock your bad self out. I'm just going to sit here. I've seen it already."

I get up from the couch and walk around. Theresa stays on the couch. From the corner of my eye, I notice her secretly pull out a paperback that was on the floor beside the couch. Before she folds back the cover, the same way I always do because I don't like people seeing what I am reading (I judge people by what they read and I assume they do the same to me), I catch a glimpse of the title. It is *Under the Volcano*, a book I have always meant to read, but never gotten around to.

As I walk around, I am surprised at how little attention I have paid to the things in the apartment up to now. That probably means something. There is all sorts of cool stuff. The living room is a total jumble of styles, just the way I like it. There is really almost too much to get into: a Forties office chair here; macramé plant hanger (and cat swing); a shelf of tiki mugs; the line of hubcaps; a great old wrought-iron LP holder filled with weird old mambo records next to an old console stereo complete with a stack of eight-track tapes; a disco ball hanging from the middle of the ceiling. Plus, Cass Corridor downtown art—a dark, smudgy painting, despair scratched into the surface (I'm not being poetic here; the word "despair" is actually scratched into the surface of the painting); a metal table welded together from car parts; found objects nailed onto a whitewashed board. The kitchen is less impressive, perhaps because this is where the litter boxes are and I decide that I want to get out of there pretty quickly. Still, there is a beautiful collection of old kitchen clocks there, about nine of them, everything from the classic fat chef clock to a long-necked Sixties kit-kat klock to the standard Telechron. I also spot a Fifties Toastmaster toaster a lot like the one my parents had, now in a box in the basement of my house.

"Wow," is all I can utter, as I emerge from the kitchen. "Good junk."

"I'll take that as a compliment from the master," Theresa says from behind her book.

"No, I mean it. You really have some great stuff."

"Thanks."

I am still looking around in the living room when I see the door to her bedroom. "May I?"

"I hope so," says Theresa.

I turn, so she doesn't see me blush. I walk in, leave the light off for the moment. Of course, my attention is drawn immediately to the bed. It's unmade, which normally would bother me because of that very conventional, bourgeois side of me, but right now I just want to jump into that bed and smell her smell, inhale her pillow, put my feet where her feet lie when she sleeps. But these thoughts cease when I find the switch for the overhead fixture. A light ticks on, not so much illuminating the place as animating it. The bedroom is painted dark blue with a black ceiling—a midnight cave. My eyes are pulled to one wall, a mural of a cemetery painted in luminescent paint, candles glowing gold, eerie blossoms of red and orange flowers, skeletons in hats and shawls, eating and drinking between tombstones. Along the bottom, there is something painted in Spanish:

> *Venimos solo a dormir, solo a sonar*
> *No es cierto, no es cierto que venimos a vivir en esta tierra*
> *—Netzahualcoyotl*

Theresa enters the room, walks up behind me, as I futilely attempt to interpret.

"'We come only to sleep, only to dream,'" she says. "'It is not true, it is not true that we come to live on this earth.'" She crosses her arms. "It's part of an Aztec poem. Don't even ask me to pronounce that cat's name."

"Oh. Okay."

"An old artist boyfriend of mine did the mural. It's in the style of Posada," she says. "You know him?"

I shake my head.

"Posada did all these incredible engravings for scandal sheets in Mexico in the eighteen hundreds. But he's sort of known for the skeleton stuff—the *calaveras*."

I keep looking. Everywhere in the room, there are skeletons—paintings, drawings, little figurines. Over in another corner is a table crowded with candles—short squat ones, tall glass cylinders decorated with Spanish words and images of saints. Dark photographs are scattered on the table as well—people and dogs and cats and even a bird or two. Then more skulls: bright-painted papier-mâché ones, translucent white ones gaily decorated like birthday cakes.

All right, I have to admit here, I wig out slightly. I don't know if it's because of all this death stuff and my mother or because I'm seeing something way too personal of Theresa's or just because this is all kind of creepy. (Or maybe it's the "old artist boyfriend.")

"Lots of skeletons," I manage to spit out.

"Yeah, it's a little problem of mine," she says, chuckling.

"Yours and Jeffrey Dahmer's," I say, not sure if I mean to be funny or cruel.

She stops smiling. "That's a mean thing to say."

"It was just a joke," I say, dread welling inside of me. "I'm sorry."

"You mean like I'm some sort of fucking killer?" I watch the energy leak out of her again, like at the restaurant.

"I didn't mean it that way, really."

She turns around, walks toward the living room. I walk behind her—close behind her. I frantically address the back of her head. "I'm really sorry, Theresa."

"I think you ought to go, J."

Panic. "Oh shit. Please don't do this, Theresa. I didn't mean it. I don't even know why I said it." I can see her getting numb on me.

"Can I call you?" I say, losing all semblance of a cool that never existed in the first place.

"Just go," she says. Then she remembers the question. "Yes. Call me in a day or two." Theresa sits down on the chair she was sitting in at the beginning of the evening. She tugs at the cuticle of her middle finger with her teeth. A cat jumps into her lap.

I let myself out.

The Morning After

In the morning, I have a doozy of a hangover. Not an alcoholic one, because I didn't even drink last night. I tend to get these emotional hangovers. Anytime I expose myself in some way or do something embarrassing or say something stupid—all of which I did in spades last night—I wake up with a head-banging, paralytic, so ashamed I don't even want to think about it, can't stop myself from thinking about it, emotional hangover.

When this happens, I know that all that day, I'm going to be thinking about the stupid things I did the night before. I will view them again and again. (There will be continuous showings every fifteen minutes.) I will be in a constant state of cringe. Dread will sour my stomach, clutch my throat, twitch my eyelid. I will think about things that I said, the things that I did (one thing in particular), and I will suddenly, spontaneously blush. (No one who encounters me during these times will know why. They will think I am having hot flashes.) All day long, I am fucked.

It used to be that when this would happen, I would simply stay in bed. A good indicator of my condition was how far under the covers my head was. Head completely exposed meant mildly paralyzed, out of bed by two. Head half covered—out by four. Head fully covered—see ya tomorrow. But this is the advantage of having your own business. It makes you get out of bed every morning no matter how miserable you are. Because no matter how horrible you feel, you would feel worse as a homeless person living in a refrigerator box beneath an overpass.

It being Friday, there are a bunch of estate sales happening this morning, but I just can't bring myself to get out of bed at six. Or seven. Or eight. Or nine. At nine-fifteen, I yank my so-very-sorry ass out of bed, head throbbing, face burning. I tell myself that everything will be fine, but I don't believe me. I know that keeping myself busy is the only thing that will help. I pass Tom the mannequin on my way to the shower. I raised his hand a few days before while I was changing his clothes (straw hat, snappy tropical print cabana suit). Now it looks like he's pointing at me.

Late or not, I head over to a sale on the east side of the city. It's in an old house; obviously the couple that owned it are dead. Everything has been picked over by the people who got there early. There are still lots of things for sale like respirators, toilet seat raisers, walkers—not what I need to see this morning. I am just about to go when I find a cache of souvenir items—an old pillow cover from Atlantic City, a Las Vegas plate (depicting Hoover Dam, the Sahara, Caesars, the Dunes, the Stardust), and a Moishe Dayan tip tray (I have no idea why such a thing exists). There are also some weird old Fifties vases that will sell, plus an old bar glass from Frank Gagen's nightclub. As I snag it and put it in my sack, I remember that one of my father's photographs was taken in front of Gagen's. This is part of the wonder of junk, these collisions in time, moments when the present catches up with the past. This puts me in a slightly better mood.

By the time I get to the store, my hangover is fading a bit. Unfortunately, today is really slow, so I have plenty of time to dwell. I try to think about other things, business, stuff I want to do to the store, how I should finish going through the things from my parents' house. Today, though, it will send me into the canyon. Mostly, I keep thinking about Theresa.

At five-fifteen, some guy tries to get me to lower the price on a Stork Club ashtray that I've got in my showcase. At twenty bucks, it's one of the more expensive items in the store.

"This ashtray's worth about five bucks," he says.

"I don't think so," I say.

"You must be out of your mind charging that much."

I want to I tell him if he doesn't like it, he can get the fuck out of my store. But I don't. "That's the price, sir," I say. Then this guy looks at me like he's going to belt me.

"You're fucking nuts, man."

I try to stare him down, but this doesn't work. He just stands there for three or four minutes, then he storms out. After five minutes, I am still shaking. After ten minutes, I release my death grip on the official Mickey Mantle Louisville Slugger that I keep behind the counter.

Gone, Gone, Gone

I decide to make it a perfect day. When I get to my parents' house that evening, Linda and Stu are there with a Ryder van. The front door is propped open. When I walk in, I notice many more things missing, just little things like the stereo, the living-room television, the kitchen table and chairs, and most of the Early American furniture in the family room.

"Well, this is nice," I say, approaching Linda. "What about our agreement?"

"Richard, it's been almost a week. Have you done anything? Have you sold anything? Have you gotten anything accomplished?"

"Sure, lots."

"What? Besides cleaning out the basement, which, by the way, rendered our agreement null and void."

Stu walks by, carrying a portable radio and an empty entertainment center. "Hey, Rich," he says to me.

I don't say anything. I sulk.

"Richard, don't worry. I'm not taking anything you'd like."

"I know. But shouldn't we sit and talk about this?"

Linda rolls her eyes at me. "Fine then, let's talk."

I frantically look around for somewhere to sit. "You've taken the fucking kitchen table and chairs, Linda. We don't even *have* anywhere to sit down! What are you going to do with all this stuff? You don't need any of it."

Linda takes an exaggerated breath, the accompaniment to her "I'm dealing with a child here" expression. "Calm down, Richard. We're giving some of it to Stu's brother and his wife. They just got married."

"Oh. Well, that's cool. Why didn't you say so in the first place? I just want stuff to get used. What about everything else?"

Now Linda smiles indulgently at me. "Richard," she says, half laughing. "What are you so worried about? The basement is yours. And don't think I didn't know what was in the storage room. I didn't want any of it. I talked it over with Mom a long time ago."

Linda brings the palms of her hands together as if she were

praying, except all the fingers are all pointing at me. "Now, here's what's going to happen, Richard. The estate sale people are coming next Thursday at one o'clock."

"You called the vultures?"

"They're coming, Richard. You have six days to take whatever you want. Everything else, we sell."

"But—"

"It's done, Richard."

The Longest Day

After all this, when I get home, all I want to do is call Theresa.

How did this happen? I barely know this woman, yet I have to call her after a bad day? How can it be that this person whom I just met, whom I hardly know, this cat lady who sleeps in the Temple of the Dead, could have such a hold on me? The real problem is, I know I can't call her. I truly believe that she meant it when she said "a day or two." I keep saying to myself, "It's been almost twenty-four hours. That's a day, right?" I know this is not what she meant. I am also scared to call, for what I will hear.

I sit down at the kitchen table and try to take a deep breath. All the day's dread has concentrated and compressed itself into a bright hot sphere about the size of a Ping-Pong ball right between my lungs. Every time I try to breathe, I feel heat and pressure, weight and pain. I don't know what to do. I stare at the pattern on my kitchen table. I follow the designs with my eyes, but they just keep leading back to me. They are, after all, boomerangs.

I Dream Again

It's a great mess of a night, a wide dark pile of images that I trudge through. I am walking around in my parents' basement, walking for a long time through rows and rows of junk, none of which I can actually identify (strange for me). Finally, I see a furnace in front of me, but I can't tell if it's the furnace in my house or theirs. It is outlined only by its own pilot light, glowing behind the ribbed iron door. I can just barely see the arms reaching for the floor above, yet they still scare me. But I can't run away because when I turn around, there's more junk behind me. It's closing in.

I keep moving. I walk past the furnace and see the door to my parents' storage room. When I walk in, it's not the storage room at all, but a darkroom. There are long pans of developer and a gigantic old enlarger on one side of the room. My father is sitting there at a desk, the desk where I used to build model cars. He is sorting photographs. The desk is covered with piles of photographs—8x10s, 10x12s, black-and-white, color. Around him there are cabinets full of pictures, boxes overflowing. My father is buried in photographs. I can only see his head above them all. When he notices me standing there, looking at him, he glares at me. "Go away," he says. Then he disappears into the pile of photographs.

"Richard," my mother says, appearing at the doorway. "Leave your father alone. Don't you have something else to do?"

I leave the darkroom, walk past my mother, back into the basement. The junk starts to change. I can identify it now and it becomes a lot of things that even I wouldn't collect: broken chairs, jars of grease, brown paper bags, balls of tied-together pieces of string, cardboard boxes, stacks of empty Cool Whip containers, and old newspapers—piles upon piles of old newspapers, stretching on for what looks like miles. I continue on a path between the newspapers. The type on them is faded and antique-looking. I start to smell something bad. I recognize rotting fruit and body odor, but there are many other fouler odors, layers of stench, each awful in its own unique way. It grows worse as I walk on, then I look to my right—in a nook between newspapers and a stack of empty milk cartons (missing children staring empty-eyed at me) is an old, old man, rail-thin, dressed in rags, surrounded by pieces of gnarled and dried orange peel, and I realize that he is where the smell is coming from. Slowly, he lolls his head to one side. His eyes are milky gray. I think he may be trying to say something to me, but his lips stop moving. I start running, but everything behind me is now in my way.

I wake with a start, as if I have just caught myself before I fall into something. Once I get my breath, I turn on the light. I lie there, sweating still, trying to rerun the whole dream before I forget it all. I don't know what the hell to make of it. It's the first dream I've had about my mother since she died. (She's scolding me, natch.) I didn't think I'd start dreaming about her so soon. It was at least a year before I started dreaming about my father, and he would pop up in this same way—cameo appearances. Still, it was good to see them both. I'm not even mad at my father for telling me to go away. I don't blame him. As for the old man, he gave me the willies, but not as much as all that bad junk.

It's quarter after five, my eyes are sandy from not enough sleep, but I'm not at all tired, so I decide to take advantage of it. If I get up now, I can actually get to an estate sale early. So I get out of bed and head for the shower. I throw on my Kar's Nuts work shirt and some Bermuda shorts. I snag the paper from the front porch, head into the kitchen, check out the classifieds while the water boils. There is a very promising estate sale in Dearborn. Another one on the northwest side of the city, not too far from the Dearborn location. I can hit that one second, then if there's any time left, I know a couple of good Salvation Armies around there.

I feel surprisingly okay. My hangover is finally gone. I pour a mug of potent tea, dump the rest into my thermos, say a brief thanks to the junk gods for what looks to be a promising day. On my way out, I check the turquoise Telechron on my kitchen wall: five-fifty. Too early to call Theresa, right? I'm sure it is. Yes, of course it is.

I Score

Getting to the sale early pays off. Since I am first in line (twice in a month!), I hand out street numbers from my truck to everyone who shows up. Just before eight A.M., a man drives up in a station wagon, goes in the back door. A minute later he comes out the front door and starts handing out his own numbers. We exchange our numbers for his corresponding numbers, thus determining who gets first plunder. For the last half hour, all of us—store owners, dealers, collectors, and assorted lunatics—stand single-file in front of this postwar ranch, half asleep, sniffing and scratching, Styro-cups of four-sugar tea in our hands, like junkies waiting for the methadone clinic to open.

Finally, the door opens and the estate guy lets in the first five.

I've seen him at dozens of these things, but he never acknowledges me. Once inside, the hunt is on. I find a dandy old ottoman-style "Breeze-All" floor fan with a brown marble plastic top; a Sixties Op Art light fixture; a "Letter Hound" spring-loaded dachshund memo-holder; a cache of Three Suns LPs; a Cuban cigar box of bottle caps; a church sconce that I can make into a cool candle holder.

A pretty darn good score. I fill up the truck and head to the sale in Detroit. The chances of finding anything are probably slim, but you never know. Junking is like gambling—when you're winning, you keep playing. But when I get there, I am amazed by how crappy and depressing and shabby everything in this old Thirties colonial is—chairs worn through the stuffing, kitchen appliances caked with the kind of grime that comes from decades of cooking food that's not good for you, mounds of dirty clothes—but in the midst of it all, in the basement, beneath a threadbare chenille bedspread and a large box filled with forty years' worth of crusty bedroom slippers, I find an early-Sixties Motorola television (fourteen-inch screen, maple cabinet), an absolute replica of the one I grew up watching, the one that caused all this damage. After I run upstairs to get my dibs, they tell me that the TV doesn't work, the picture tube is a goner. I don't really care. I know some electronics guys that may be able to get it working again, and if not, I can rip out the guts and use it as a display in the store or I can take it home and plunk my actual TV inside the cabinet. I tell them I'll give them five bucks for it, and they say okay. I have no idea where I'm going to put it, but there's just some things you've got to have.

I get back to the store about quarter to eleven. No time for much of anything before I open, maybe a little lunch, except I'm not hungry. I decide that after I open, if I have time, I will work on cleaning the things I picked up today. (My parents' things are still sitting untouched in my basement, I remind myself.) Just as I flip the sign on the door, the dread hits me again. I don't know why. I should be in great spirits after the excitement of scoring, but instead, I feel depression stomp in and take charge. It sends an alternate me out to meet the world—one with clay limbs, a brain bogged in Karo syrup, a throat that traps words like Chinese fingercuffs. I consider turning the sign back and not even opening today, but that would be a very bad idea. Aside from the fact that absolutely nothing would get done, I know that before long I would not have it in me to call Theresa. She is what keeps me from tumbling into the abyss. The problem is, she is also one of the reasons why it could still happen.

I park it on the bar stool behind my counter and wait for the deluge of customers. There is no one. It will be a slow day, of course. I go over to the hi-fi to put on something upbeat. I choose Perrey and Kingsley's "The In Sound from Way Out," one of the first Moog synthesizer LPs. All *boops* and *dwarps* and *beeeoo*s. Basically, it is such silly music that if you listen to it for about ten minutes, it will really cheer you up. Any longer than that, though, and you may end up going quite mad.

The Junk Gods Laugh at Me

At six, I lock the doors and flip my sign to "Closed." I unplug the Christmas lights around the front window, turn off my lava lamps, switch off the turntable ("Zounds! What Sounds!" by

Dean Elliott and his Swinging Big, Big Band!), and go back behind my counter. Normally, at this point, I would cash out and go over the day's receipts. Not today. I did not make a cent today. A grand total of five customers and zero sales. Usually on a Saturday, people are out, they just got paid and are in the mood to spend a little dough, but this—this is probably the worst Saturday I have ever had in the store.

Surprisingly, though, I feel a little better. I enjoyed not having to talk to anyone. And I did manage to clean up some of what I scored this morning and even put a few pieces out. Now, I'm simply putting off calling Theresa. I don't know why, because I've been wanting to call her since I left her place on Thursday. But first, I need to steel-wool the louvers on the ottoman fan, clean the LetterHound with Goo Gone, look through the box of bottle caps for the fourth time.

Finally, at about six-thirty, I call Theresa's number. When she answers, she sounds upset again, and before I even say anything, I think, if this works out, which it probably won't, we will be the most depressed couple on the face of the earth.

"Theresa, it's J."

Her voice brightens discernibly. Immediately, I feel better. "Hey, you," she says. "I've been waiting for you to call, you rat bastard. I thought you were being Mr. Cool on me."

The whole idea of this is so supremely absurd to me I can't keep from snorting into the phone. "I thought you just didn't want me to call for a couple of days."

"I said a day or two."

"Well, this is two days."

"If you really loved me, you would have barely survived one without talking to me."

I don't know what to say to this and she can tell I don't know what to say to this.

"J, I'm kidding."

I start babbling, then I can't seem to stop. "I wanted to call you last night. I didn't want to scare you away. That's why I didn't call. I didn't mean to upset you. I wanted to—"

She cuts me off. "God, J. Shut up." She is laughing a little, but I can tell that she is touched. I don't know why, but she is. "Can you come over, like right now?"

The urgent tone of her voice has a interesting effect on me. Of course, I can't just be aroused, I have to be terrified while I'm at it. "Um. Sure. I could bring something to eat." I am trying here to make this sound like a nice TV date, but I sense she has other plans.

"No. Just you."

Gulp.

I Want to Be Your Tee Na Nee Na Nee

When I get to Theresa's place (I bring some Chinese takeout just to be on the safe side), I don't have to let myself in this time because she isn't parked in the Chair of Gloom with a quilt of cats. In fact, she greets me at the door (thrifted kid's striped shirt, work pants), telling me that it's sooo nice to see me again, kissing me before I can say anything back, which is fine with me, because I never know what I'm going to say. It's wonderful, but I am nervous and experiencing that sense of watching myself do everything, when she pulls my glasses off (I think she really likes doing that), and for some reason, this helps. Maybe that other self that watches me can't see so well then.

I gently extricate myself from Theresa, under the pretense of catching my breath. It's not so much a pretense, really. I think I'm hyperventilating.

"Can we sit for a second?" I say. At first, I think that maybe someone down the hall has turned up the bass on their stereo, but then I realize that the sound is originating from my chest cavity.

Suddenly, Theresa becomes very helpful and supportive. She is the Doctor of Love treating her problem patient. "Of course, J. You're right. We're going too fast again."

After we park it on the couch, she looks at me and I swear she knows that I get rubbery when she flashes those cow eyes at me. I try to fight off the shiver. I am incredibly attracted to Theresa, but still kind of jumpy about the whole thing. A subject change seems in order.

"So tell me about work," I say. "What did you do today?"

She sighs. "Boy, you sure know how to kill a mood."

Theresa is quiet for a moment. She obviously doesn't want to talk about work. So I decide it's time to try to redeem myself after the other night. I touch her knee lightly. "Hey, how about explaining all that skeleton stuff to me?" I mean to say this casually, but it comes out like stilted dialogue from a late-night commercial. "I really am interested."

Theresa eyes me suspiciously. "Yeah, right."

"No, I mean it."

Eyebrows arched. "J."

"I swear."

She thinks about it a second. "Okay, fine. It's mostly Mexican folk art. A lot of people love it. It gives some timid souls the creeps."

I move a little closer to her, till my calves are touching hers. "How did you get started with it?"

"I picked up one of the *calacas* at some funky little thrift once and it kind of got me started."

She runs into the bedroom, grabs something, then runs right back. She holds it in front of my face. It is a small figure, a skeleton in a little uniform, riding a cart with a box on it marked *Helado*. "See, he's an ice-cream man."

"I've never seen anything like that at a thrift before."

"Well, it wasn't like a Salvation Army or anything. Sort of vintage store with some art. More hoity-toidy than yours."

"Oh."

"After I got this one, it kind of got me hooked on all the Dias de los Muertos stuff."

I'm nodding my head, but I must have a bewildered look on my face.

"Days of the Dead, J. Where people welcome the dead back into their homes? It happens on November first and second every year, All Saints' and All Souls' Day?"

"Oh. Okay. I don't really know about any of that. I'm not Catholic or anything." I refuse to act like I know something when I really don't.

"Too bad. You would have made a good one. You're very guilty. So, what are you?"

"I'm non sequitur." My standard joke.

She smiles. "I'm not much of anything myself. I was brought up Catholic, but I got fed up with that. They're not real crazy about women."

I can tell she's going to talk more, so I just clam.

"Anyway. Days of the Dead. It's kind of a combo deal—Aztec and Catholic. Once a year, the souls of the dead come back to the land of the living to visit. So anyone who's lost a loved one can build an altar, an *ofrenda*—offering. They decorate them with flowers and photos and candles, and they put the dead person's favorite foods or drink on the altar, or anything they enjoyed while they were living, so the deceased can come and enjoy the essence of them. And the families gather and people visit—"

"Wow," I say.

"—and there's skeletons everywhere. The windows of the stores. Bakeries baking bread crossed with bones. Kids wearing masks, eating sugar skulls with their names on them. You eat death, isn't that wild? But you mock it, too. Because that's all you can do. I know it all sounds kind of gory, but it's really, like, life-affirming. There's parades and dancing—"

I am nodding my head like a madman.

"And there's a vigil at the cemetery all night. And they decorate the graves with candles and burn incense. You ought to see it, J. It's beautiful."

"When did you go?" I say.

She stops, looks at me. "What?"

"When were you there?"

"Oh, I've never been."

"I thought you had. It just seemed like—"

"I'm not exactly rolling in dough here. But I've seen tons of photographs."

One of the tiger cats jumps on my lap.

"Billie, down."

"It's okay," I say, wrapping my arm around the cat. I actually welcome the diversion. Theresa watches me cuddle the cat. She smiles. I am getting the feeling that, like my father, maybe she sees something in me that isn't there.

"I got some beer, J. You want one?"

"Yes, I'd love one," I say. Things are cooling down a bit and I can feel myself start to relax.

Theresa goes into the kitchen, comes back with two Motor Citys and hands one to me. I immediately chug down half. The beer is ice-cold and I can feel my eyes start to water. I am this far from one of those cold headaches.

"Why are you so afraid of me, J?"

This catches me off guard. (There's a surprise.) In fact, I nearly demonstrate the classic spit-take. "I'm not afraid of *you*," I sputter. "I'm really attracted to you. It's just that I'm . . ."

"Afraid in general?"

I nod, down the rest of the beer. The cat jumps from my lap, choosing an unfortunate place from which to kick off.

"So it's nothing in particular?" she says, looping her hair behind her ear.

"Everything in particular," I say, still wincing.

She laughs at me, leans close to me, kisses me, tongue tip first, then rubs the tops of her fingers under my chin, down my Adam's apple. She is petting me. I am one of the pack now, her only boy feline, her 'fraidy cat, too nervous to purr. I kiss her back, and for the first time, I feel completely relaxed. I finally let myself be pulled in. My defenses have been beaten back, I stop thinking about me, and five minutes later, after we shoo four cats off her bed, we light some candles and settle deep into the sandalwood soft Temple of the Dead.

I'm not sure exactly what to say about what happens next.

Except that we have what is probably the clumsiest foreplay two people can have. It is one long ridiculous sequence of accidental hair pullings, zippers that won't unzip, head butts, frozen bra clasps, tooth collisions, cats that won't leave the bed, packets that won't tear open, near falls-out-of-bed and charley horses. I probably apologize about forty times until Theresa tells me to stop apologizing and start performing my manly duty.

I happily oblige, finally forgetting about everything but the lovely task at hand. I am about to say something here that may not sound very nice, but I will say it anyway. In the middle of sex, with this dear dear woman, this hepkitten Aphrodite, I am suddenly flushed with masculine exultation over the fact that I am actually having *sex!* Yes! (I can't help it. It's been almost five years. If I said four before, I lied.) Here I am, having sex, and here's the part I'm ashamed of, I would have felt this way no matter who I was having sex with, even some sleazy B-girl. (Are there even B-girls still?) But then I look over (we were on our sides, you see, trying it that way) and see this woman, this junk angel, of flushed full face and body (whose bottom I am clutching, fingers touch-melting into her flesh), of sweet if inconsistent disposition, with whom I am sharing the aforementioned blissful relations, and I realize that it is much more than just fucking, that I am most certainly and ridiculously and brilliantly in love with her. But somehow, this only fuels my manly euphoria and I experience a testosterone epiphany. Suddenly, I am Superman. (DC Comics', not Nietzsche's.) I am Shaft, Superfly, and the Mack all rolled into one. I am Dean Moriarty making fast time, Henry Miller after absinthe and raw eggs. I am the Tchotchke King, collector of the arcane, lover of women, spy in the house of junk.

Things Work Out

Theresa actually seems to enjoy herself. That way, I mean. I did not necessarily expect this to happen. I must say, in my limited experience, I have not always had good luck in this department, but between the two of us, the four of our hands, and considerable direction on Theresa's part ("There, Junk. Ow. No not there. Ow. There. Yes there. Now you've got it, cowboy. Keep doing that until further orders"), we are able to do the do. Don't get me wrong, I don't mind direction at all. I am not a good improviser. I am not the Thelonius Monk of the clitoris. I need assistance. If I could, I would call AAA and see about getting a road map, a Trip-tik: *Your Vacation Guide to the Female Orgasm.*

Anyway, after she enjoys a cheery interlude ("Please stop, J! My brain will explode!"), she flips me over (I am learning how strong she is), and what little will I have left dissipates. (Not that this whole thing has taken that long. Believe me, it hasn't.) As I slide into pure supercharged hemi-powered ecstasy, I glimpse skeletons dancing on the walls, slash-mouth skulls, empty sockets staring at me from shelves and tabletops, wide-eyed, head-cocked death grins. Tonight, they do not bother me. Far from it. Tonight, I become one of them. All my emotions of the past few awful weeks are pulled from my body, thrown into one funky weird miasma of sensation and glee, glory and pain. I am stripped to the bone, falling into it now, screaming all the way down.

After the Lovin'

This is what happens: We are just lying there, holding each other. Theresa seems fine. I, of course, am feeling stupid and self-conscious, not knowing what to say, not having done this for so long. Then, I don't know why, I ask Theresa if I can tell her about this dream I had last night.

"Sure. I guess," she says, a little hesitantly.

"It's kind of weird," I say. Then I tell her the whole thing, at least what I can remember, with my parents and the photographs and all the smelly junk and the old guy and the orange peels.

"Wait a second," she says. "You say the guy was blind?"

"I think so, yeah."

"And you walked through big stacks of newspapers and garbage?"

I don't know where she's going with this. "Uh-huh."

Theresa turns to face me directly. "J, have you ever heard of the Collyer Brothers?"

"I, I don't know. They sound sort of familiar."

"This is so bizarre. J, I think Homer Collyer was the guy in your dream. You must have heard of him and just don't remember, because it sounds like you were in their house."

"Really?"

"Yeah, I think it was in the Forties. These two brothers lived up in this big old house. In Harlem? Anyway, the cops wound up there one day and they go in the house. There's junk piled up to the ceilings. I'm not sure if there was anything good."

"Some of it would be good now, I bet."

"Yeah, probably. Anyhow, they start digging through all this junk and old newspapers and stuff, and they find old Homer Collyer, blind as the poet he was named for and dead as a fucking mackerel. I don't think they ever found his brother, but they think he's the one that called the cops."

"What happened then?"

"It's a pretty famous story. They spent, like, the next month clearing out that house, tossing out literally tons of debris. They just kept finding more and more and more. They're the original junkers, J. That's what you could turn into if you're not careful."

"Oh boy," I say.

"Didn't your mother ever say, 'Get up there and clean your room. It looks like the Collyer brothers' house'?"

"I don't know, maybe."

"I think it was a popular thing for mothers to say." Theresa smiles at me. "So clean your room, J."

"Great. Thanks a load for the analysis."

She purses her lips. "Hey man, it's better than my dreams."

"Why? What happens in your dreams?"

Theresa throws out her hands, then brings them together in mock gaiety. "Oh, you know, the usual," she says, her voice all happy and chipper. "I dream that I wake up and that my hands are covered with blood. Silly me! Then I get all scared and run to the sink to wash it off? But more blood just keeps appearing from nowhere. I wash and I wash, but the blood just doesn't go away no matter what I do."

Right here, Theresa cocks her head, shrugs her shoulders, and smiles broadly, a horrible grimace. "Gosh, in fact, there's lots of blood everywhere, on the sink, on the floor, and I'm screaming and I'm crying. And before long—Land o' Goshen—I'm covered with blood! I'm swimming in it! Whee! That's my dream. And I must love it because I have it just about every night. At least on those nights when I actually fall asleep." At this point, Theresa looks at me, but she isn't smiling anymore.

"Please let's fuck," she says.

Knob & Bob

I left Theresa's at about midnight. All right, she kicked me out at around midnight. After our second encounter, of which I'm not going to say any more because I've already talked way too much about sex, way more than a person like me should talk about it. Let's just say that we enjoyed ourselves together and leave it at that. Afterward, we forgot about dreams, gobbled cold egg rolls, and watched *Out of the Past*, a great old *noir* film starring Robert Mitchum, who truly is one of the coolest guys to ever walk the earth. But as we sat there on her couch, I was having a hard time keeping my eyes on the movie. I was watching Theresa there in ragged shorts and an old Seventies "Mickey Rat" T-shirt, full of holes (exposing delicious fleshy treats here and there), legs crossed beneath her, watching the movie. I kept wanting to do weird animal things, come up to her on all fours, rub my head up against her legs, wedge my nose into her crotch. When I did these things, she would laugh, but she was still a little withdrawn.

It is now eight in the morning and what I would really like to do is give Theresa a call, hear what her sleepy, early-morning voice sounds like, but I am worried that she is worried that I am already too hung up on her.

I can't understand why she's worried.

I will call her at a reasonable time later. I will be Mr. Cool. I will play hard to get. I will try not to love her too much. I will try to be the person I need to be, so to be the person I want to be, the person that is with her. But for now, it is Sunday morning and I must go junking.

I Am Tardy

I arrive at the only new estate sale in the paper at about ten-fifteen. I really should have been here earlier. I would normally be feeling bad about this. But today, I have an excuse: blessed sexual fatigue! My lower back hurts, my legs are shaky, and my muscles are aching in places where I forgot that I had muscles, thanks to years of involuntary celibacy.

Yet I am bright-eyed and bushy-tailed, there is a spring in my step, a twinkle in my eye, and all that other crap that people say when you actually don't look like hell warmed over for once. So notices Mona, the woman who is handing out the numbers.

"You look perky today, Richard," she says, smiling. She is an older lady, quite nice actually, for someone who handles estates.

"I guess I feel pretty darn perky, Mona. Any good stuff today?"

"Oh, yes. I think there's some things you'll like, if they last."

"That's a big if."

She hands me a number, my place in line. I am number 21. This does not bode well. There are twenty other people who get to go in before me, vying for much the same junk. From here I can go sit in the truck and read the paper, or go get a cup of tea at the 7-Eleven. I decide to cop a few Z's in the back of my truck.

When I wake up, it is horribly hot in the back of the truck. I have sweated through my undershirt. I look at my watch. It's past noon. I scramble out and observe the general public entering and leaving the house at will. I've missed my measly number 21 position. When I go in, I see Mona at her table set up just off the vestibule. She looks at me, confused.

"What happened to you?"

"Fell asleep in the car."

Mona *tsks* me. "Too bad."

I shake my head, grunt, head into the dining room. There are some scattered pieces of crystal, chafing dish—nothing. Kitchen—nothing. I decide to forsake the bedrooms and head straight for the basement. Downstairs, I spy a couple of funky paint-by-number landscapes and a menu from the Chin-Tiki, an old Polynesian restaurant in downtown Detroit, closed since the Seventies. I scout the basement. There is nothing more of interest.

Upstairs, just to be on the safe side, I check the bedrooms. My instincts are correct. Zilch. I pay Mona for the stuff, grab my receipt.

On my way out, I give the garage a look-see. It's a mess—rusty garden tools, paint cans, a box of old magazines that practically have mold growing on them. (When will people realize that it gets damp in a garage?) I flip through the box quickly and find a few issues of *Like*, early Sixties, so I snag them. They're in rotten shape so the guy in the garage just charges me a quarter each.

In the car, I pull out the copies of *Like* and tear through them. They are from July 1961, August 1962, and March 1964. I can't seem to remember what year my father's photograph was accepted. I keep turning wilted pages. The magazines are full of nifty old photos of bomb shelters and Richard Nixon and stuff like that. But nothing that looks like my father's photos. I shouldn't have bought the magazines, but I got so excited I wasn't thinking.

A Garage Sale Incident

I spot a garage sale sign on the way back to the store. I hit the brakes, turn down the street. In front of the house, some kid is selling lemonade at a little stand. Never a good sign. I park the truck. I try to smile at the girl as I walk up, but I think I just scare her. She doesn't ask if I want to buy a glass like she asks the other people who walk in around me. I notice everyone looking at me as I walk in. They are all squeaky-clean white suburbanites looking at me like I'm some sort of freak—the ratty-haired, horn-rimmed-glasses guy who looks like he just rolled out of bed. (So I'm wearing an old pajama top. It's better than what passes for shirts nowadays.) I walk by them all, look around the garage. There is nothing the least bit good there—all baby clothes, crappy Eighties lamps, McCall's patterns, and two air-popcorn makers. I flip through a box of LPs and somehow know that I will see a copy of *Frampton Comes Alive*.

In the garage, there's a man in a lawn chair, reading a newspaper. "Hi! Looking for anything in particular?" he says. He's probably not a whole heck of a lot older than me, but very dad-looking. A spare tire, golf shirt, and walking shoes will do that for a guy.

"Do you have any older stuff?" I say.

"Sorry. This is it."

"Thanks."

I turn to leave and notice a shirt on a table, a Kmart flannel shirt, a frayed brown plaid with a sewn-in tan dickie. It is truly one of the ugliest shirts I have ever seen. I pick up the ugly shirt, realizing that I am about to have a junk moment. I know this ugly shirt. I know it because my mother gave me a shirt like it for Christmas when I was twenty-one.

I had just discovered the Salvation Army and had already thrown myself into thrifting. I hated everything that was new and "bourgeois." (I had just learned this word. It was before I realized that I was as "bourgeois" as everyone else.) I opened the shirt and could not disguise my complete and utter disdain for it. It was so ugly and so new and so Kmart. Part of me knew that she had really tried and that this seemed right to her, but it was completely wrong. It was so wrong, and so completely not *me,* that it made me mad, brat that I was. At least I didn't yell or throw it back in her face, but I whined and sulked and complained all day. I don't know why. I just did.

My mother never bought me anything personal again after that Christmas. Only generic stuff—socks or underwear or gloves or slippers. It was right around then that the troubles started with my mother. It wasn't because of the stupid shirt, I know, we just didn't get along. She wasn't getting along very well with my father either. She was just starting to master the art of being a very unhappy person.

And now, standing at this garage sale, holding this ugly shirt, Sunday depression invading my bloodstream, I start to gasp for breath. I try so hard to hyperventilate quietly, but it is not working very well. A couple of rather loud, subhuman sounds escape from me, and soon everybody at the garage sale is looking at this goofy fuck, one hand clutching a flannel shirt, the other his chest, face streaming tears, wheezing like a Stanley Steamer. The dad guy who I had talked to approaches me. (Why, why must I do these things in public places? Why can't I just have my emotional *grand mals* at home, behind closed doors, like everyone else?)

"Hey, are you okay?" the dad guy says to me.

I nod. I am breathing through my mouth, very shallow and heavy-like. I need to swallow, but can't, and when I finally do, I start getting the hiccups.

"Sit down, okay?" The dad guy is being very nice. "Honey?" He turns to his little girl. "Could you get me a glass of lemonade for this gentleman?"

A Dixie cup appears in front of me. I drink it down. It's awful, like lemon water, but I drink it all because I don't want to hurt the kid's feelings. It helps. I start to calm down a little.

"I'll pay for this," I wheeze and reach for my pocket.

"It's okay," he says. "It's on the house."

I hiccup. "Please, I want to, and I want the shirt, too." I pull a couple of crumpled dollars from my pocket and hand them to him.

He gives one of the bills back to me.

"I'm sorry," I say. I get up and run out of the backyard of this nice man and his family.

In my truck, a few blocks away, I can finally breathe again. I look at the shirt on the seat next to me. Then, right there in the truck, still panting, face still smarting, I realize something. It's kind of a cool shirt.

Crackpot Theory #3

In my business, eventually you come to the horrifying realization that you like the same things your parents liked—not things similar to the things your parents liked, but the exact same things. Maybe you don't necessarily like them for the same reasons, but does that really matter after a while? I don't think so. I mean, who really knows why we like anything?

This is what happens: You think everything's oh so amusing and you're so above it all, then one day you realize that you really enjoy Polynesian music. At first, you listen to it because it's so kooky and hokey and so weird. But you keep playing it. Then little by little, you start to understand. You decide that it makes you feel good. It's relaxing. It really is *exotic*. So what if they're playing a Japanese koto, Mexican marimbas, and Burmese gongs all on the same song? Are there electric organs in Polynesia? Does Polynesia even exist? Who cares?

These days, everything is grist for the irony mill. If you start thinking too much about why you like black velvet paintings or panther TV lights or those Shriner dolls with the bobbing heads, you'll make yourself nuts. Next, you'll be worrying about how people will react to the stuff at your estate sale after you're dead. (Here's the answer to that: They will laugh. Oh yes, they'll have a good time. No matter how cool you think you are. I see this already in the shop when I notice late-thirties boomers cooing over some great winged mid-century monstrosity, then I look over and spot some twenty-year-old slackers exchanging glances and stifled smiles. *Check out the geezers.* The thing is, the kids are buying Bicentennial junk from the Seventies. I ask you, just when does the statute of limitations on irony run out?)

So I say, like what you like, ugly or beautiful or beautifully ugly. Stop thinking about it. Try not to laugh at everything. Ignore Susan Sontag's "Notes on Camp." Create your own codes. There is a taint of death in all irony.

I Kid Myself

Today there's a fair amount of business, but it drops off at about four o'clock. At five-thirty, I close the store early, knowing the work I have ahead of me over at my parents' house. As I sweep up, I notice that with yesterday's score, the store is looking a tad crowded. I tell myself that maybe I should lay off the junking for awhile. After all, my basement is full of salable items, though I'm not sure I can even get to any of it, what with all my parents' junk.

Then there's the question of my parents' junk. I have no idea what I will do with it all. It's great stuff, but I probably won't be able to keep most of it. Yet I haven't quite gotten around to really looking at it, sorting it out. I know the easy answer would be that I have some sort of sentimental attachment to the stuff, but I haven't seen most of it in decades. A lot of it even predates my birth. I just can't seem to do anything with it. Except what I am about to do, which is go get more of it.

Linda Gets Busy

When I arrive, I am shocked to find that my parents' house has been stripped of all character. Linda's been doing preliminary work for the vultures. Not really necessary, unless you're a control freak. Everything is still here, it's just been taken off the walls and tables—all the frilly little knickknacks, all the candle holders, all my mother's dreaded "country" stuff, has been rearranged for easy assessment on folding tables and counters. Now they can just swoop in, mark everything from the spatulas to the half-burned logs in the fireplace, sell everything they can, sweep out the rest, and Linda can get to what she really wants: the house.

I take a shallow breath and tell myself to shut up. Linda's obviously been doing a lot of work here. I mean, it's true that she just wants to sell the house, but she's at least handling the situation. I am the one that just comes in and bitches about the way she is handling the situation.

I walk around the living room and dining room. The dining-room set, the coffee table, the lamps, are all much too nice for me—they're not scratched, they're not weird-looking—they're tasteful. I am not used to tasteful things. With all the people I know, I suppose I could easily enough find somewhere to sell them, but they are too big and too unwieldy and too much my dead parents' dead things for me to want to go to the trouble of taking them. The same goes for the other rooms. I'll take the little tacky items, but the rest of it is better off just sold to some dealer. I decide to head for the basement. It is more my territory. I am a burrowing man.

Downstairs, things are more the way they were before, a familiar jumble. The door to the storage room is wide open. I had cleaned everything out, but now there are some more boxes in there. Apparently, they are for me. I am touched (and amazed) that Linda would do something like this. I realize that the only way Linda and I can be nice to each other is when one of us isn't there. On top of one of the boxes is a pink Post-It note written in Linda's dainty hand:

> Richard—
> Thought you might like these.
>
> —L

I peek inside one of the boxes. There is an old "Campus Queen" thermos, a few more Mickey Spillane books, and a great old electric mixer with a jadite bowl. I am surprised at how well Linda can pick out things I would like. Perhaps I've been underestimating her. In another box, there are more of my father's photographs, curled and yellowed slightly, and another one of his calendars. Once again, the photographs are different from the last batch. These, much to my surprise, are black-and-white family photos, pictures of my mother and my father, Linda as a toddler, and a baby which would have to be me. The odd thing about these pictures is that they remind me of my father's serious photography, but also of the snapshots that fill our family photo albums. It's like this was the period when he made the big change from photographer to insurance salesman and father.

There are pictures of the family under an umbrella at a beach somewhere; one where I am a little older, at what looks to be the Thanksgiving Day parade; the obligatory first-birthday cake-all-over-the-face shot; first haircut, two barbers holding me down while I scream hysterically; all of us at the zoo; Linda wearing a Halloween monster mask, holding her hands out as if to grab me. Once again, I am screaming.

Then I flip to a beautiful sepia-tone photograph of my mother, dark-haired, looking almost beatifically at a newborn infant she has in her arms. Her left arm is cradled beneath the baby, the right wrapped around it. Although a blanket obscures it, I can tell that her right hand is squeezing the child's tiny fingers. In the unfocused background, I can make out a fan-shaped window of a front door. I have never seen this photograph before, yet somehow I know that it was taken on my first day home from the hospital, on my first day here in this house, where I stand now, holding this picture, getting ready to haul away the debris of my parents' life together.

I experience a junk moment of great intensity, and I don't mean to belittle it by calling it that. I just don't know what else to call it. Maybe it's nothing. Maybe I'm just standing here in a basement, feeling my mother's touch, unable to realize that this is simply how you feel when a particular part of your life is over. The strange thing is, I have felt this presence before or something like it. Not just with my mother and father, but with people I've never known, whom I've never seen, whose things I've received or purchased or sold or given away. I've felt them in some infinitesimal way because my hands touched where their hands touched. So maybe it is a junk moment, after all.

I walk over to the downstairs extension and dial a number. The phone rings once, twice. I have no idea if she is going to be there or if she even wants to see me, but I decide not to think of that right now. I just want to talk to her. I just want to talk to her.

"Theresa, it's J," I say, as soon as she picks up. "Can I come over?"

"You want to talk to Theresa?" the man on the line says. "Just a second. She's in the shower."

I Figure Out Some Things

When I get back to my place at around ten, weary, head pounding, there are three messages on the loathed answering machine, all from Theresa. I listen to them, while holding the last of my parents' basement stuff.

1) "J, did you just call my place? Dorr says there was some guy on the phone who said he wanted to come over, but then hung up. Call me crazy, but this sounds like you. Call me back."

2) "J, it was you, wasn't it? You're such an asshole. I can't believe it. Was this because there was a *man* here? No, that's just too stupid to even think about. Call me anyways, you big dumb hunk o' jealous male."

3) "Junk, aren't you home yet? If you get this and it's not too late, why don't you just come over?"

I drop the boxes and head back to the truck.

The Long Hello

Theresa answers the door in an old green-and-black flowered rayon dress, barefooted, pearl-pink barrette in her hair. She looks great.

"You are such an ass," she says, shaking her head. "I can't believe you. What did you think, I was fucking someone here?"

"I—"

"Let's get this out of the way. You spoke to my friend Dorr, the artist I was telling you about? I used to fuck him, but I don't anymore. We're pals, okay? And currently, I'm not fucking any-body but you. That doesn't necessarily mean anything, it just hap-pens to be the situation at this moment. Got it?"

I nod sheepishly.

"Now, don't ask for any more details or I'll to give them to you."

I'm already getting way too much information. I try to squeak out a few words.

"J, don't say anything. Just come in and knock me a kiss, you goof."

I am a good little pup, so I do as she says. Then, well. Obvi-ously, we are caught up in the blush of new love (at least I am), that period where we can't seem to get enough of each other, where we are sexually insatiable. Don't get me wrong, this is nothing I've actually experienced. But I've done some extensive reading about it in old *Penthouse* Forums.

Postcoital Depression and You

Afterward, we make a tent under the sheet in Theresa's bed and hold each other. I have always liked playing tent, and it is even more fun with Theresa there. Between my astigmatism, the black light, and the toxic shimmer of blue passing through the sheet from the lava lamp, she has the iridescent glow of a living black-velvet nude. It's quite wonderful to look at her actually. Having my head under the sheets is good also because tonight I'm not really in the mood to look at the painting on the wall or the skull stuff on the tables and shelves. Frankly, they still kind of give me the screaming meemies.

Then quite abruptly, Theresa starts crying. I don't know what to do, but totally self-involved man that I am, immediately decide it has to do with me.

"Theresa, what's wrong?" I say, pulling the sheet back from my head so I can sit up. "Was this a bad thing? Shouldn't we have done this?"

She looks up at me, tears streaming, face flushed from I don't know what, crying or coming, and laughs a weak sobbing laugh at me. "No, J. It's just me. This just happens sometimes after sex."

Throat clench. Don't need to hear she's been having sex, when I've been out at estate sales, getting excited over uncovering an old box of Swedish nudist magazines. I shake it off, tell myself that some people actually have normal lives, where they do normal things, like have sex. Try to be normal, just for a second, Junk. Try not to receive images.

Cats join us on the bed. After she started crying, they just filed in, one by one.

"Is it work?" I say. A calico quietly slips into my lap, sniffing first. I throw her off. (I don't mind the cat itself, it's just that I'm naked here, for crying out loud.)

Theresa crosses her arms, holds herself. She is cradling her breasts in a most alluring way, and I'm trying desperately to concentrate on what she's saying.

"Yes. It's always work. Oh, the other day, some woman gave us her five-year-old cat, this big beautiful white cat, nothing at all wrong with him."

"Why did she have to get rid of it?"

Theresa takes a deep breath before speaking. "Because it kept getting fur on her couch. Fur. Like it's the cat's fault it had *fur*. That poor thing was so scared, it just sat in the cage and cried all afternoon. It was just awful. And it never got adopted. Nobody wants a fully grown five-year-old cat. Everybody wants kittens. So yesterday I had to put it to sleep."

"I'm sorry."

"What's to be sorry about? I do it practically every day. Why is this one any different? I don't know. It's just that some of them affect you more than others."

"Like people."

"The only time he ever really calmed down was right before. I held him for awhile. He was such a sweetheart. I gave him some hot dog and he was purring. He seemed so happy to be held." Theresa stops to blow her nose. "This is going to sound weird, J."

"What?"

"He knew. Right before I gave him the shot, he turned and looked at me. I thought, *He knows that I'm going to kill him*. Then he touched my hand with his paw. It was like he forgave me. He was purring when I killed him."

I guess I'm crying a little too, at this point. "God, I don't know how anyone can do your job."

Theresa grabs another tissue from a box next to the bed. She wipes my eyes, then her own. The darkness beneath them is accentuated by the wetness. "I can't seem to *stop* doing it. It's fucking me up, J. I feel like I owe them my guilt. My nightmares. I don't have anything else to give them," she says angrily, then coughs. "I can't sleep. I'm always in a pissy mood or freaking out about something. It's what will pull the two of us apart, I suspect."

"Don't say that, Theresa. I . . . I—"

"It's what always happens."

The calico jumps back onto the bed, climbs into her lap, puts her nose to Theresa's. "Oh, thank you, Sylvia." She snuggles the cat, half laughing.

"Please don't talk about us being pulled apart, Theresa. I'm not even sure you like me yet."

Theresa frowns at me. "You think I do this with someone I don't like, J?" Then she shrugs slightly. "Well, it's not like I've never done it with someone I don't like, I have, but—"

"Please, I really don't need to hear about your other people. I'm not exactly the most experienced person in the world."

She laughs. "Gee, I'm really disappointed, J. I was hoping you were a total slut, like most men."

"I'm sure I would've been if I had the chance. Look—I just, it's just that, I'm kind of smitten with you."

Theresa smiles at my choice of words. Then when I look as though I may continue down this same road, I watch the terror rise in her eyes. I start to feel shaky for what I might say here.

"In fact," I say, "I, I think maybe—"

Theresa lets out a scream and all the cats jump off the bed. She leans over and kisses me hard, over and over. "Please. Please. No," she says, pushing slick salt lips against mine, pushing me down, hushing me with her body.

Say What?

(So I was going to tell her I thought maybe I loved her. Is that so bad? I wasn't expecting her to say it back to me, or anything like that. Let's not be ridiculous here. We've only known each other a short time, I know that. It's just that most of the time, I don't know how I feel about anything. But every once in a while, in the middle of all the dithering and futtering around that is my life, occasionally I get a crystalline glimpse of how I actually feel about something. When that happens, I try to acknowledge it. That's all. But if she doesn't want me to, I won't. I'll never say it if she doesn't want me to say it. I will not say it for as long as she'll let me be there to not say it. I am starting to wonder, though, how long that will be.)

Spending the Night—Do'⋏ and Don't'⋏

An hour later, Theresa turns on the poodle lamp clamped to her headboard and announces that I have to go. This time, I protest slightly.

"I don't like people to stay overnight," she says.

I look at her, thinking that she's kidding at first. After all, what difference could it make? We've just shared the most intimate of acts. (Actually, that's not true. We haven't gone junking yet. I'm thinking of asking her very soon.) Soon I can see that she's not kidding. At that point, I ache a bit, if only because I have rules about junking and what I eat on particular nights of the week, and she has rules about people sleeping over after sex.

"Okay," I say, thinking I'm being a good little soldier about the whole thing. "I'll leave."

Big sigh. "J, stop looking so hurt. Look, I'll never be able to sleep if someone is here. I mean, I probably won't be able to sleep anyway, but if someone is here, it's practically an impossibility."

"Like insomnia, huh?"

"I guess you could call it that."

"I don't mind. We could stay up together. It'd be fun."

Theresa affects a big fake grin. "Yeah! We can listen to records and bake cookies and tell scary stories."

"You're mocking me."

"Very perceptive, J. I'll thank you not to turn my sleeplessness into a fucking pajama party."

"I'm sorry. Maybe I could help. I could give you a massage." I raise my hands and put them on her shoulders.

"Stop it," she says, twisting her bare shoulders away from me.

"Please let me stay," I say. I guess I'm kind of begging at this point. I don't know why this means so much to me. Yes I do. I'm tired of sleeping alone, especially lately. Also, I desperately want to be different. I want to be the guy she lets stay over. It's all I've got. It will keep my mind off those other guys, if I can be the special one.

"J, I said no. Goddamn it, this is not up for discussion."

"Okay, fine. I'm sorry." I whip the sheet off me, swing my feet over, and start searching for my underwear. "I'll leave."

Theresa takes a loud and dramatic breath. "Oh shit. J. Don't get all huffy on me." First she sounds pissed, then just exasperated. "Just hold on for a minute, okay?" She grabs my wrist.

I twist it away, concentrate on finding my boxers. "I thought you were in such a hurry for me to leave."

"J, I just— It's just not a good idea for you to stay. Don't be mad, please? It has nothing to do with you, okay? Please?"

She scoots over to my side of the bed to give me a hug. I stop being mad and hug her back. I find it difficult to be mean to a naked woman asking for my forgiveness. I am a man, after all.

So, in typical man fashion, I say, "Then if it has nothing to do with me, why not let me stay?"

"J . . ."

She seems so stressed here, I know I shouldn't push her, but I can't stop. "Please let me stay. Maybe it will help that I'm here. Please, Theresa. I don't want to go home."

Where that came from, I don't know. Maybe I made it up. But I can tell I've struck a nerve.

"Your parents' stuff?" she says.

There is nothing to do but nod my head.

"All right. You can stay, J. But don't say I didn't warn you."

I Stay Overnight

After Theresa warms up to the idea of me staying over, things are fine. After she curls up on one side of me, cats curl up all around us. The sheet that covers us is taut, a tent staked by felines. I can't sleep this way. And every five minutes, Theresa lets out an exhausted sigh. This doesn't help. I have nothing else to do, so I start rubbing her head. I wait for objections, but there are none. I even hear a slight murmur of pleasure. I am actually quite good at massaging heads and necks and shoulders. My mother used to make me rub her back when I was a kid. I would try to stop and she'd say, "Just a little more." I'd practically rub my little digits to bloody nubs. Still, it was good practice.

I continue massaging—temples, crown, base of the skull. After about a half hour, the sighs become less pronounced and less frequent. A few minutes later, Theresa's breathing changes, the breaths get shallower. By the time she starts snoring, it is about three-thirty by the old Westinghouse next to the bed and I am actually starting to feel as though I could fall asleep myself. A short time after I stop rubbing, Theresa begins to mumble in her sleep. At first I think that she is talking to me, yet I can't understand a word of it. It sounds like a conversation, almost as though she is trying to convince someone of something. I fall asleep to the sound of her burbling, content that she is at least getting some sleep.

It is about quarter to five when Theresa's wrist smacks me upside the head. I start to rouse when her hand hits me. I feel the thick silver band on her thumb bite into my cheekbone. At this point, she is flailing around pretty good, talking like crazy.

"Theresa, are you okay?" I know she is still asleep and I don't want to wake her, but I think I'm bleeding. "Theresa?"

Then, well, she kind of screams. Not incredibly loud, but loud enough.

I throw my arms around her from behind to keep her from hurting me again or herself. "Theresa, wake up," I shriek into her ear. "You're having a bad dream."

"Who is that?" she says.

"It's J, Theresa. It's J." I try to concentrate on the terror she seems to be feeling and not on the fact that she's not sure who's in bed with her. "It's J. Are you all right?"

She turns around and clutches me, as hard as I've ever been held. I can feel the tears on the nape of my neck, rolling across my shoulder blade. She is crying, but there is no sobbing or any noise at all. "Theresa, please. It's okay, it's okay." She is still squeezing me. (I know it's awful of me, but I'm happy about this. She's glad I'm here.)

"The dream?"

I feel her nod. "You want to talk about it, or would you rather not?"

"Not."

"Okay."

She pulls her head back and looks at me. Even in the dim morning light, I can see the terror and fatigue in her eyes.

"You're bleeding. Did I do that?"

"I'll live. You want to go back to sleep or do you want to get up? It's getting light outside."

"I think you should go, J."

This I did not expect. "I'm worried about you."

"J, this happens all the time. I wish you had listened to me last night. I don't like that you saw this."

"But I don't mind."

"J. *I* mind. Please go."

Funk and Junk

So here I am at home, wide awake at six-fifteen on a Monday morning. I make a pot of tea and I spend part of the morning studiously avoiding the stuff from my parents' house. Instead, I listen to Seventies dance eight-tracks (Ohio Players, Chic, B.T. Express) and clean up estate sale things that I've brought in from the garage. There is some good stuff—Tom and Jerry cups and bowl, Arizona souvenir napkin holder, Fifties fold-out wooden condiment tray, a set of brushed aluminum kitchen canisters. This junk will sell.

At around ten, I give Theresa a call at home. There's no answer. Either she's not there or she does not want to talk to me. I think about trying her at work, but I'm pretty sure the shelter is closed on Mondays.

I give myself a choice, a lesser-of-two-evils type of choice. I can either go over to my parents' house and do my final sweep of the main floor and upstairs, or I can go downstairs and start to deal with the stuff I've brought back. I really don't feel like driving, so I opt for the basement.

I have to do something about my parents' things soon. This becomes eminently apparent as I plod downstairs with a cup of tea. When I reach the bottom of the steps, I recall that I can no longer move around in my basement.

I set my teacup on the last step. With my foot, I push a few of the cardboard boxes away so I can make it over to one of my parents' studio chairs. The box next to the chair is one that I put there days ago (though it feels like weeks). I can tell by the way I crisscrossed the flaps to keep them closed. When I fumble them open, I have no idea what's inside until I see the copy of *Everything You Ever Wanted to Know About Sex* and realize it's the box with the stuff from my parents' Sex Drawer. I want to just put it aside, but I am immediately drawn into it again. Beneath the book, there are a few old magazines from the Seventies—*Woman's Day, McCall's, Family Circle*—but stashed between them is a thickish envelope, flap curled, gum yellowed, edge of the envelope slightly soiled as if handled often. When I pull it from the box, I see scribbling along the back, a long list of years: 1958, 1959, 1960, 1963, and continuing on. The last date is about six years ago.

When I open the envelope, there is a flowery sweet scent. Somehow, I know that it's Jungle Gardenia. I don't know why this envelope would have a scent or how I know what it is, but I know, as if I have summoned this information from a secret olfactory fold of my brain. I put my hand inside the envelope and feel the cool slick surface of a photograph.

The first one is a moody sepia-tone shot of a nude woman. She is sitting in a chair, leaning forward, looking down and to the right, dark hair over face, legs slightly spread. In the photo, the woman's body (a very nice body) is really all that is illuminated, the source of all light in the photograph. I have to admit, I am a little surprised here. I seem to have stumbled upon a cache of ancient erotica left there by, I would presume, my father. I have heard about this sort of thing from estate sale people. But then I look at the photograph again and feel a kind of fear surge through me. The woman's face is obscured, but there is something familiar about her. I know the hair. I know the arm. I know the chin. Before I even remove another photograph from the envelope, I know that the woman in the picture is my mother.

I lean forward in the chair. (Apparently, I've been forgetting to breathe.) With the shift of my weight, the bands that support the bottom cushion creak, which makes me realize that, in the photograph, my mother is sitting in the same chair I'm sitting in right now.

The second picture looks as though it was taken sometime in the Sixties, with the reddish, vaguely artificial color characteristic of photographs taken around that time. My mother's hair is fuller, blonde now, styled in a French twist, looking more the way I remember her when I was a child. She is posed, standing against a doorframe, one foot resting on the frame, knee jutting. She is completely naked again, looking dreamily somewhere to the left of the camera.

I can hardly bring myself to look at the third picture (full frontal, perched on a tub, my mother with a sponge), yet when I do look, I can't seem to stop. I keep trying not to be surprised. I put the photographs down, stand up from the chair, thinking I will go upstairs (for more tea? For what?), but I just sit back down. I reach again into the envelope and pull out the rest. There are eleven others, all of them nudes (all of them artfully shot, yet quite explicit). I discover that each one is dated on the back in my father's script. The earliest photo is from 1958, two years before my parents got married. My mother is sitting on a beach somewhere, legs outstretched, arms bent behind her to support her upper torso, nipples tipped skyward, an erotic version of the pose of the girl in the old Coca-Cola ad, the one with the headline that reads *Yes*. My mother is looking straight at the camera, twenty-three years old and obviously proud of the wild project in which she is participating, in which she is the sole subject.

The other photos range anywhere from one to five years apart, according to their markings. Some are color, some black-and-white, in various poses, usually indoors. The most recent is from six years ago, shortly before my father died. My mother at age fifty-seven. The pose is slightly tamer, in a rumpled bed, yet still extremely revealing. I make myself look at this photo. My mother does not look like she is enjoying herself in this picture, not like the others. I don't think it's because her breasts sag or that her pubic hair is sparked with white or that her legs are twined with purple, but because she knows this will be the last photograph. Along the left side of the picture, almost invisible, there is a gray strip that I recognize as the edge of an oxygen tank.

I gently place all the photographs back in their envelope. I am not sure what to do with these, whether to show them to Linda or not. I don't know how she'll feel about them. Yes I do, but that doesn't mean she wouldn't want to know. I don't know how I feel about them. I am not a prude, and I am certainly not disgusted, but it is a tad weird to find nude photographs of your mother. The truly weird thing is, my parents didn't really get along for most of my childhood, yet apparently they still had this ritual they performed, a ritual that long outlasted my father's photographic career.

I decide that I'm done. I head back upstairs, try to call Theresa again.

An Off Day

Even though I have been opening the store the past few Mondays, I decide to take this one off. I check the newspapers. There are a few garage sales around (this is the peak of garage sale season— you can find them pretty much seven days a week), most of them in far suburbs, in areas way too new to have anything truly good. Further examination reveals, however, a small concentration of sales in Pontiac, where there are some promising old neighborhoods, as well as a few good thrift stores. I opt for them and hope for the best.

By three-thirty, I am a beaten man. I have pissed away all afternoon getting lost, driving to five different garage sales and not one of them has had anything worth purchasing. There is one more that I have circled in the paper, but I decide to blow it off. This is a risky thing, I grant you, because sometimes the last sale is the one that changes your luck. But most of the time, it isn't.

Either way, I can't go home empty-handed. My last hope is the Salvation Army. As I head down Wide Track Drive, I start to feel my luck change. But what this is really is the realization that no matter what's there, I will buy something, if only just to break the curse.

Crisis Averted

I am in luck. There is a pair of painted plaster fruit wall hangings (apple and grapes) and a full place setting of pink Melmac that I'm sure I can sell. The whole thing runs me $2.83. And I walk out a happy, still junk-lucky man. This may sound silly, but no one, from the lowliest Tuesday-morning trash picker to the toniest antique dealer, can afford a dry spell. I've had them and they are not fun. Once it happens, there's nothing you can do but ride it out. That ride can take days, weeks, even months, and will most surely drop you off at the Depths of Despair, searching anywhere and everywhere for that something of value that will change your luck. That's why I always buy at least a trinket, just as tribute to those capricious gods of junk fortune. Also, if you start thinking that you're never going to find something, then you won't find anything. Whatever happens, the true junker cannot be desperate. Like dogs, the junk gods can smell fear. You will most surely be punished.

On the way back home, I call Theresa again, leave another message. I try the shelter, but as I suspected, it's closed today. I decide to go over to her apartment.

In front of Theresa's building, there are usually some old men hanging around, sitting on ancient kitchen chairs (beat to hell by constant use, unfortunately), whose job is to scowl at everybody who enters the building. After I pass through this phalanx of dour geezers, I stand in front of her door for just a minute or two and listen. There is a meow, but no footsteps. When I knock, four or five or more cats all chattering at the door. No Theresa. I pull out my notebook, the one where I keep my list of things I actually need for my house (magazine rack, floor lamp, bookshelf), and write a short note:

> T—
> Stopped by to say hey. Give me a call.
>   —J

After I fold the note and wedge it in her doorjamb, I pull it out again and scrawl "Miss you" at the bottom. Of course, I immediately regret doing this. I almost tear it off three times, then I decide to leave it.

Why I Hate Answering Machines Part II

"Richard, I hope you're getting everything you want from the house, because, don't forget, the estate sale people are starting Thursday."

This is the message on my machine waiting for me when I get home. I hit "Erase," head into the living room, put Bob Wills & The Texas Playboys on the turntable, and meander into the kitchen in search of food.

Monday's Dinty Moore Beef Stew does not taste very good. Perhaps it's a bad can, though I've never had one before. I look through the boxes of Mom and Dad's canned goods, thinking about eating something else, but the stew has already filled me up, albeit unhappily. Then Bob Wills's whining on "Roly Poly" sends me running into the living room in agony. I try a Provocative Percussion LP, hoping it will relax me. Enoch Light usually works, but not tonight.

All night long, I feel unsettled. I try not to wait for the phone to ring. I try not to keep wondering why Theresa doesn't call me. I know it's only been a little while, but we have been, well, intimate, and I just want to talk to her. She's acting like it's no big thing, which maybe it isn't to her. I turn on the TV. There is nothing on. I turn off the TV. I don't feel like reading. It's just been a stupid day all around.

The Next Level of Intimacy

Tuesday, I am awakened by the phone at about eight. It's Theresa and she seems pretty excited.

"J. Guess what? I've got the day off. I thought we'd go junking. What do you think?"

"That'd be great," I say, drowsily.

"Would you drive? I mean, you've got the truck and all."

"Sure. Okay. I'll pick you up in an hour."

I'm pleased at first, but after I hang up, I start to have second thoughts. Fred's the last person I went junking with, and although it was fine, there is still something that changes the experience for me. You have to adjust to someone else's junking style, go at their speed, spend time on stuff you might not care about. There's also the fact that I've never actually gone junking with a woman. I'm not sure what to expect. The closest I've ever come is with the woman from the Salvation Army. (That's just because we both worked there. She never would have dreamed of going to a thrift store in her spare time. If I had even suggested it, she probably would have clobbered me.)

When I pick up Theresa, she is all smiles and caffeinated jollity. She says she needs this day off, and I agree. It will be good for her. I quickly warm up to the whole idea. After consulting the papers, we decide to head for a freak Tuesday "estate sale" in Rosedale Park, an interesting neighborhood in northwest Detroit, a pocket of swank in a prairie of blight. (I put the quotes around "estate sale" here because I suspect it's more like a garage sale. Still, it's a cool old neighborhood and Theresa has never seen it, so it's worth hitting.) We are heading down the Southfield freeway, jabbering away, when Theresa starts screaming at me.

"J! Pull the car over! Hurry, pull over! *Now!*"

This, not surprisingly, scares holy hell out of me. And since I happen to be in the middle lane, pulling over isn't all that easy to do. Finally, I manage to cross over and get up on the shoulder, Theresa screeching at me all the way. She jumps out of the truck and yells to me, "Get the license number of that gray Pontiac up there! Hurry, J!"

"What's going on?" I plead.

"Those fuckers just dumped a dog. Go, J!"

Suddenly, I'm involved in some sort of high-speed chase. I didn't even see anything happen. I get back on the freeway and drive like a lunatic for a few miles, but there's no gray Pontiac anywhere in sight. When I exit and double back to pick Theresa up, she's nowhere to be found either. I get out of the truck at the area where I had dropped her off. (This does not make me happy: deafening engine roar, putrid diesel fumes, cars rocketing past at seventy-five mph two feet away from me. Yikes.) Theresa then appears at the top of the embankment. She walks down the steep hill to my truck, looking discouraged, obviously not a thought about the danger.

"He got away from me," Theresa says, disappointed. "Can we just stay for a little while to see if he comes back?"

"Sure."

"Sometimes they'll get in the car if you just open the back door. Any luck getting the license number?"

"No. I couldn't even spot the car. I'm sorry, Theresa."

She pats my arm. "It's okay, J. You tried. Let's just see if we can get the dog. The poor thing looked so scared."

I open the passenger door. We slide in. "Is this common?" I say. "People dumping animals on the freeway?"

"All the time. It's a popular disposal method. Dump the dog, it freaks, runs into traffic, no longer a problem." Theresa shakes her head in disbelief. "I've just never had it done in *front* of me."

We wait. After a half hour, Theresa spots the dog, a beagle, at the top of the embankment. When it sees my truck, it runs away again.

After an hour, we have drunk all my tea, eaten the tube of Pringles I bought specially for our little junking expedition. (I usually don't eat while junking, it slows you down, but I made an exception today.) Traffic thins out considerably. One car pulls over and a man in a business suit asks if we want him to call a tow truck. We thank him and tell him that we're waiting for someone.

Later, I put in a sick comedy cassette I made from Rudy Ray Moore, Lenny Bruce, Pigmeat Markham, Rusty Warren, and Moms Mabley LPs, but then I turn it off. Somehow "The Signifying Monkey" doesn't seem appropriate, considering our mission.

"Just a little longer, J. Okay?"

I must be looking antsy. Theresa smiles at me, a worried smile that asks me to please understand.

"Sure. It's all right."

After another half hour, Theresa gives up. At least, I think she's going to give up. "Look," she says. "Do you mind if we go up to the next exit, turn around, and drive past again? I have a feeling he'll be back."

"Okay." At this point, all my hopes of going junking have flitted away. I'm just happy for something to do. I start the truck and we head up to the next exit, which is about two miles away. We then circle back, get back on the freeway again, and pass the area where we were parked.

"Shit. No sign of him," says Theresa.

I am dying to hit some thrifts, but know what I have to do. "You want to take one more lap?"

"Thank you, J." She puts her hand on my knee, and I realize that I would drive in circles for this woman all day.

After two more laps, we head over to the big St. Vincent de Paul store in Lincoln Park. We walk around and see objects from our childhoods, titter at the ugly stuff, marvel at the truly ugly stuff. She wants to explore areas that I don't usually think of—light fixtures, typewriters, bowling balls. I score a Chinese junk boat TV lamp, a lightly chipped Fifties plaster wall hanging of a gaucho, and a Bermuda souvenir plate with hibiscus and golfers on it. Theresa unearths a starburst clock from the Sixties that still seems to work and a wooden tiki mug. We do well. Afterward, we hit the Council for the Blind and the Salvation Army, but no luck. Even still, I have decided that I like doing my rounds with Theresa. It is a good junk combination. I am happy as pie by the time we get back on the freeway. I can tell Theresa is, too.

"Did you see that biker chick that ran the place?" she says, scooching up next to me on my jumbo bench seat, placing her hand on my arm. (My hands, however, remain safely on the wheel at the ten and two positions. What can I say? I'm a disgustingly conscientious driver.) "Man, she was a trip! She had on all that leather, then the Lee Press-Ons, the gold rings, the gold bracelets, the gold necklaces, then the tatts on her fingers. Did you see those?"

I laugh. "A definite fashion statement. They didn't say 'Love' on the left and 'Hate' on the right, did they?"

"I wanted to see, but I was afraid to get too close."

"Incredible."

"J. Turn the truck around."

"What's wrong?"

"Just turn it around. At the next exit, okay?"

I keep asking Theresa what's wrong, but she won't answer me. When she directs me to get back on the freeway going south, I figure it out and have enough sense to shut up. When we approach the same area where the people dumped the dog, I know I am right. There on the shoulder, body twisted impossibly, blood at the maw, is the beagle. I pull over. Theresa opens the door to the truck, walks over to the dog, and kneels next to it. I turn off the engine.

"He was waiting for them to come back," she says, as I kneel down next to her. Her voice is quiet, but unquavering. Theresa runs her fingers through the dog's fur, strokes its head. With her other hand, she pushes the body into a natural position on the gravel. "They always think the people are going to come back for them. That it was some sort of mistake."

"Theresa—" I say, but I don't think she hears me. She is in a different place. She doesn't even seem to notice the blood on her fingers.

"Do you know anyone that trusting? I don't."

Five or six cars roar past, but no one stops.

"Do you have a blanket or anything?"

"Yeah." I walk over to my truck, open the tailgate, pull out the moth-eaten blue-and-green Pendleton that I use to protect fragile junk.

I give it to Theresa, and gently, methodically, as if she were wrapping a present, she drapes the dead beagle in the blanket. In the truck, she cradles it in her lap on the front seat. She tells me I will drop her off at the shelter, that she will catch a ride home with somebody. She will not debate it with me.

The only other thing Theresa says is, "This is my fault."

Still Life with Green Beans

Wednesday morning, there's nothing of junk promise in the papers, so I go back to bed. At ten, I shower, fill my thermos, and head to the store, where I sweep up, then go out for a hamburger. Nothing really happens until about three-fifteen, when I actually sell something. A beige fiberglass Herman Miller–style shell chair (somehow selling a knockoff doesn't bother me) that I bought for two dollars. I sell that bad boy for fifteen! Plus, the same guy buys a chartreuse pagoda lamp and some weird wine goblets from a place called LUMS.

Afterward, feeling good about making a little money, I try Theresa at the shelter. They tell me she is busy and can't be disturbed. I don't know how to take this. She does not return my call. Or the one after that. Or, I'm afraid, the one after that. At six-thirty, I leave for home, a little depressed, a little pissed. I tell myself that I cannot call her again. I tell myself that I have to wait for her to call me back.

At home, my Ramen Chicken Noodle Soup is inedible. I pitch the whole thing and search again through Mom's groceries. I uncover cans of Campbell's Cream of Mushroom Soup, Hunt's French Style Green Beans, and Durkee's French Fried Onion Rings. Suddenly, I crave a bowl of Zesty Green Bean Casserole. It doesn't make me all weepy or anything this time, it just sounds good. It sounds *zesty*. I mix the soup and beans up in a shallow dish with a little pepper and some margarine, throw the onions on top, and put the whole kit and caboodle in the oven at 350° Then, as if by concocting this slop I have summoned up some powerful gastronomic necromancy, the phone rings and it is Theresa.

"Hi baby," she says to me, chewing gum with mouth open (didn't her mother tell her?), voice all sweet grape and purple velvet.

No one has ever greeted me this way. Suddenly all is forgiven. I forget to be annoyed. I forget to be aloof. I just want to crawl into the receiver with that voice.

"Sorry I didn't call sooner. You feel like coming over?"

"Hi," I say, still dumbly reacting to her greeting.

"Hi." She sounds a little down, but I hear her smiling at me, at my swooning. "So you want to come over?"

"Okay. I just put some Zesty Green Bean Casserole in the oven. I could bring it over when it's done."

She laughs, halfheartedly, but sincerely. "How cute. That's the recipe you were bawling over when I met you."

"I remember." I can't explain why, but this hurts a little.

"Okay, Betty Crocker. Just make it snappy, okay?"

I Make a Joke

I arrive at Theresa's, casserole in hand. I stand there at her door for a moment, enjoying this moment of not being all that nervous, of actually feeling pretty comfortable going over to a woman's place, a woman that I am seeing (my girlfriend?).

I knock. Theresa opens the door (shrunken white T-shirt, Fifties dice skirt, pearly-blue barrette, barefoot) and smiles indulgently at me, at my foil-wrapped offering.

"How thoughtful. A hostess gift."

"Hot dish for a hot dish," I say, rather pleased with myself. I thought it up on the way over.

"You ass," Theresa says, laughing. She gives me a grape kiss. "Come on in."

While Theresa puts the casserole on the table, I am greeted by cats. Three of them come right up to me, a tabby, a marmalade, and yet another that I have never seen before, a dalmatian. The marmalade rubs herself against me and purrs loudly, while the others sniff.

"I think Sedgwick has a crush on you," says Theresa, back now, slinging her wrists over my head, behind my neck. "I'm kind of glad to see you myself."

"How was your day?" I say, asking the question for the sheer prosaic pleasure of it, for the couple-y sound of it. Behind her, I see that her mannequin has more Post-Its on it than ever.

"I don't think I want to talk about it," says Theresa, suddenly looking exhausted. She rests her head on my collarbone.

"What happened?"

"Let's not talk about it, J. Really. I've been talking about work way too much lately."

"Okay." I am slightly miffed at this. Here I am thinking that I might be part of a couple, yet she won't even tell me about her crummy day.

Theresa kisses me, then slides her lips over to my right ear. "J, let's go to bed."

"I, uh—"

"We'll have your lovely casserole after. I need you right now."

"I . . ."

"Let's consider that a 'yes.'"

Sex Problems of a Voluntary Nature

I'm not sure all my hemming and hawing truly did constitute a yes, but I certainly didn't put up much of a fight. What follows is the loudest, most acrobatic, and probably the wildest sex I've ever had (I realize this isn't saying much). During it, Theresa is on top of me (forgive me these graphic details), eyes closed, slamming me against the headboard of her Fifties maple bed painted black (a junk sin). Now all this is fine, but something starts to nag me (between shimmering, prickly whitecaps of pleasure). I sense that all this—activity—is not borne of a raging desire for yours truly, but something else entirely. This really bugs me after a while. So much so that I actually stop *in medias res*. (An amazing feat, I think, for someone with a penis.)

"J, what's wrong? Why'd you stop?" says Theresa, panting, eyes open now, focused yet bewildered.

"I'm fine. I just get this weird feeling that you're not really having sex with me. That it doesn't even matter that I'm here." Am I really saying this?

"Come on, J. That's not true."

"It's like you're trying to fuck something away."

"Oh, please." She hooks a damp lock of dark hair behind her ear and peers down at me, annoyed.

"I'm not kidding."

"Well, what do you care?"

"What do I care? You don't need me, you just need a cock."

"Well, it's your cock. Doesn't that count for anything? Come on, J."

She starts to rock on me again and I can't believe that I stop her again. "No. I don't like this. You might as well be fucking your pals Roger or Dorr or whoever else." I disengage myself.

"Maybe I will next time," she says, rolling off of me.

I move to the other side of the bed, staring at the table filled with candles. None of the candles are lit, but from the light of the lava lamp I can make out tiny framed photos of dogs and cats. I've noticed them before, but this time I really look at them. Some of the pictures are pocked and discolored, like they were cut from

Polaroids. The weird thing is, the little frames that hold the photos are not old or junked at all, they are the kind that you buy new in, like, Hallmark stores—goldtone and brushed silver, some of them bordered with little bones or fish. This is very uncharacteristic of Theresa, and I forget for the moment that I am having a sex argument (my first!).

"Why don't you just leave?" Theresa says, back turned to me, facing the mural.

I turn to her, curious now, talking to the back of her head. "Who are all these animals, Theresa?"

"Go *away*." She curls her knees to her chest, shutting me out further.

For some reason, I just keep pressing her. I am annoyed now, but I feel stupid too, mad at myself, even though I know I was right about the sex.

"Then tell me what happened today," I say, my head over hers. "Or was it yesterday? I told you that dog wasn't your fault. He was afraid of us. There was nothing you could do. There was nothing anyone could do."

"Shut up, J. You don't know anything about it."

"Just tell me what's going on. I'd be happy to let you do whatever you wanted if you'd just let me know what was going on."

She turns around now, trying desperately to look normal, but her eyes give her away. "Let's go out and get something to eat, J, okay? Or go to a movie."

Her voice has gone dead and flat. I should recognize that this obvious change of subject means that I have gotten to her. I should stop here and comfort her, but I don't. "Theresa, just tell me. What happened?"

"I told you I don't want to talk about it."

"Why not?"

"I just don't want to."

Tears are starting to well, but I see something else happen there too. A change. She is giving herself over to something. I feel regret rise in my throat. It starts swelling in me, giant waves of it, a tsunami of regret. I know that it is too late.

"You asshole," she says, starting to sob.

"What?"

Theresa has wrapped a sheet around herself, is holding herself, the way I should be holding her. She is starting to rock in the bed. "I killed fifty-one animals today."

"Oh shit."

"They brought in all these cats from this one house. This woman's husband hated cats, so she kept getting more and more, just to spite him. Then they started to breed. Seventy-three cats all living in one house. The cruelty investigator found one litter box and one food dish."

"God."

"When they brought them in, it was so horrible. Most of the cats were so feral they wouldn't even get near a human. They were all diseased and inbred and starving. It was just awful." Her eyes are still closed.

"Did you—"

"That's all we did all afternoon. Elliot set up another table in the Euth Room. Then we did one after another after another. Like machines."

"Oh."

"There was a mountain of dead cats by the furnace. We could have used a shovel."

She sits back in bed, staring at the wall. "Then, at the end of the day, we had to do all the animals we were scheduled to do. I had to put down eight dogs, then a litter of cats that was perfectly healthy."

Theresa wipes her eyes with the sheet. She continues to speak like I'm not there. "I had the mother on the table, a big tabby, and while I was shaving her paw and wetting the vein, all her kittens were chasing each other, playing around my feet. Then I started to do the kittens one by one. I was just numb by then. But there was this little sweet runty one who was so cute who just kept chirping at me—these little clipped meows." Theresa coughs, covers her face with her hands, takes a couple of quick shallow breaths. She pulls the sheet tighter.

"She kept doing it, even while I killed her brothers and sisters. Finally they were all gone except for her. And when I picked her up, she stopped, and I thought she knew what was coming, then she started purring, and I thought to myself, *I just can't do it, I can't do it*. Then Elliot said, 'What's wrong?' I told him I was going to take this one home. And he said, 'You can't, Theresa. You've got too many. You want me to do it?'"

"So you let him do it?" I say.

"No. I did it."

"Oh."

"After I did it, I kept thinking, *I've changed my mind. I want her after all*. I'm standing there holding this delicate little corpse and I change my mind. I want her to come back. I want to take her home. I want to give her a real name instead of the ones we just make up at the shelter so all the animals have names and we can call them something as we kill them. I want to give her a real girl name, Amelia or Flannery or Jayne or *something*. I'm just standing there, holding this dead kitten, then Elliot just takes her out of my hands and carries her over to the furnace room and lays her down with all her others against her mama."

"I'm so sorry, Theresa."

She stares at the wall with the mural as she speaks. "There's this look in their eyes when you kill them. Suddenly there's just nothing there. Their eyes ghost over. There was a beautiful animal there and now there's nothing. And you did it. And at the time, you can't even stop long enough to realize what you've just done. You just go on and do another one and another one. But each one does something to you. They burn you inside. Pretty soon, there's just this mass of scar tissue where your soul is supposed to be."

Theresa closes her eyes and starts crying again. "I don't know if I can live with myself anymore for what I do."

Then something happens. This naked, vulnerable woman with tears streaming down her face, who a moment ago was sharing the warmth of her body with me, looks up at me and starts to scream.

"Are you fucking happy now? Are you done fucking interrogating me? Want some more details?"

"Theresa, I'm—" I don't know what to do here.

Theresa turns from me again, hunches over in the bed, twists the sheet off herself, starts heaving, having what look to be convulsions. I lie on the bed, wrap my arms around her, try to comfort her. She explodes into motion, a cartoon cloud of flailing arms and legs. Her silver thumb ring lashes my chin (my second ring-related injury), her head collides with my collarbone, and the pearly barrette flies across the room.

"Ow. Theresa, I'm so sorry. I didn't—" She shoves me away, pushes me right off the bed. I fall on my tailbone and it hurts like hell. I knock over an old glass from Cregar's Pickwick House. It shatters against the leg of the bed. She turns around completely, junk demon now, face red, tops of breasts red, whole body red with rage at me. I can smell her rage mingled with the juices of our sex.

"Get the fuck out of here! Why did you keep pressing me? Couldn't you see that I didn't want to talk about this?" Theresa starts throwing clothes at me, and when all my clothes are gone, she begins rocking herself on the bed.

"Theresa—"

"Get out!" she wails at the wall, in a way that must have hurt her throat. Someone pounds on the wall next door.

I scramble off the floor, grab my glasses, my clothes—pants from the dresser, shirt from the table with the lava lamp, which has been jostled and probably suffered irreparable damage. I run out of the room. She slams the door behind me.

Nothing More Than Feelings

At home, I can't begin to believe what happened tonight. So many different emotions and sensations that I haven't even finished experiencing yet: I am still gleeful from hearing Theresa's voice on my phone; still melting from seeing her at the door in dice skirt and pearly barrette; still scared and aroused by her question; still clammy warm and flushed euphoric from making love with her; still amazed by my stopping it; still humming with sick power from pushing Theresa to tell me something she didn't want to tell me; still nauseous at what she told me; still aching from my fall from the bed. Yet none of this compares with the abject throat-clenching terror of the idea that Theresa may not like me any-more.

I pick up the phone and go through the whole B-movie drill of trying to call her, to get her to talk to me. I let the phone ring and ring and ring, finally she picks up, I frantically say her name, and she hangs up. When I call back, the phone is busy, and it stays that way all night.

I am up all night. I fret myself sick. I throw up three times and eventually assume the fetal position on my sweat-soaked bed. I have felt this bad before, but never in this way. I begin to realize that there has been a certain advantage to being an emotional retard for all these years. No one has really managed to do this to me so far.

This sounds so stupid, but I have never missed my mother so much before. Even if she were alive now, I doubt that I would have called her or gone to see her, and even if I had, I'm certain that she would not have had any sage advice for me. She would have simply showered me with platitudes. All through my child-hood, my mother met all of my disappointments, childish heart-breaks, frequent beatings by bullies, with an arsenal of clichés: *There, there, everything will be all right; If he's going to act that way, then he's not really your friend anyway; This too will pass; Everything will seem better in the morning; Better luck next time; You only get as much out of something as you put in.* They wouldn't have helped really, but why do I suddenly miss them so? What I truly miss is the mother of my youth. Because I know what the mother that we just stowed in the earth would have said to me: *You probably deserved it, Richard.*

Why do I even wish I could hear that?

I drag myself from bed and sleepwalk to the bathroom for a

shower. Showers always make me feel better, except for this one. I also manage to cut a huge gash in my cheek while shaving. You might wonder why someone who feels as bad as I do would want to shave. The first thing a man is supposed to do is to stop shaving when he's upset. You'd say, if I was really so crushed, I wouldn't be shaving. Well, you'd be wrong. I needed to shave, so I shaved. That's the way I am. Plus, I am about to go over to Theresa's and throw myself at her mercy and although it might all be more effective if I go over there all grubby and red-eyed and unshaven and torn-up-looking, I seem to be hanging on to some old-fashioned courting notion that I probably read and laughed over in *A Teenager's Guide to Dating*. "Always look your best if you want to make a good impression."

I Stand Up for Myself

I discover that even the crabby old guys are not sitting in front of Theresa's building at seven o'clock on a Thursday morning. I climb the grimy staircase to Theresa's apartment. I knock at the door and hear a chair move inside. She is up. This seems like a good sign. Maybe she is as upset as me. I hear footsteps and meows from inside and I can tell that Theresa is looking through the peephole at me.

"Go away," she says from behind the door.

I address the peephole directly. "Theresa, please let me in. I just want to talk to you. Please."

"No. Go away. I don't want to see you anymore."

"Please, just let me in for a minute, Theresa."

"Fuck off."

I start banging at the door. This is really not like me. I am slamming at the door. "Please. Please. Theresa."

"Go away. I don't *like* you anymore."

Oh shit. I sort of collapse there at the door, weeping and coughing and wheezing. Despite my clean shave and overall tidy appearance, I am not a pretty sight. The people in the surrounding apartments start opening their doors to look at me, this pathetic wretch lying in a heap on their cat lady neighbor's doorstep. I pull myself up into a sitting position, back against Theresa's door, and try to summon the strength to actually stand. When Theresa opens the door, I almost fall backward into her apartment.

She towers over me. I am a caterpillar waiting to be trod upon.

"Why were you so mean?" she says.

"I'm sorry. I'm so sorry, Theresa." I grab her legs, sob into the hem of a faded mint-green chenille bathrobe. I am disgusting even myself here, but I can't seem to help it.

She steps back from my reach. "God, you are fucking pathetic. Close the door," she says.

Snuffling, I pull my leaden legs around and shut the door. I'm not sure I can get up from the floor yet.

Theresa's elbows are flat against her torso, arms crossed at the wrists, as if protecting her vital organs. As she leans down, her red-rimmed, dark-rimmed eyes burrow into my flesh. "Why were you so mean? I've never done anything like that to you. You just kept pushing me and pushing me."

"I know. I know."

"Why?" She is staring down at me.

"I don't know. I just wanted to."

It doesn't take long for me to realize that this is the wrong thing to say. I think she might actually step on me.

"You prick."

"I just feel like I'm totally at your mercy. It scares me."

Finally, the expression of complete loathing on her face gives way to something else, to bewilderment. "Why would you feel that way?"

I hesitate, but only for a moment to wipe my nose before I say it. "You know why. I'm fucking in love with you."

"Shit. Shut *up!*" She claps her hands around her ears, turns away disgusted, walks over to the Chair of Gloom and sits. Two cats jump into her lap.

Sedgwick comes over and plops in my lap. I brush her away and get up from the floor. I walk over to the chair. Another cat, a big white one with pink eyes, jumps up on the arm. Theresa looks like she's in shock. She tugs at the skin of her forefinger with her teeth. A dot of blood blossoms on her cuticle. "I asked you not to say that," she says.

I don't know where it comes from, but suddenly, I am Mr. Glib about the whole thing. "Well, not technically. You asked me not to say something, but it was never actually determined what that thing was." I try to smile, but it makes me realize my nose is running.

Theresa sighs, so very tired. "All right. Maybe I was using you to forget my day and my life, but I still wanted it to be with you. I could have just as easily fucked Roger, you know. I had just seen him. It probably would have been a better idea than calling you."

"Why?"

"Gee, I don't know, J. Could it be 'cause we wouldn't be going through this right now?" Big exhale. "Besides, I can't be calling you up every time I have a bad day. I'll start to depend on you."

I sit on the arm of the chair. "So? Is that so bad?"

She looks at me. "Apparently so, considering how you acted."

I decide that shooting myself right now would really hit the spot.

"Look, I'm sorry about last night," I say, pleading. "I can't say it enough."

"You should be sorry. You were really mean."

"I know. It's just that you never seem to let me in all the way. It kind of made me mad. And the other thing, not letting me say it."

"Why, J? Nothing's going to be gained by saying it."

"Oh. Why not?"

"Because I'm not going to see you anymore."

Color Me Gone

Theresa practically tells me that she loves me, then sends me on my way, almost cheerily, like I'm some unpleasant chore that just needed to be taken care of and now she can go about her business. (Dumb things I gotta do: **1** Pick up cat food. **2** Return library books. **3** Vivisection on J.)

It doesn't make any sense. Maybe I should have made more of a stink—started screaming or breaking things. (But why destroy some innocent junk, just for the sake of a tantrum? That would be wrong.) She was just so matter-of-fact about disposing of me, I didn't know how to act. I just said good-bye and left.

"Have a good life," she said, closing the door behind me. I can't believe she said that. It's like "Have a happy day."

Sitting in the car, still numb, I get this strange lucid sense of things actually having ended, but it's nothing like last night's *I've really blown it. How am I going to live with myself?* kind of terror. Actually, I'm quite calm, especially when you consider the gibbering heap of protoplasm I was a half hour earlier at her door. Surprisingly, I'm not even feeling embarrassed about that. I just feel like there's nothing I can do about any of this.

I start to head home, but, eminently sensible and clear-headed, I know that I can't go there right now. I don't want to go to work yet either. Yet I don't want to be alone right now, so I wheel over to the Rialto for a touch of breakfast. The Rialto is one of my favorite places to eat. It looks as though it belongs in an old train station from a Forties film—weird old chrome fixtures, lodgepole pine paneling, mirrored pie cases, varicose-vein career waitresses with names like Bea and Vernice. On two separate occasions, tragedy has struck the Rialto. The first time, an elderly couple at a window table were killed when a car jumped the curb and crashed through the front window. Then a few years later, some guy pulled out a gun and took a few waitresses hostage. He killed two people. Finally a policeman took him down.

Somehow, the Rialto seems an appropriate place to go this morning.

The Most Important Meal of the Day

When my waitress, Susie (apron button: *When life gives you lemons, make lemonade!*), sets the Rialto Breakfast Special (AKA the Widowmaker—three eggs, bacon, sausage, ham, hash browns, toast, and grilled pineapple ring) down in front of me, I eat like some sort of crazed, rabid animal. I eat and eat and eat. I celebrate my Midwestern roots by putting catsup on everything, including the pineapple ring. Before long, I am a member of the Clean Plate Club. After my fourth cup of bottomless tea, I pay my bill and head out.

It doesn't occur to me that maybe I feel a little *too* good after what has just happened. Of course it doesn't. I still don't want to go home, so I hop on the freeway and head for the parental estate one more time, like I've been meaning to do, just to make sure everything is in order. After all, today's my day for getting things done. Meanwhile, I'm feeling tip-top. I'm the cat's pajamas. I'm the bee's knees. I'm totally in denial. I'm vomiting on the side of the freeway. Oh you kid. Up, up, up it all comes.

After, I start driving again, but am still pretty woozy. Then it gets worse. Being sick has lowered my resistance, and I start the descent into my time-delayed funk. It's a short trip. Before long, I am truly down with the funk. I am the grandmaster of the funk. I have to busy myself soon or else I most certainly will cave in upon myself, a walking sinkhole. Panic clutches my vitals, wrings the air from my lungs, and I strain to keep the truck on the road. I keep driving, nothing else to do.

At my parents' house, I am almost happy to see Linda's car there. I remember the nice thing she did for me by leaving the good stuff there in the storage room downstairs, and I experience warm familial feelings for her. I want to be with someone who likes me, but I will gladly accept someone with whom I have nothing in common, but who is related to me and feels some social and moral obligation to like me just a little.

I walk into the house. Linda is sitting at a card table, writing things in a spiral notebook. She looks up at me and actually smiles. I can't explain how much better this makes me feel, though I'm not sure it shows. I wave to her, in that way you wave to people who are five feet in front from you.

"Hello, Richard," she says.

"Howdy, sis." We are both obviously on our best behaviors.

She puts down her pen. I park it across from her.

"Consider yourself warned, Richard. The estate sale people are going to be here in two hours."

"I'll be gone by then."

"Did you get the stuff I left for you?" she says.

"Yes, I did. Thanks a lot. How did you know what I'd like?"

"Oh, just a guess." She knits her brows, gives me a look, almost maternal. "Are you okay?"

It worries me a little how well she seems to know me. I don't feel like I know anything about her, except bad things. I guess I stopped trying a while ago.

"Uh-huh." I'm trying not to say anything.

"Are you sure?"

I am not going to say anything. It will not help. I will just feel stupid afterward and she'll use it against me.

"You can tell me."

"Oh, I've been seeing this woman and she just dumped me."

I'm not known for my resolve.

Linda is surprised, but apparently not by my being dumped. "Richard, you've been dating?"

"If you want to call it that. I liken it more to bloodletting."

"I didn't think you did that. You've been alone for— I mean, the only one I even remember was that trashy little blonde. I just thought you . . ."

Now she is starting to sound like my sister. "What?" I say, getting kind of steamed now. "Lived like a monk? Cruised little boys? Boinked barnyard animals? What, Linda?"

"Nothing. I just thought you had convinced yourself that you had *evolved* beyond all that."

Ouch. Linda keeps surprising me. I'm impressed that she can dredge up something this insightfully nasty. I've definitely been underestimating her. I can't come up with a searing rejoinder, so I skitter uncontrollably toward the truth. "No," I say. "I'm just not very good at those kinds of things."

My sister gives me her patented look of disgust, which is exactly like my mother's patented look of disgust. "Oh bullshit, Richard. You have to *try* before you can determine something like that."

I am taken aback for a second, but only a second. "Well, excuse me, Madame Freud. Who the fuck slipped you the clever pills?"

Linda crosses her arms, also just like Mom. "Don't be mean, Richard. I'm just telling you what I've noticed."

"Well, stop noticing things. It doesn't suit you."

"Everyone sees it, Richard. You sit around locked in your house and your little unprofitable store, with all your old junk, spouting off your little theories, acting like you're better than the rest of us. But at least the rest of us are out living our lives."

(What is going on here? My big sister, who is usually dumb as a sputnik lamp, is busting my chops big-time. Excuse me, but here is where I lose it.)

"Oh, so your life is the one I should be judging myself by?" I say. "That's hilarious. People like *you* kill me. You think everybody should be living the exact same nine-to-five Wonder Bread strip-mall life as you. And anyone who doesn't is wrong or *weird*. Yeah, all we want is to be just like you, Linda. Thanks, but if I have to become you, I'll just slash my wrists right now."

"Fuck off, Richard."

Is it just me, or is pretty much everyone telling me to fuck off lately? I don't care, I'm out for blood now. "So, if you're so busy noticing everything, did you happen to notice the photos of Mom?"

"Oh, I saw the pictures. So what? Dad's big dream. That's probably where you get all your pretentious artsy-fartsiness."

She doesn't know what I'm talking about. "I'll be right back." I run out to the truck. (What can I say? I put them there for just this sort of occasion.)

When I come back into the kitchen, I drop the envelope on the table, where they land with a nice, hostile *blap*. "Go ahead, open it."

All right, as soon as I see Linda's face as she sees the first photo, I feel like a fink. My sister, who was always the biggest prude in our family, followed by my mother (apparently I was wrong about that one), looks like she is about to start bawling. All thanks to me. I'd been wanting to do something mean to someone and Linda was the perfect someone. Now I feel even worse.

"Pretty wild, huh?" I say, in damage-control mode, kind of laughing, hoping maybe she'll join in. "I mean, it's no big deal. They're art photos."

"I hate you, Richard." My sister throws down the packet, gets up, and leaves the house. I hear her car start and then she is gone.

So much for that one person who is socially and morally obligated to like me just a little.

Penetralia of the Bungalow

After Linda leaves, I walk around the house, taking a last look. I am amazed at how well organized things are. Linda has really been working at this. All clothes are hanging in the closets or on the closet doors, accessories neatly displayed on the beds, bric-a-brac lined along the dressers and tables. She has thrown away the underwear, made sure no important documents will be destroyed, no family heirlooms sold. I'm willing to bet that she has a checklist for the estate people. I realize that I haven't done anything except look for all the cool stuff, or pick up the things she's left for me. All suspicions are confirmed: She is the responsible one, I am the layabout.

In the basement on the unfinished side, the things that are left are all the usual items, stacks of boxes of years-gone-by— crusted objects of infancy; broken stuff of childhood; hoarded, superfluous debris of abundant middle-class middle-age; corrective, supportive refuse of late life. Shame on us: unwanted gifts (still in cellophane); things saved for, then never used; spares of things for which there was no need of singles; clothes outgrown or never worn; equipment for sports never played; devices for foods never cooked; games played, then forgotten (Life, Clue, Trivial Pursuit). I have seen all these things before in countless other basements, in countless other homes. I have seen too many things of too many lives too many times.

I don't feel very good. I want to go home.

I Fall Back on an Old Friend

I decide to not open the shop today. This, of course, is a very bad idea, yet that doesn't seem to stop me. When I get home, there are no messages on my machine. Tom the mannequin stands over in the corner, in his cabana suit and jaunty hat, waving at me. (He's glad to see me. After all, we've got so much in common. We both look a lot like men.)

It is only one in the afternoon, but I swear I'm ready for bed. Depression has settled around my head like a conical hair dryer from a Fifties beauty salon. I am viewing everything from beneath it, insulated from the rest of the world, pressurized hum in the background. But that hum I hear is not really a hum, it's an endless eight-track tape that whispers the sounds of my wailing on Theresa's doorstep this morning, her dumping me, my Vesuvian retching, the argument with Linda. It plays them over and over, at an almost inaudible level, a bombination, the white noise of failure.

I am so tired, so very tired. But when I lie down on my bed, the pressure intensifies and the volume of the hum goes up a notch. I start hyperventilating and so I have to sit up again, but as soon as I sit up, I get tired again. I go on like this for about a half hour before I give up. I sit there thinking about how tired I am of being me. I'm tired of having to eat every day. I'm tired of having to shit every day. I'm tired of making tea, of drinking it. I'm tired of walking through the same rooms, driving the same streets, going to the same garage sales, going to my store, talking to the same people, going to estate sales, buying the same dead people's same dead junk. I am tired of thinking.

I turn on the television.

All my life, television has always been there for me. Whenever I've been depressed or anxious or sick or unhappy, I've always been able to turn the television on and feel better. You don't have to tell me how sad that is. But I bet if you talked to some other people, *really* talked to them, you'd find plenty that felt the same way. Television just has that effect on people. Yes, yes, I know about those people who don't even have a television and they're so proud of it, how they lord it over everybody. I don't care. I like television. I will shout it from the rooftops—*Television is my friend!* I want the whole world to know. There is nothing that gets your mind off personal agonies better than television. It is my drug of choice. Some folks like heroin, some like booze. Just give me some old reruns from the Fifties, Sixties, Seventies and I'm happy. (Or at least not noticing how unhappy I am.)

But right now, remote control in hand, there's not a damn thing on. I blast through the channels, which is in itself a diversion, but not as good as actually watching something. At first, I settle on an old science fiction movie, some piece of celluloid junk from the Atom Age Fifties, where a guy (after being exposed to radioactivity, no doubt) shrinks down to the size of a wedding cake ornament. He's lost inside a house, and everything he encounters there is a hazard to him. I come in at the scene where he is trapped in a dollhouse, trying to escape the cat. I watch a little, but the cat starts to upset me, so I switch channels again.

I watch television for the next ten hours—sitcoms, cops and robbers shows, talk shows, even a couple of music videos—anything I can possibly stand. Because I cannot possibly stand being conscious of myself right now.

The Anti-Cruelty Shelter Is Neither

Friday morning, I am awakened by my dread, which has now settled over my entire body. I am already exhausted, yet I know that I will not be sleeping any more this morning. I sit up on the couch (television still on, blaring insipid cheery morning chat), try to get used to the idea of waking up in a Theresaless world. (I was not even used to the idea of waking up in a motherless world, and now this.) This fact weighs on me like—oh hell, I'm too tired to think of a simile. Let's just say it gives me very poor posture. I click off the television and suddenly the house is deadly quiet. I turn it back on, change it to the Weather Channel (those graphs and maps and tidy hairdo's somehow soothing), then head for the kitchen. There I stand at the counter for two or three minutes, unable to decide if I want Japanese Green Tea to ease my jangly nerves, or Morning Thunder to jolt me awake, possibly out of this malaise. After more painful deliberation, I decide on the Morning Thunder, knowing I'll regret the shakes it will give me later and the inevitable crash.

Making tea is an excruciatingly tiring process, and I fight off the urge to flop back on the couch to watch more TV or to work myself into yet another sniveling frenzy. Since it is about seven, it occurs to me that perhaps I can put this early rise to good use. I check the papers. There is nothing much going on today, a couple of estate sales in Bloomfield Hills, which will be way too expensive, and a few crummy garage sales. It occurs to me that I really have nothing to do except go through my parents' stuff. I know it's a bad idea, but I simply don't know what else to do with myself. I decide that if I take some to the store, maybe I can get some of it sorted or cleaned up or even out on the shelves. This is not a good time to do this, part of me realizes, but I desperately need to occupy myself.

I load a few large boxes of stuff into the truck. I start to drive to the store, but soon I find myself heading south on Woodward Avenue, into the city, to the Anti-Cruelty Shelter. I know it's stupid, a bad, bad idea, but I can't stop myself. I realize then that I had been thinking this all along, that this was the only reason I could even get myself out of the house. I just want to take a look, just a look. It's eight o'clock, way too early for anyone to be there. No harm done.

Before long I am in a pretty bad part of town driving down John R, right near the Hamtramck border. The street is lined with gutted, burned-out buildings and empty, overgrown fields that used to contain gutted, burned-out buildings. The only businesses that seem to be thriving are the party stores, cinder-block bunkers slathered with ghetto colors—lemon yellow, titty pink, electric blue, slashed by banners for malt liquors and cognacs and cigarettes. On the right, I spot the shelter, a dull brown brick box with another dull brown brick box behind it. Between the two, there's an open space surrounded by a tall fence, lined with razor wire. As I pass, I notice the small gravel parking lot along the opposite side of the first building. There is a long moment where I forget to breathe when I spot Theresa's rusty silver Volare. I suppose I wanted this to happen. Of course I wanted this to happen, but now that it has, I wish I had just gone to work. I park my truck next to Theresa's car.

The battered old wooden front door has no window, but is retrofitted with a peephole. The door is so thick, my knock barely makes any noise, so I must pound on the door, but even that doesn't do much. I press a button I find hidden along the jamb. I think I hear a buzzer sound inside. Swollen minutes pass and I decide that she can't hear, or she just isn't going to come to the door, or she sees me and just won't open up. I buzz once more, then head back toward the car, relieved, yet disappointed.

As I'm rounding the building toward the lot, I hear the wood-on-wood shriek of the door opening. When I turn around, Theresa is standing there outside the doorway in jeans and a work shirt. She has a large dog on a leash, a pit bull. She just stands there, looking at me. I walk toward her. Part of me is thinking about some hokey scene from a movie where the two estranged lovers hurl themselves back into each other's arms, but the expression on Theresa's face does not prompt this sort of action. Also, the pit bull is growling at me. I think he'd take great pleasure in noshing on my windpipe. Theresa tugs his leash, and he settles.

"Why are you here?" she says.

Why am I here? I am an idiot, that's why. *Punish* me. "I was on my way to work and I just wound up driving over here. I don't know why. I'm not stalking you, I swear. I'm just having a hard time with all this. I'm sorry."

"Stop apologizing, J."

"Right. Sorry. Look, I know it was stupid coming over here. But I think what you said yesterday was a really bad idea. If you like, I will not ever say that thing and you certainly don't have to say it, not that you feel it anyway, but—"

"J, shut up. This is not about you. You don't know what I've been through, you have no idea."

"Right. Sorry. This isn't about me. Then why am I here?"

"I don't know, J. Just go home. I can't do this with you. I can't—"

I am actually getting very mad at her. "Look, I'm sorry you have this job that makes you feel so bad. But maybe you should just find a new job."

Suddenly, her anger catches up with mine.

"Is that what you think I need to do? Just find a new job? Who's going to do *this* job? Who's going to take care of these animals?" she says, tugging at the leash. The pit bull growls again as if on cue.

"No one else can do your job? You're not that important, Theresa. None of us are."

"Given. But who, J? Who? I can barely get volunteers down here to take care of the cats."

"Why does it have to be you?" (Now we are just standing there, yelling at each other. People drive by and they don't even seem to notice. One of the advantages of a bad neighborhood.)

"Because it just *does*."

"You can't let someone else do it? Bullshit."

"Everyone wants someone else to do it. But who?"

"Why does that have to be your job? You've made it so you'll never get out of here. The whole world will collapse without you. Except you're a mess. You can't sleep, you're always upset, you've screwed up your life—"

"Oh, because I'm not staying with you? If I hang with you, I'll be fine, right? Is that it? Yeah, you're my salvation. Mr. Self-Esteem. Come on, pull me out of this, J, back into the land of the living. Where you spend all your time so usefully, digging through other people's remains like some ghoul."

I don't know what to say, so I settle for an old favorite. "Fuck you, Theresa." I suppose I am crying by this time.

"Fuck you, too," she says, only she's not crying. I guess she wins.

I turn to get the hell out of there. She follows me all the way to the car, yelling at me, holding the dog back, who is now pissed as hell, barking, gagged vicious gnarls from the throat. He wants to kill me for trying to lure away his precious mistress. I'm surprised she's not letting the thing go after me.

"Save me, J!" she yells after me, all irony now. "Save me from myself!"

I get into my truck and roll up the windows, but I can still hear her and the dog. I start the engine, put in a homemade cassette, and soon Martin Denny's "Quiet Village" is blasting so, I can't hear anything except lush piano and fake bird calls.

I Catch Up on My Rest

I don't really want to talk too much about what happens next. Let's just say I don't spend the next couple of days productively. I don't open the store. I don't go to any estate sales. I don't take care of things around the house. I finally take that much-needed vacation from personal hygiene.

The rest of Friday I spend in bed. Saturday I spend in bed, but I manage to stretch the cable television into the bedroom. On Sunday morning, I sleep in till noon, then decide that now's a good time to explore this whole thing about drinking after getting dumped. I've noticed it's what everyone does on television. Over-all, it seems like a reasonable plan. The problem is, I don't drink that often, so I don't have any liquor in the house. (Not counting the blackberry brandy in my bowling ball liqueur dispenser, which has evaporated into a brownish goo.) This means I actually need to leave the house.

I get in the truck, stop at the first party store that's open, and pick up a half pint of Five o'Clock vodka. (I do not require much alcohol to achieve intoxication and it need not be expensive.) There in the parking lot, after a few bilious capfuls of hooch, I have the brilliant idea of going to the estate sale that is happening right now at my parents' house. (Linda, even furious at me, is so orga-nized that she keeps me apprised of all the estate sale goings-on with dispassionate, yet detailed phone messages. This drives me nuts. Why can't she just be mad at me and let it taint all the other aspects of our relationship? No, she has to be mature. I hate that.)

I nip at the short dog on my way to the estate sale. The Five o'Clock vodka has a piquancy not unlike creosote. Nevertheless, by the time I get to my parents' house, I have a snootful, I am four sheets to the wind, I am crocked, sotted, blotto . . . (I can't think of any more old expressions for being drunk because I am.) I cruise the block, do some reconnaissance, while I finish the bot-tle. I do not see Linda's tidy little Buick anywhere, nor Stu's rugged four-wheel-drive penis substitute, so I am safe. There are a lot of cars, so I park pretty far down the street.

I get out, throw my shoulders back, and strut just as straight and proud as I can. I proceed carefully up my parents' front walk, past the sign that says: *Estate Sale Today*. The company running the sale is not one that I recognize. (That Linda, always looking for the bargain.) Despite the sign, as I walk up onto the porch, I have a moment. I don't know if it's the time of day or that I'm drunk, but this action seems so crucially familiar to me that I believe when I get inside I will see my mother at the kitchen table, cup of tea in front of her, ready to start in on why I am wasting my life. I even believe for a warm nanosecond that I will see my father sitting in the adjoining room, quietly reading the paper.

When I walk in the front door, all I see is a strange woman sitting at a card table with a metal cash box in front of her. (This seems familiar to me as well, but in an entirely different way.) The woman behind the table gives me a strange look. Yet she couldn't possibly know that the swaggering dipsomaniac in front of her is one of her clients. (The advantage of being the irresponsible sibling—I may travel incognito.)

I walk into the living room and it is full of people. There is not that much stuff left. Apparently, our estate sale is a success. I head for the kitchen. There is a box on the counter filled with the items from my parents' junk drawer. The kitchen table is still there and it holds what few items are left from their cupboards and cabinets. Their dishes are gone. Their toaster oven, their blender, their crockery canisters, their saucepans, their butter dish—all gone. Next to me, some fat young woman holds up my mother's favorite mug, a flowered china monstrosity that Linda gave to her, and shows it to her even fatter companion. (Friend? Mother? Daughter?)

"What do you think of this? Do you like it?" she says with a lazy drawl.

"God, that's so ugly."

"Really? I think it's pretty. I'm gonna take it."

"How much?"

"Fifty cents. I'll see if she'll go a quarter."

"Might as well."

I walk into the family room and my father's Early American La-Z-Boy has a tag on it marked twenty-five dollars. That's a pretty good price, I think. What's left of the family-room furniture is priced to move. All the shelves have been stripped bare of books and everything else. When I walk into the dining room and living room, I see where it all has gone. It is all gathered on card tables that line the walls. (All the Danish Modern furniture is long gone to the dealers.) All the little knickknacks my mother collected over the years, pottery from all the road trips we took, her collection of ceramic cats, the china (used once a year, on Thanksgiving), it is all still there.

When I walk back into the kitchen, the two fat women are discussing the merits of nonstick coatings for cookware. The younger one has a cast-iron frying pan of my mother's in her left hand. With all the estate sales I've been to, it has always amazed me that there were people who would buy old frying pans. There are some things even I won't buy used, like underwear. And although I do have a few thrifted items that I cook with at home, I mostly have just cheap stuff that I bought new a long time ago. But this, I decide, is one frying pan I should own, one that I shouldn't have to buy. This woman is holding in her hand the cast-iron frying pan of my youth, my mother's frying pan, the frying pan that cooked the eggs I ate on Saturday mornings, the grilled cheese sandwiches I devoured at lunch with Campbell's Cream of Tomato Soup, the hamburgers that were fried and placed between two slices of Wonder bread. (We did not acknowledge the existence of buns in my family—bread was bread.) Then and there, I know that I must have that frying pan, and I go about devising a plan to rescue it from this troglodyte. (troglodette?)

"You think food'll stick to this, Dee?" says the young fat one about my frying pan.

"Sure will. You'd be better off getting some Silverstone. Nothing sticks to that. God only knows what these people cooked on that thing."

"Indeed," I say, affecting an English accent. I am trying to sound like James Bond, but it is coming out more Monty Python. "God himself only knows. Especially considering the people who must have once lived here."

The younger fat one looks at me. "What? It seems all right. I been in worse places than this."

"You're joking, I'm sure, madam. Look at these people's furnishings. They are undoubtedly the trashiest of white trash. They were probably cooking up a *mess o' possum* in that very pan you hold in your hand."

"You really think so?"

"Indubitably. Were I you, I would put down that pan and exit these premises with the utmost alacrity."

The older fat one looks at me, then looks at the other one and says, "I think he wants your frying pan, Joyce."

The younger fat one looks at me. "No, he doesn't, Dee. Do you, mister?"

I nod my head. "She's quite right, you know."

Joyce frowns at me. "Well, you can't have it," she says, mortally offended. Two seconds ago, she couldn't have cared less about the stupid pan, but now, since someone actually wants it, it's the holy fucking grail.

"Give me the pan, Joyce," I say quietly, still British, but as threatening as possible.

Joyce appends the pan to her ample sweatshirted bosom. It

obscures almost all of Mickey Mouse's torso, but only a fraction of hers. "I will not."

I'm getting tired of this accent, but damn it, when I do something, I carry it through all the way. I try to look mean or crazy, like I could do anything. And even though I feel that way, I don't think it's quite working.

"Joyce," I say, "William Seward Burroughs once said, 'No one owns life, but anyone who can pick up a frying pan owns death.' Don't make me prove it to you, Joyce. Give me the pan."

"I'm getting the manager," says the older fat one.

"Give me the pan, you hog!" I scream in my own voice, trying to wrest it from her grip. The few people who are in the kitchen with us exit rapidly. "Why do you want it, anyway? Go cook your depressing meals on someone else's frying pan!"

I am still trying to yank the frying pan from Joyce when the cash-box woman from the entrance shows up with another older woman. They both try to pull me away from Joyce and the frying pan. There are four women, two of them over the age of fifty-five, trying to restrain me. All women are trying to control me, I decide, and that makes me fight for my frying pan all the harder.

"Sir," she says, grunting from the strain of trying to pull me away from death-gripped Joyce. "I'm afraid if she had the frying pan first, it's hers. There are plenty of other pots and pans available."

"I want this one!" I say.

I am not proud of what I do next. But I do it because I know it will get the job done. I employ a massive head-butt on Joyce. She screams and grabs her forehead with one hand. I grab the pan and charge out of the house. The two estate sale women chase after me not because I have given some lard-ass a possible concussion, but because, after all, I have exited without paying the one-fifty for the frying pan. They run after me for a few houses, but quickly give up. Far down the street, I jump in the truck with my prize and peel rubber out of the neighborhood. I say to myself, *I will never come back here again*. And I won't.

Part 2

My Gradual Return to the Human Race, More Crackpot Theories

No matter what you do, the days pass and pass, pile into weeks, months, years, and soon decades (when you get into your thirties, you start noticing decades) and you realize that your life can't go on forever. (Yet you keep hoping that it might, perhaps due to some clerical error.) Even with the years I've lived, all I really have is this vague notion of temporal accretion, this translucent mound of images, like my father's negatives, the ones I've been sorting and stacking, each memory imposed upon the others, distorting all those above or below. At best, it all could be a pile of brittle, curled photographs held together by a crumbling rubber band. Or else these things, these incident images, these yellowed memories, occurred, but during someone else's life.

We mutter clichés about time flying, marching on, healing all wounds, when in reality, time just makes the wounds terminal. I've noticed that during the ordinary passage of days, the only time I truly feel aware of being alive is when something bad happens. The rest is just the oblivion of normalcy. In the three months that have passed since my mother died and I met/lost Theresa, I have felt awful more often than not, but I have been more aware of my life occurring right in front of me. Painful, but a good thing. After all, do we squeeze as much meaning from our days as we can? Of course not. Too often, we throw away our days just like our junk—half used, three-quarters good. That's what junking is, a chance to go back and use some of what is left over. (*Zut alors!* Were there only some way to do that with time.) Though I still revel and take great comfort in repetition, I know that bad things must happen every so often in order to intensify the experience of the familiar. I suppose I am as at ease with this as a person can be.

Two important things have occurred. First, I tried to sort my parents' things, but it was a waste of time. I felt like a louse for even thinking about selling any of it, even the things that were originally mine. All I could handle was going through my father's photographs. Which was awful at first, then, as I settled into it, a great comfort. I've decided that my father had talent, but hadn't found himself yet. As for my part in the matter, I'm sorry I ruined his career, but there's also a lot to be said for a childhood where you get fed once in a while. You see, I happened to find my father's big publication. There was a stack of copies in another box with photographic stuff—*Like* magazine, December 1964. Ironically enough, the photo was not one of my father's "Work" series or his "Night and City" series, but a color picture of my mother, silhouetted in front of a Christmas tree, glowing all beatific, pregnant as all get out with Linda. I realized that he had made his choice well before I came along.

As for my parents' junk, I finally called up Fred, who has helped some people handle their family's estates. He told me that my problem is not uncommon. At first, everything is sacred, nothing can be given away or sold, much less thrown away. The winnowing process may begin only once a person sheds himself of the emotional weight of objects. To arrive at this takes time, the amount of which varies according to the personal sensibilities of the individual and respective square footage of available storage space. So I decided not to rush myself when it comes to my parents' things. I will do something, but when I'm ready. For right now, it's all in storage. (How can I afford to leave it there? This has to do with the second thing that happened.)

My Ascent to the Bourgeoisie

I have become rich. Yes, I am quite a wealthy man, at least wealthy for me. I discovered that sister Linda has quite the knack for real estate. (Mom would have been proud. But then, she was already proud of Linda.) She managed to sell the house for a handsome sum, and I got half. I let Linda keep everything from the estate sale. (She did all the work. I got the frying pan. It seemed fair.) That made her sort of like me again, at least as much as she ever did.

I'm not exactly sure of what to do with all this money, really. I don't need anything. I have my store. (Though it took a while to get my customers back after the three weeks I was closed due to depression.) I have my house. I have lots of good junk. I'm happy. That's not entirely true. In regards to Theresa, I can at least say that I haven't been completely pathetic about the whole thing. I haven't been calling her day and night or sending her flowers or driving by her apartment at all hours. I haven't left any gifts on her doorstep, like those statuettes I see all the time at the thrifts—the little munchkin holding his hands far apart and saying "I wuv you this much." I haven't done that. I have simply done what comes naturally. Nothing.

I guess it's working, because I don't feel sick every day like I did for the first month and I actually sleep okay for most of the night. I am back on my schedule again, junking most every day (earlier and making good scores), though we're well into fall. There are plenty of estate sales (other people's dead parents, thank God), a few garage sales (though by this time of year, most of the good stuff is long gone), and the thrift stores are full. I have also made a discovery: Junking is even better when you don't need to do it.

Have a Happy Estate Sale

Today's sale is on the northwest side of the city, an older area called Redford Township. I haven't explored there as much as I'd like, but it's kind of a neat area. Miles and miles of smallish, alarmingly identical postwar ranch houses, Detroit's own little Levittown. The estate belonged to an elderly couple, but here's the surprise. They're both still alive and healthy. Max and Bernice are moving to a retirement village in Florida and "getting rid of every goddamn thing we own," as they put it.

They really have some pretty good stuff. I pick up a nice Fifties coffee table, sleek sort of design (McCobb?) with a glass top that you could display toys under or a collection of ashtrays or shot glasses or snow domes or anything you wanted, really. It's the kind of thing I can actually sell for probably a couple hundred bucks if I don't keep it myself. Also a great old Russel Wright pitcher and gravy boat; an early-Sixties striped demitasse set; an old Japanese transistor radio, which is disgustingly collectible these days. All in great shape. I know this stuff sounds suspiciously like "vintage resale" merchandise, but I can now afford to buy some stuff that's going to sell for more. That's the way it is with money. And even though I don't really need any more money, it's fun buying a better class of junk.

All right, maybe I've sold out a little. You can say I'm forsaking my junk roots, but I'm actually buying more cheap junk than ever. The store is looking good these days. Too good. I'm having more problems with shoplifters. Last week, I caught some accountant-looking cat trying to steal a Hawaiian shirt. I noticed this guy slip it into his jumbo recycled plastic bag after he bought a big tiki spoon and fork. I don't know if it was an impulse thing or some sort of experimental larceny or what, because he didn't really look like the type (for tiki or thievery), but I actually watched him rip me off. I was almost tempted to let him get away with it because I admired the theme to his theft. When I stopped him at the door and grabbed his bag, he bolted. So I sold the spoon and fork a second time later that day. I put an extra-low price on the set and sold it to a couple who had just gotten married. They were sweet, in an aging, middle-class hipster sort of way.

The Trouble with Chairs

After the estate sale, I head for a couple of Salvation Armies that I know in the area. There is mostly nothing, but at the one on Grand River I spy a pair of Fifties kitchen chairs that are extremely cool. Chrome tubular legs, red-flecked vinyl upholstery, both like new. Usually, I'd snap up something like this without a thought. The real problem with these chairs is that I know that Theresa would love them. This happens to me all the time, seeing stuff she would love, but with these chairs, I don't know what happens, the impulse is too strong to resist. Then I realize that they actually match her kitchen table. As you know, matching tables and chairs are not mandatory, but even she would be pleased.

As I purchase them, I know it's a completely wrong and pathetic and unhealthy thing to do. I tell myself that I can sell them easily at the store, which is certainly true, but I know what's going to happen. By the time I get the chairs in the back of the truck with the rest of my purchases, I am thoroughly disgusted with myself. I have been doing so well lately in regards to the Theresa thing. And then I go and do something like this. I decide right there in the truck that I will sell the fucking chairs at the store and that will be that. I have done enough groveling, enough whining, to last me for the rest of my life. It's just so stupid. What was I thinking? *"Theresa, here's some kitchen chairs. Now do you love me?"*

Return Trip to Hell

I get back to the store at around quarter to twelve and immediately realize that I have cracked open some ugly door of fate by buying those kitchen chairs. Because damned if Theresa's car is not parked right behind my store when I pull up. I cannot believe this. But I did it to myself. I should not have bought the chairs for her. I have summoned her from my past to come make me unwell again. She could tell there was something here for her and she came round to pick it up. The junker's instinct at work.

My heart sinks, so far down that it hides beneath the seat of my truck, wraps itself in the greasy rags I use to wipe my windshield. I ask it nicely to come out, but it says no. It begs for mercy, starts to weep blood all over my floorboards. Apparently it doesn't want to go out and get stomped on again. I really can't blame it. She's probably got those big Red Wing stormtroopers on and it will hurt like hell.

When I finally get out of my truck, she gets out of her car. Things take on a slo-mo, auto accident pre-impact effect. I try not to look too much. I go around to the back of the truck and open the tailgate without looking at her. I act like I haven't seen her yet. I pull out the two kitchen chairs and set them down carefully on the gravel. I keep my head down. I keep looking at the gravel. When I finally hold my head up, she is standing there, smiling at me. I think that I will have to try very hard to keep from throwing myself on the gravel and begging her to take me back. But the grovel on the gravel doesn't seem to happen. I'm not sure why.

For one, Theresa doesn't look as good as I thought she would.

No exotic thrifted clothing, just jeans and a Cramps T-shirt. She has let her hair grow out a little, but it's lank and dirty. Her hands are scratched-up, nails down to the quick, natch. The circles around her eyes are darker than I remember. Don't get me wrong, she still looks good, but then she always was the kind of woman that could pull off that sullen, dissipated look.

"Hey, J. How's your bad self?"

I go from completely expressionless to big smile, zero to happy in 2.4 seconds. I smile and smile, becoming slowly aware that it is a forced, strained, clown-from-hell kind of a smile. "Theresa," I say, through my teeth. "Copacetic. How's about you?"

"Okay."

There is a bottomlessly long pause. I want to scream just to break the silence and have something to do. I look up at her. "Well, here's your chairs. Maybe you should just take them and go."

Confusion twists her eyes and mouth. "What are you talking about, J?"

I take two short shallow breaths which provide no oxygen whatsoever. "Against my better judgment, I bought these chairs for you today. I had not really planned to give them to you, but it didn't matter. You obviously knew they were here, so you showed up. So take them and go, please. That would be a good thing."

Theresa looks at me as though I am quite mad. "J, you're tripping. I don't have any idea what you're talking about," she says, now actually noticing the chairs. "Hey, but they do match my kitchen table." She looks back up at me. "I really just came by to say hey."

I close my eyes and start taking deep deliberate breaths that I believe are quite beneficial to my brain and vital organs. The only problem is, after a few of them I can't seem to stop. Soon I am panting like a terrier on Benzedrine.

"Oh shit," says Theresa, as she sits me down on the tailgate of my truck. I should resist, just out of spite or something, but I seem to go wherever those hands lead me. I am helpless, hapless, hopeless. Fuck! She sits down on the tailgate next to me and I smell her smell, her wonderful flower child patchouli/hint of cat piss smell. My throat clenches and the hyperventilating triggers a coughing jag. It's like when we met, only far worse. (Then, I didn't know what agony was ahead of me.)

"Holy cow, J. Are you all right? I shouldn't have done this. I didn't think this would happen."

"Apparently, I am not as sophisticated as you," I wheeze, between coughs.

She gets up. "Maybe I should just split, okay?"

My breathing is starting to slow down, though I'm wishing it would stop altogether, although that would mean I could no longer smell her. "No, wait. It's okay, it's okay. What did you want?"

She hesitates for a moment as if she is still considering leaving, then just sighs. "Oh shit," she says. "I just felt like talking to you. I've been real depressed—"

"Really?" I am just foolish enough to think she's telling me she made a mistake about us.

"I haven't slept in weeks. Work has been so bad. I don't know if I can take it much longer." She closes her eyes, breathes, tilts her head toward the ground.

I say nothing. It's work that's bumming her out, of course, not missing yours truly. How could I have thought such a thing? How quaintly amusing of me.

"I just want to go to sleep—"

I watch Theresa open her eyes, gaze at a tree in the alley, at anywhere but me. Just then, I feel a change occur. It's as if atmospheric conditions have suddenly reversed. A cold front has pressed forward and the barometer has plunged dramatically. There is a shift in power.

"But it's so great to see you," she says, finally turning to me, smiling weakly.

"Now I get it," I say, the cough suddenly gone. "I've been deemed worthy. I've been chosen for the coterie of ex-boyfriends with whom you're so friendly. I get to be the junk store ex-boyfriend. Gosh, what an honor."

"J—" Theresa is not smiling anymore. She is not so happy to see me now. Because it is not me, but someone else entirely, my doppelganger, my evil twin, my bad self.

"What, are Roger and Dorr and the others on vacation? Is there some sort of ex-lover strike? You need to recruit me?"

"J, quit it."

"This is swell!" I say gleefully. "I get to be one of those guys about whom you can tell your next victim, *We used to fuck, but we don't anymore.*"

"Shut up!" Theresa looks ready to cry. I hope I'm happy with myself. (I am.)

"Well, am I right?"

She is shaking now. "Yes, you're right," she says, voice cracking. "I came here for just what you said. I missed you. I thought maybe we could be friends."

Theresa stands up, walks over to her car, and gets in. She drives away.

I couldn't be happier. At least for a few minutes.

I Ponder the Future on My Tailgate

After Theresa has been gone those few minutes, I am in a dither. Seeing her has dredged up all my stupid feelings all over again. Of course, it's not like they were that far from the surface to begin with. I feel bad for being so nasty to her, even though I was totally on target. The worst thing is, I still have those fucking chairs. I sit there on my tailgate for awhile, glaring at them. Were I moved to write a bad poem, I would have to say that the empty chairs mock me. I just want to crawl home and lie in bed or maybe watch television for twenty-four hours straight. But I don't. I get up and take the chairs inside along with the other stuff.

It's a quiet day, so I spend most of the next four hours cleaning stuff up and either replaying the encounter with Theresa or trying to banish it from my mind. I scrub, I shine, I spray things with Windex. Even though they really don't need it, I rub down the legs of the accursed chairs with Nevr-Dull. They, of course, look great. I put it all out on the floor. Nothing gets marked, but at least it's out there and that makes me feel better.

At around four-thirty, I am rewarded for my diligence. A woman comes in, an attractive woman, I might add, but a type you don't see much of in this kind of store. A perky blonde, dressed very tidy, very khaki, definitely not a hipster, but apparently a woman with discriminating taste in junk. She looks like she has just gotten off of work, maybe an ad agency, but probably not the creative department. She looks at the chairs, then goes over to check out the Shawnee planters that I picked up from Fred ages ago.

"This is a great store," she says to me, as she browses. Then she comes back, sits down in one of the new chairs.

"Thanks," I say.

"Have you been open long?"

She gets up, then sits in the other one. She is interested. *Yes! Let's get rid of those things!*

"Yeah, for a few years."

"You've got a lot of cool stuff."

"Thanks. Nice chairs, aren't they?" I say, nodding toward them. "I just picked them up recently."

"Yes. Very cool." Am I imagining things or is she smiling at me?

She stands up and looks at them both. She is trying to imagine them in her kitchen or wherever. I'm thinking thirty-five for the set. (Did I mention that since I became rich, I have raised my prices, too?)

"They're not marked," she says. "How much?"

I'm still thinking thirty-five for the set, but that's not what comes out of my mouth. "You know, I just realized that someone put some money down on those this morning. I'm really sorry. I completely forgot."

I watch the smile wither. "Oh, really?"

"Look, if you want, I'd be happy to give you a deal on any other chairs in the store. I could go twenty percent off."

I watch her start slowly for the door. "No, it's all right. These were the only ones I really liked."

"I'm so sorry."

She heads for the door. I continue talking. "Come back again. I get new things in all the time—" But she is gone, probably never to return. You don't want to do that to people in this business. You don't let them get their hopes up only to dash them. The ring of the bell on my door lingers in the air in that annoying way it has.

I feel like hell. Not only because I have lost a potential customer, a foxy mama at that (at least a conventionally attractive mama), but because now I know I'm going to give those infernal chairs to Theresa, because the curse is on them and there's nothing left to do but get them out of here and out of my life.

I Address the Chairs

At five-thirty, I close up the shop early and throw the kitchen chairs into the back of the truck again. This is a bad idea, I tell myself. I keep telling it to myself during the drive to Theresa's apartment building, as I park next to her car in the dirt lot, as I lug the chairs past the scowling old men with nothing better to do, who still sit in front of her building. I keep telling myself as I walk up the stairs to her apartment. It doesn't do any good. I knock on her door. There's no answer, so I knock again. I hear various meows from various cats, but no voice cooing to them, telling them to hush.

"Theresa, it's J. Could you open the door? I've got those chairs for you. I want you to have them," I say. I flash on the last time I was at this doorway, then push it out of my head. I've made myself crazy enough for one day.

"Theresa." I knock some more. A big yowl from, I think, Sedgwick the marmalade.

"Theresa. Open up. I just want to give you these chairs and split. That's all. Really."

I can't decide if I am relieved or disappointed that she doesn't answer the door. I consider just leaving the chairs in front of her door, but they'll probably be stolen. Besides, it sort of scorches me that she won't even answer the door. I decide not to leave them. I'm just going to split. Of course, I will now have to schlep them all the way back downstairs, back to the truck, back to the shop.

By the time I klonk my way to the bottom of the stairs, I have had it with the chairs, curse or not. I must be rid of them. Outside, the old men sitting on the porch scowl at me again, even worse this time, as I approach. I excuse myself as I stumble through, cutting a wide berth for my cargo. One of them mutters something in Arabic, throws his cigarette butt into an old Maxwell House can. Then I have a brilliant idea. I turn to address them all.

"Excuse me, gentlemen. I noticed that your chairs are in pretty rough shape. Would you like a couple of new ones?"

Suddenly, these grumpy old farts' faces brighten up like I've just told them they've won the Lotto. It's probably the first time anyone's paid any attention to them in years.

"Sure," one of them says, a doughy, red-faced guy with a little straw stingy-brim that rests on his noggin like Mr. Potato Head. He's got about thirty-five years' worth of gin blossoms, the Route 66 of alcoholism, across his nose, but he's smiling like a maniac.

"Here you go, my man. Enjoy." I hand him the two chairs and I suddenly feel unfettered, free of my burden. I am Atlas on a coffee break.

The Curse of the Chair Lingers

In the car, I start to feel bad. They were great chairs and now they're just going to be used for chairs. They've lost all their meaning, all their coolness. Plus, the chairs were meant for Theresa and now they are not hers. She's going to have to look at them every day when she comes home from work. It's going to seem like I purposely did a mean thing when all I really wanted to do was get rid of the damn things. Still, it's done and I don't have to think about it anymore. That's all I care about.

But the closer I get to home, the more it spooks me that Theresa didn't answer the door. If she didn't want to see me, she would've just yelled through the door. "Fuck off, J" would be a pretty good guess. By the time I get to my house, my tough guy attitude has completely wilted and I am genuinely concerned. So, always the sap, I turn the truck around in my driveway and head back over to her place.

When I get there, I have to run the gauntlet of old guys again, except now they're my new best friends.

"Got any more stuff for us?" says Mr. Potato Head.

"Not today, chief," I say, trotting past.

All right, by this time I have freaked myself out. I keep telling myself everything is fine, I'm just being a worrywart, a nervous Nellie. But at her door, I find myself pounding and yelling.

"Theresa! Open up! It's J! Are you all right?" Nothing still. More cats yowling, but no sound of Theresa.

I pound some more. I hear a door down the hall click open. I am being peeked at and I don't care. She might be out for a walk, I tell myself. It's entirely possible that she is out for a walk. There are a lot of places she could walk to around here. Nonetheless, I unsnap my summer-camp wallet, flip past the photo of my dad (trench coat) and the one of my mom (Sixties portrait, clothed), finally locating my laminated library card. I can see Theresa doesn't have the dead bolt on, so I slide the card into the ancient doorjamb and flick it under the latch. (I'd like to say I learned this from some old ex-con junker who taught me all his tricks, but in fact I learned it from television.) It clicks up just the right way, but at this point, I have no desire to congratulate myself on my lame street smarts.

I push open the door and immediately see that Theresa is not taking a walk at all. She is in the Chair of Gloom passed out with four cats lying on her. At first I think she is drunk, but she is extremely pale. It looks like she has thrown up on herself as well. Her breathing is very strained, very slow. There is a suspicious bulge in her T-shirt pocket. I reach for the bulge and even though I know I am going to pull out an empty pill bottle, when I reach for it, my hand touches her breast and I'm ashamed to say I feel aroused for a moment. (Men can manage it just about anytime.) The prescription label on the bottle is in her name. *Zulinski, Theresa. For sleep. Take one before bed as needed. Dalmane 100mg.*

I put it in my pocket, run to the phone, and call 911.

I Am No Help Whatsoever

Before the ambulance arrives, I don't know what to do with myself. All I can think of are all the things I've seen in the movies when someone takes an overdose of sleeping pills. I want to rouse

Theresa, slap her, pump her full of black coffee, get her up and spend a torturous night walking her around in circles, and in the morning, she will start to come around. Then I will be the first person she sees with a clear head and she will realize that I am her salvation. This time, she will let herself fall wildly in love with me, etc., etc.

Instead, I just sit there, talking to her, telling her not to die, telling her she's going to be fine, reassuring this unconscious woman with everything in my mother's repertoire of clichés. Luckily, the ambulance arrives amazingly fast and I am relieved of my useless duties.

"Please get out of the way, sir," the paramedic says to me, because I don't seem to be moving away from Theresa. The same guy checks her pulse, breaks some sort of inhalant under her nose. Theresa stirs a little, then he gives her an injection of something. I watch the needle slide into that tender pale arm. Helplessly, I hold the empty pill bottle out to him.

"We know what she took, sir. You told the dispatcher over the phone."

I nod. Then, within seconds, he and his partner have slipped a stretcher under Theresa and start to wheel her out of the apartment. When they pull her out of the chair, I notice a paperback book stuffed between the cushion and the arm. It is Theresa's dog-eared copy of *Under the Volcano*. I grab it, then rush to catch up with the paramedics.

As the door locks behind me, I realize that I have no idea where the keys are, but it's too late to worry about that. Out in the hall, everyone in Theresa's building is gawking at the two men carrying their neighbor down the stairs. There are hollow-eyed mothers and sorry soiled toddlers, half-wit busboys, widows living on their dead husbands' disability, lonely old men who talk to anyone on the bus. They are thrift shop people. I think I recognize a couple of them. The whole thing is also just like a scene in a movie, except no little kid approaches me and says, "Is she gonna be okay, mister?" No one asks me anything, they all just stare. I'm not sure Theresa even knew her neighbors all that well. But I know that after we leave, they will all stand in the hall to speculate about what has happened, feel better about their own situation, however hopeless it may be. It will be the most they have spoken to each other in years. Then, in a day or two, everyone will go back to passing each other silently in the hall.

We Go for a Ride

This is not the first time I have been in an ambulance. We had to call for one a few times with my mother, when she got really bad and we were afraid to move her. I suppose it could be fun, zooming in and out through traffic, siren blaring, except for the fact that there is usually someone you're fond of lying there sick or unconscious. I look at Theresa. She is on oxygen now and breathing a little more regularly. The paramedic has her hooked up to all sorts of equipment and monitors. He doesn't seem overly concerned. This fact neither scares nor comforts me. For some reason, I cannot seem to imagine Theresa dying. I don't know if this is just lack of imagination on my part, or that I am in some kind of shock.

At Beaumont Hospital (Hugh Beaumont Hospital, as Theresa used to refer to it) we slide in through the emergency entrance toward the back, and by the time I get out of the ambulance they have slipped away with Theresa through some doors and I am left standing there, left holding a clipboard with a few thousand questions on it to answer. I don't know the answers to any of these questions.

The Wait

While I sit in the waiting area of the emergency room, I witness all sorts of horrific things, people walking in dripping with blood, moaning on stretchers, panicked families screaming at each other. I hear an attendant say, "There's a lot of blood today." And many people holding odd things to their injuries—dishtowels, sanitary napkins, pajamas, you name it. I guess you just tend to grab whatever's nearest to soak up that pesky life fluid.

While I sit, I start to look through Theresa's book. There are lots of pages folded, sentences highlighted—passages about pariah dogs that follow people around, the Days of the Dead, the Mayans, the unpronounceable names of two Mexican mountains, but what strikes me most is one particular passage she has underlined:

I think I know a good deal about physical suffering. But this is worst of all, to feel your soul dying. I wonder if it is because tonight my soul has really died that I feel at the moment something like peace.

I read this passage over and over, until I realize a nurse is calling out Theresa's last name and I walk up. "The doctor wants to talk to you," she says to me, turning around. I nod and follow her into another waiting room. I wait for a few minutes until a doctor walks in. He is tall, black, bespectacled with graying temples. Except for the hundreds of freckles that cover his face, he looks just like you'd expect a doctor to look.

"She's fine," he says. He tells me that they got to her in time, that they pumped her stomach, that she is a lucky girl, that she is resting comfortably, that she will have to undergo psychiatric care. Somehow, I already seem to know all this. I ask if I can see her. He says not yet, but soon.

I Give Theresa a Good Talking-To

It is a few hours later when they let me see her. At least it seems like just a few hours later, but when I look at my watch, I realize that it's three in the morning. I have been at the hospital almost nine hours. I have read many sections of *Under the Volcano*, as well as every *People*, *Newsweek*, and *Time* on the table in the waiting room, not to mention the *Star*, the *National Enquirer*, and *Weekly World News*, which some people have so thoughtfully left in a pile on the floor. Once again, someone calls Theresa's name. I stagger up.

"You can see her now briefly," a different attendant says. "She's very tired." The attendant leads me down a hall through a series of doors, well out of the emergency wing, past a bunch of nurses' stations. I'm not sure where we are, but I'm wondering if it is some sort of psychiatric care unit. Finally we walk into a room with two beds in it. The first bed by the door is empty, Theresa is in the second one. She does not look up when I come in.

"You've got five minutes," says the attendant, then exits. Part of me wants to rush up to Theresa, drop to my knees, embrace her, kiss her, start bawling like a baby, etc. This is not what I do.

"You asshole," I say to her.

Theresa looks up at me. She has a little color back, but not much. Her face is gaunt and oily. There are large dark rings around the hooded eyes. There is a welt on her bottom lip. "I was going to say the same thing to you," she says languidly.

"If I hadn't come back, you'd be dead by now."

Theresa takes a long, ragged breath.

"Was this your idea of like, the solution to something?" I say.

A dim spark appears in Theresa's eyes, then she just turns her head like she doesn't have time for me. "Why are you here? I thought you didn't give a shit."

"I— Is that—?"

Sluggishly, she turns her head. She gives me a wilting look, then snorts. "Please. I didn't think even you were capable of that kind of egotism."

I smile. "All right, but— Theresa, why did you do this?"

"Oh fuck. I don't know, J. I'm so tired. I don't know. Everything. I wasn't really planning this. It seemed like a good idea at the time. I just wanted to sleep."

This makes me want to grab her shoulders and give her a good shake. "Gee, when did it stop seeming like such a good idea?" I say, trying unsuccessfully to keep my voice down. "When you vomited on yourself? When you woke up in the hospital? As they were pumping your stomach?"

Theresa closes her eyes as if that will make me disappear from the room. "Go away, J. You're making my head hurt. When did you become such a jerk?"

"I didn't tell you. I'm rich now. In America, it's like a license to be a jerk."

"I don't like you anymore."

"Doesn't matter," I say, slipping my hand over hers. "I saved your life. Now we're friends."

We Adjust

I spend the night in the waiting room. From about four o'clock on, I get a little sleep. As much as one can sleep in one of those ugly sticky vinyl hospital chairs. I'm surprised that I've never seen one of these pop up at a rummage sale. If one did, I'd probably think it was *cool* or something. But here in its proper environment, it is as ugly an object as one will find anywhere.

At about eight in the morning, I talk to a doctor. By this time, I have learned to lie and tell people that I am her half brother. The doctor, this one a woman, tells me although the number of pills Theresa took might or might not have killed her, this still must be taken seriously. She tells me that Theresa will be staying there for at least a while. They'll keep an eye on her and she'll see a therapist, then they'll make some sort of recommendation. That's the procedure in cases such as this. She doesn't say it, but she means attempted suicides. But I don't know to whom they're going to make recommendations. As far as I know, Theresa has no family. Will they just make their recommendations to Theresa, or to her friends, or will they just send them out into the air? The doctor tells me that I can see her for a few minutes, but that's it.

When I walk into Theresa's room, she is dozing. I settle into the chair next to her bed.

Suddenly Theresa starts talking to me. "Are they going to put me under observation?" she says drowsily. Her eyes are still closed, her eyelids like burnished lead.

When she speaks, it takes me somewhat aback. "Uh, maybe a smidge," I say. It disturbs me that she seems to know the drill. Still, I don't ask. She turns to me, eyes slitted, faint crooked smile, apparently amused by the idea of being observed.

"They're just going to keep you around, make sure you don't do anything stupid again. You're not, are you?"

"Are you really rich?" She tips her head back in the pillow, eyes wider now, assessing me.

I give her my "I'm serious here" stern expression. "You didn't answer my question."

Theresa rolls her eyes like a pouty teenager. "No, I probably won't do anything stupid again, Dad."

"Promise me you won't."

"All right, I won't."

"Thank you. Then I will tell you. Yes, I am rich. Not only in health and good junk, but in the pecuniary sense as well. You'll also find that I'm not afraid to share it with my friends."

The eyebrows arch mock-quizzically, but I can see she is very fatigued. Even after all that has happened, I can't believe how much fun it is to see her again, to kid around with her. I suddenly get a jolt of reality, recognition of what the world would be like without this woman in it. But if she hadn't done this colossally idiotic thing, it would have been like that for me anyway.

"J, are you all right?"

"I'm fine." I give her the trooper's smile, the one you give instead of bawling.

She is a little more alert now, wanting to chit-chat. "So how did you become rich? Did you make some incredible score?"

I try to keep from laughing. "Please. I think you know better than that. Linda just sold my parents' house for a bundle. I got half. That's all."

"Just like that. Did you ever do anything with that stuff from your parents' basement?"

"Not yet."

"Maybe I'll give you a hand with it when I get out of the bughouse."

"That would be swell."

Then Theresa looks down at the sheet and exhales. "J, man," she says. "I'm so sorry about how things got all fucked up. I'm sorry about all of this."

"Sorry, sorry, sorry," I say, *tsk*-ing her. "You sound like me. Are you sorry you're still alive?"

"Ask me later."

A nurse appears in the room and gives me the look. I grab my bowling shirt and put it back on over my T-shirt. "I'm going to take off for awhile on some business. You going to be okay?"

This time, she gives me the trooper's smile. "I'll be fine. Hey, would you mind giving Roger a call? I left him kind of a weird message about coming over to feed the girls. I lent him a key a while back. Call him, would you?"

"Sure."

"I'm not really ready to talk to anybody, but I don't want him to worry."

I can't help thinking, *But you weren't worried about letting him find your body, were you?* But I don't say anything.

"He's in the book. Pinkel."

"Pinkel? He's a Pinkel?"

"J."

"I'll call him," I say, as I head for the door. "See you later."

Then Theresa actually musters a real smile at me, the first one I've seen there in a long time. "J," she calls to me. "Find something good, all right?"

I Go to Church

I pick up a paper outside the hospital and turn to the classifieds. There are a couple of estate sales, but I am really too late for them and they are too damn far away. Some days I am just not in the mood to drive, and this is definitely one of them. But there is a promising church rummage sale a few miles away. I start up the truck, but as I put it into drive, a full-body fatigue rolls over me and I have to put the truck back into park. Suddenly, I am so tired that all I want to do is go home and go to sleep for about fifteen hours. But I don't feel like sleeping. I need to go junking and that is what I will do. I take a deep breath, put the truck back into gear, and head to the nearest 7-Eleven for a jumbo extra-sugar tea.

The tea helps and I get my second wind (perhaps my third or fourth by now) and I head for the rummage sale. Evidently the junk gods are pleased with me, because I get there just in time for the nine-A.M. "Early Bird." I have to wait in line and pay a buck, but I do get first crack at all the stuff—a Sixties two-domed coffeemaker; a stash of great old flowered and fruited dishcloths from the Thirties and Forties, still with the bands around them; a ceramic Winchester six-gun ashtray. I pile all this up on a table in front of one of the cashiers.

Then I see it. I immediately want it. The sensible part of me says it is way too big and bulky and heavy and just too plain stupid to even mess with, no one will ever buy it, but the other part tells me I have to get it. It is simply too weird and cool to pass up. It is an old stand-up Walton Belt Vibrator like the kind people used to use in reducing parlors. It's something like you'd see in old Thirties movies, a pedestal with a big U-shaped strap that people wrapped around themselves to vibrate all their fat away. I love things like this, an object that's time is so far past it moves way beyond useless. *Say, you don't have to exercise to get rid of that unsightly flab. Just vibrate it away!* It just goes to show you that sixty, seventy years ago, people were just as deluded as they are today. I point to the contraption, ask the old lady behind the table, Virginia Slim dangling from her chops, "How much?"

"Myrtle, how much for the reducing machine?" she yells into a back room. "There's a young man here who would like to buy it. God knows why. He's skinny as a rail."

Myrtle. God, I love this business.

"We'll go ten on it," she says, after returning from a brief private consultation with the mysterious Myrtle.

"Sold," I say, hoping I can even lift the thing. They didn't make stuff very portable in the old days.

I take another lap before I go. I find a Sixties glass juice decanter with fruit painted on it. I put it with my other items and pay up. Without too much trouble, I get it all in the truck. (Myrtle's husband, George, gives me a hand with the vibrator. I decide it would make a great display for the store. I envision Tom the mannequin, in a gaudy Eighties jogging outfit, strapped into this bad boy.) I head home, satisfied with my haul. I decide it's been a good morning's work and that I deserve a few hours' sleep before going in to the shop.

What Time Is It?

When I get home at about eleven-thirty, I remember that I'm supposed to call Roger, not a task to which I look forward. I dial information for the number. When I call, all I get is his answering machine. For once, I am incredibly thankful for this. I leave a long, rambling message about who it is that's calling, about Theresa being in the hospital, that she's fine, and that he should definitely ignore anything he might hear from the neighbors. Then right after I hang up, I remember something else. So I call back and ask him if he would go over there and feed the cats. If he can't, to please let me know. I leave my number. It's one of my epic two-part phone answering machine messages. This is why I hate those things so much. Afterward, I settle in for a very short nap.

When I wake up, it's five-fifteen and my head is pounding. I can't believe that I've slept this long. It's way too late to go in to work. I'm really angry with myself. But there's nothing I can do. The day is gone.

I decide to whomp up some dinner, my favorite starchy meal, Kraft macaroni and cheese. As I'm boiling the macaroni, I notice the price tag on the box is not from my supermarket. It confuses me for a moment, then I realize that this mix is from the box of food I took from my parents' house months ago. It saddens me, but I do not experience one of my meltdowns, even after I figure out that my mother probably bought this box especially for me. Before she got sick, she would try to lure me over for dinner once in a while. I would go, but these dinners always ended badly.

Judging from what I do next, it might appear that I suffered a series of mini-strokes while I slept, rendering me loopy. Because suddenly I have the urge to call my sister. Which is what I do.

I can safely state that Linda is surprised to hear from me.

"Richard?" she says. "Is that you? I didn't expect to hear from you."

"How are you?" I say.

"I'm fine."

Well, there's no real need to get into what we actually talk about. It's just dumb brother and sister stuff. Linda hasn't changed a bit, she is still as conventional as the day is long, she still thinks I'm nuts, but I can tell she is kind of glad to hear from me. She has some good news, though she does not realize that it's good news. She's had a falling-out with Aunt Tina. Apparently, Tina stuck her nose where it didn't belong (Mom's affairs, most likely) and big sister tweaked it. I am exultant. We hang up, after making promises of getting together for lunch. We probably won't actually do it, but maybe we will.

A Leather Encounter

It's about six-thirty by the time I get to the hospital. When I walk into Theresa's room, she's sitting up in bed, still connected to the IV. She still looks groggy and pale, but basically better. She has a visitor. It is the infamous pierced, tattooed, and leather-clad Roger Pinkel. I can't really see any of the tattoos now because it's October in Michigan and a guy needs to keep his limbs covered. But there is plenty of leather, not to mention piercings (and probably a few that I can't see). Rog is sitting on a chair next to the bed talking to Theresa. He looks up at me and there is no real recognition at first. I notice that his eyes are red and puffy. Could it be the big palooka is all choked up? Call me crazy, but suddenly I'm starting to like him.

"Hey, Theresa," I say.

"J," says Theresa softly.

I give ol' Rog the standard greeting. "Hey, Roger. How you doing?"

"Richard," Roger says, standing up. He's got his hand out for me to shake. I try to shake it, but I can't really move it much. Roger sits back down. He is being very quiet, but not in a hostile way. (Oh, let's face it. The guy has never done anything to me. It's just that he's big and tough and good-looking and tattooed and bohemianish and he used to sleep with Theresa and he can also beat the snot out of me ten ways from Tuesday.)

"Uh, Roger—did you get the message I left for you? Messages, actually."

Roger shakes his head no.

"They let me get to a pay phone a little while ago, J," says Theresa. "I called him at work."

I nod my head in an exaggerated manner. "Oh." Then I start to feel sort of self-conscious, like I'm interrupting some sort of special friend/ex-lover thing. I smile weakly at Theresa, then look over at Roger. "Look, why don't I come back in a little while. Let you two talk."

"J, it's okay," says Theresa. "We talked."

"Yeah, I was just leaving. It's cool." (Of course it is.) Rog stands up like he's getting ready to leave. He gives Theresa's hand a squeeze. "Don't do anything like this again, Tre. We need you." He looks over at me with sad, garage-sale-painting eyes. In agreement, I shake my head like a lunatic. "Okay, I should go." He moves for the door.

"Say hi to the girls for me," says Theresa. She gives Roger a kiss on the cheek. "Tell them I'll be home soon."

"See ya, Roger," I say, hands in pockets.

Roger looks at me ominously. "Richard. Can I see you out in the hall for a minute?"

This is it. He's asked me to step outside. He's going to pummel me. He's never liked me, always thought I was a little junk-picking weasel who didn't deserve Theresa and never treated her right, which means he will just have to teach me a manly lesson. Right there in the hallway of the psycho ward at Hugh Beaumont Hospital, there will be a testosterone-fueled punchfest with me as primary recipient. The only upside I can see is that I'll already be in the hospital, and with any luck, I'll be spotted by a passing candy-striper who'll flop my broken torso onto a magazine cart and right into intensive care.

We're out in the hall. "Look, I—" I start to babble, trying to save my heinie, coward that I am. But in mid-quiver, I am interrupted by Roger's throwing his arms around me.

"Thanks, man," he says, squeezing me to the point of pain. Then Roger heads on down the hallway, oblivious to the stares of the nurses, noticing either his danger-boy good looks or the fact that he almost just crushed that little scrawny guy with the glasses over there.

Back in the room, Theresa looks a little scared. "J, is everything all right? Is Roger okay?"

I must look stunned, because she is almost getting out of bed. "I'm fine. Stay. I just thought Roger was going to—he just gave me a big hug."

"Oh. Well, Roger's big on hugging. He's kind of New Age that way. Come on, sit down."

"How are you feeling?"

"All right. I saw the shrink today."

"And?"

"I'm depressed."

"What else did he have to say?"

"She. And that was pretty much it. I'm depressed. That's all she wanted to say right now."

"That's fucking brilliant. You just tried to kill yourself."

"Anyway, I'm going to be here for awhile yet. I'm gonna start therapy tomorrow. That should be fun."

"Yes. A riot."

She closes her eyes and turns her head toward the ceiling. She takes a long breath. "J?"

"What, Theresa?"

"I don't want to go back to work."

"Then don't. We'll find you a new job."

She turns to me, eyes open now. "But I feel like I should go back."

I move my face a little closer to hers. I expect my Theresa smell, but it is different—antiseptic and bleach and sweat. "Theresa, you've done enough for the animal kingdom. It's time to let someone else do their share."

This annoys her. I obviously don't understand. She pulls the sheet up, covering everything but her face. She links her hands beneath the sheets. "It's not that easy. They need me."

"Theresa, *you* need you, too."

"I know, I know," she says, nodding in that way people nod when they know you're right, they just don't believe it themselves. Then she looks at me, kind of scared. "J, don't go away, all right? At least, not for awhile."

"I'm not going anywhere."

"Did you mean what you said about us being friends before?"

"What do you think?"

"I don't know."

"For Pete's sake. Of course I meant it. Now just relax." And I take her hand and we just sit there, saying nothing. I wonder if it's bad that I feel so happy that she needs me. Then I decide not to care if it's bad or not, just to enjoy it. Because it probably won't last all that long.

Small Packages

On Monday, they change Theresa's room to a quieter part of the hospital. I visit her every day and every day I bring her a little trinket, something I pick up in my travels. It has to be an object I can put in my pocket, so that keeps me from going hog wild. Yet soon, I start to neglect my daily (and all-important) mission of stocking my store and making a living and my only reason to be out junking every day is to find something to bring to Theresa.

One day it is a lapel button from the Sixties: "Is there life after birth?"; the next day, a spoon with an amber Bakelite handle; the next day, a Bicentennial ballpoint pen from an old bar in Detroit called *Jordan's on the River*. Today, I couldn't find a damn thing, so I decide to go home before I head for the hospital and grab something from my personal collection of stuff. I don't really know what comes over me, but I head for a drawer that holds one of my most prized finds—a cigarette lighter made in Occupied Japan. It is a great piece of craftsmanship, a cigarette lighter that looks exactly like a tiny camera. It has its own working tripod and twirling focus rings, and when you hit the shutter button, the top pops up to expose the lit wick. I bought it for two bucks and I know that it is worth at least a hundred. (Which doesn't matter because I wouldn't sell it.)

Even as I am shining it up, I know it's a dumb thing to do, giving this away. Okay, maybe it's not dumb exactly, but I realize that it means something. This cigarette lighter is very precious to me. It's just the sort of ridiculous object that I love, from a time when it seemed like a good idea to have a lighter that looked like a camera. Still, I go right on shining it up, then I plop it in a little ziplock bag.

At the hospital that evening, when I give it to Theresa, I swear, she just about busts into tears.

"No way, J," she says, handing it back to me. She knows how much it is worth and refuses to accept it.

"Look, it's okay," I say. "I got a great price on it."

"Bullshit," she says to me. "I know you have one of these at home. You told me about it."

I lie through my teeth. "That's why I don't need this one."

"No, J."

"All right, fine. You're forcing me to tell you. It was only three dollars. I got it at one of the last garage sales of the year."

She buys the story. "Are you kidding me?" I can see that she is happy to have an excuse to take it. "Wow. Well, okay. Thanks."

"I was trying to seem like a big shot."

"This is so cool. Thank you, J. Come here," she says, grabbing the lapels of my shirt-jac. She kisses me and it's the first time we've done this since becoming amigos. But it doesn't feel like an amigos kiss, it feels like a real kiss, but maybe that's just me. I look at her and she's got a strange look on her face, like "Oops. I forgot we weren't doing that anymore." Luckily (or not) we both decide to ignore it.

"How's therapy going?" I say. Nothing like a mental health update to wet-towel the mood.

"Okay, I guess. The doctor says that I refuse to forgive myself for what I do at work."

Theresa says this as if she is conveying a weather report from television or something. I don't know what to say, so I play shrink. "What do you think about that?"

"She's probably right, I just don't know what difference it makes."

"You don't?"

"No, I don't. Lay off. Okay, J?"

"All right. No need to get snippy. What does she say about you going back to work?"

"She doesn't think it's a good idea."

"Oh."

Theresa picks up the lighter again. "This is really so cool, J. Thanks again."

Then for the rest of the time that I'm there, while I'm trying to talk to her, she plays with that lighter. She's like a child, discovering neat little features on it, like the hidden place where you squirt the lighter fluid. I must say, even though I'm a little miffed with her for snapping at me, it's just a blast to watch her.

When I leave the hospital that night, I am still buzzing from that kiss and how happy the lighter makes her, until I realize that I am in big trouble, because I am totally gone on her again. (I know, it's not like I ever stopped. I just got used to the idea of her not being around.) In any case, my problem is back and I worry that once she gets out of the hospital, she won't need me anymore.

White Zombie!

The next day, when I go to the hospital to visit Theresa, I have a tiny New York City subway token in my pocket for her. It looks like maybe it's from the Fifties. Another object from my personal collection. Nothing much in the way of estate sales or rummage sales today, and it's gotten too cool outside for garage sales. So I hit a couple of Salvation Armies. Nothing. (Actually, I did get one "Pat O'Brian's" hurricane glass just to buy something. I've decided to collect them. I'm just not sure why yet.)

When I walk into Theresa's room, I immediately sense something is different. Theresa has a television now and she is watching it intently. Too intently. Especially considering that it is just some stupid old sitcom from the Eighties. But she's so engrossed that she barely acknowledges my entrance. So I sit down on the ugly chair next to her bed. Finally, at a commercial, she turns to me. I am already wigging out because I am sure that something is wrong with her. But I try to act normal, as though everything's just peachy keen.

"Hey, Theresa," I say, smiling. "How's your bad self?"

She nods her head. (Which seems rather curious to me, considering the question.)

"How are you feeling?"

More nodding. "Okay."

I look at her face. Her eyes seem all right, but something is definitely different. "Are you all right?" I say.

"I'm fine, J. Do I seem different?"

Right now, I'm just glad that at least she knows who I am. "Well, yeah. Kind of."

"Like how?"

"I don't know. Sort of numb."

"Kind of like Jack Nicholson at the end of *One Flew over the Cuckoo's Nest?*"

I knew she was still in there somewhere. I'm probably just overreacting.

"Is that it?" I say, snickering. "Have they given you one of those pesky frontal lobotomies?"

"No. Lithium."

I stop laughing. "Oh. How is that?"

"It's okay."

The program comes back on and we both watch until the next break, a commercial for some product that's "Morning Fresh," whatever the hell that is. I am feeling very weird right now because it does not seem to be bothering Theresa that she is in this semi-zombielike state.

"So, are you going to be on it for a long time?"

"On what?"

"The lithium?"

"For awhile, I think. Maybe a long time."

"Oh. Because you don't quite seem like yourself."

"That's the idea, J. Look, I'm sorry I'm not being entertaining enough for you today, but I just don't feel like it. All right?"

"Okay. Sorry."

So we just sit there. We watch the rest of this stupid show. And after that we watch another stupid show. And after a while, I get up to leave.

"See ya, J," she says, as if we had sat around and actually spoken to each other.

"Later."

Theresa waves absently in my general direction. Then I walk out of the room. In the hallway, I realize that I haven't even given her the subway token. I almost decide to skip it, but that seems like bad luck. So I run back into the room. She looks up at me, not happy, not sad.

"Hey, I forgot to give you your present." I pull it out of my pocket. "It's a gen-u-wine New York City subway token, circus 1950." (Once, I got a stack of old photographs from an estate sale. Some poor mistaken soul actually wrote "Circus 1965" instead of "Circa 1965" on the back of one of them. I never forgot it and use it whenever I can. It was, however, completely lost on Theresa this day.)

"Hey, thanks," she says, holding out her hand. She looks at the token, then puts it down on her tray. "Neat."

"I guess I'll be going then."

"Okay, bye."

I am bothered by this whole episode, our little nonvisit. Theresa seems to know that she's one of the undead, but she just doesn't seem to care. I don't know what to do, except see how she is tomorrow. But I'm afraid that she'll be worse.

Outside, in the parking lot, it's getting like winter already, this crazyass Michigan weather. Luckily, I'm wearing my father's Seventies Ultrasuede jacket, the one I stole from his closet after he died of emphysema. I try not to think about Theresa, wrap it tighter around me, button it all the way up to the top. It's still too big for me, but very warm. I love this jacket. I jam my hands deep into the pockets, where I feel something like tiny bits of wood down at the fringy bottom. I pull out a couple. I stop in the middle of the parking lot to examine them. It takes me a few moments, then I realize that they are tiny petrified fragments of tobacco, the remnants of a lifetime of cigarette smoking. Just then, I am awestruck by the power of junk, it's inverse clairvoyance, the ability to reveal both the past and the future.

What We Carry

The next day, a Saturday afternoon, I come to see Theresa. Before I actually walk into her room, I peek in first. She is lying on her bed, fully clothed—an old Pendleton shirt and jeans—reading a book, cover folded over so I can't see it. From where I stand, she still gives the impression of looking kind of spaced, but she does seem more herself.

Even though it is open, I knock on the door to announce my presence. She puts the book down and I see that she is reading *Under the Volcano*. (She had asked for it last week. I gave it back, against my better judgment. It is a depressing book, after all.) Theresa looks over at me and smiles, a bright, wide smile, then it's as if she catches herself and the smile does a quick fade. I realize that yesterday's behavior, the aloofness, the crankiness, the general zombie behavior, may not have been due entirely to medication. Could it be Theresa is slowly weaning herself from me?

"Good afternoon, Miss Theresa," I say, my smile fading fast too, as I start to comprehend what's going on.

"Hey, J."

I walk over to the chair next to the bed and sit down. "You still reading that book?"

"Just rereading some parts."

There are other books on the table next to her. On the top of the stack is a big book of photographs called *The Days of the Dead*. I remember seeing this book over at Theresa's, because on the cover is a pair of the toy skeletons in coffins, not unlike the kind of stuff Theresa has in her apartment.

"Roger brought those from home," Theresa says, when she sees me looking at the book.

"That was nice of him," I say. "Isn't that happening soon?"

"Uh-huh."

"So how you doing?" I notice her hands. The scratches and cuts on them are healing now, the nails growing back a bit, after some time away from the shelter.

"Okay."

I can't believe how fucking genteel this conversation is. If I was a fly on the wall, I'd do a kamikaze dive straight into the linoleum out of sheer boredom. Finally, for lack of anything better to do, I reach into my pocket for today's gift. "Hey, I got you something."

Theresa cocks her head and gives me her *bad dog* look. "J, you've got to stop this—"

"It's nothing, okay? Really. Just take it."

I grab her hand and open the curled fingers. I place it in her palm. Luckily, it is practically nothing. A swizzle stick. Granted, a very old cool swizzle stick, a wooden one advertising "City Ice Cubes" with a little character on it with an ice-block head. But it's still a swizzle stick nonetheless. And nothing for her to get all huffy about.

Theresa looks at it and smiles, the one she was smiling before she forgot that she wasn't supposed to be smiling at me. "Thanks, J. You know, you really don't have to keep coming here every day. I think they're going to be letting me out next week—"

I beat her to the punch. "And after that, you don't want me hanging around so much."

"No, no. It's just that, I know it's a lot of work for you getting over here every day and I—"

"—And you'd just as soon I didn't."

"J, would you shut up?"

I feel fear and bile rising in my throat. I stand up, ready to make a quick exit. "Sorry. Forget it, Theresa, it's all right. I understand."

"No you don't, J. Shut up. And sit back down."

"Sheesh. Sorry." I sit down. I clam up.

Theresa picks up the book folded open on the bed, then puts it back down. "Oh shit."

"What?"

Theresa sits up, folds her knees up against her chin, then hides her face behind her knees. After a few moments, she pulls her head up, looks at the wall in front of her.

"This sounds stupid," she says. "But in this book, there's this part where Geoffrey Firmin sees this old lame Indian carrying around another even older, lamer Indian on his back, and later you realize that it's like he's carrying his own corpse."

"Lovely image," I say.

"'What is man but a little soul holding up a corpse?' it says." She turns to me. "J, that's the way I feel. Except I'm holding up a lot more corpses than just mine."

"The animals?"

She puts her head back on her knees.

"Theresa," I say.

She lifts her head, lowers her knees, assumes the lotus position.

"J, please. I'm leading up to thanking you. I'm not sure why. I guess I wouldn't have made it through all this if it wasn't for you. I *know* I wouldn't have made it. I'm still not so sure I'm glad I did. But thanks anyway."

"Hm. Well. You're welcome, I think." I'm waiting for that other brogan to drop.

Hands on knees. (The perfect pose for dumping someone.) "But you're right. I'm not so sure we should be seeing quite so much of each other once I get out."

I knew it. "That wasn't my idea, I just thought you—"

"I'm afraid we'll get involved again and I'll be right back where I started."

Okay, I'm hopping mad now, and I decide to say something about it. I scoot the ugly chair right up against the bed and get in her face. "Excuse me, why are you blaming me for everything that's wrong in your life? Maybe I'm the only thing that's right and it's everything else that's fucked up. I didn't do anything except love you and you couldn't fucking accept that. That was the problem."

Face to face now. "No, this is the problem right here. All this pressure you put on me."

"Oh, bullshit. I'm not putting any pressure on you. You put it all on you. I don't expect anything from you. I'd just like to hang out with you, be with you, but no, we can't do that."

"Being with me is a lot more complicated than that."

"You're just afraid. Admit it."

"Shut up, J."

I can't let this happen. There has to be a plan, a diversion. I have to blow something up.

"I want you to do something with me," I say.

"Oh no, there's no pressure from you."

"Come to the Days of the Dead with me."

"What?"

I spy a change of expression, a shift from confusion. I keep at it.

"Come with me to Mexico for the Dias de Muer—tose," I say, stumbling a bit on the end of it. "You said they're coming up, right? A couple of weeks? Beginning of the month?"

"J—"

She is considering it, I can tell. This is all I want.

"You're getting out of the hospital, right?"

"Yeah, but I don't know if it's a good idea—"

"What? To do something you've always wanted to do?"

"But I—"

"Just think about it, okay?"

Part 3

A Little Traveling Music

Let's get this straight. I am not a ramblin' man. I have actually built up a resistance to travel just from listening to other people's stories. Not horror stories, mind you, just stories. (Okay, perhaps I have heard one or two that involve pickpockets or killer viruses or hostage situations.) Basically, I just can't stand it when people talk about the trips they've taken, especially foreign trips. I overhear them in the store sometimes. (Yes, foreign travelers in my store. Did I mention that the neighborhood is "improving"? We're being gentrified against our will.) No matter how people talk about where they've been, I still feel like they're rubbing my nose in it. *I've* been there and *you* haven't. Of course, how can you casually mention to someone that you just returned from Zanzibar or Montevideo without sounding pretentious? You can't. So you're better off not going anywhere, I say. That's the whole problem with travel. It always sounds like you're showing off.

All right, I know that's stupid. I just never really got around to traveling. I never had the money and I guess I was kind of scared. But now I'm ready to actually go somewhere. The idea of foreign junk intrigues me. I guess that's what they mean about expanding your horizons.

Postcard from Oaxaca

Mexico is lovely this time of year. (We know I've never seen it at any other time. I'm getting pretentious already.) Theresa and I are in a town in southern central Mexico called Oaxaca. Right now, the town is setting up for the festival, which starts tomorrow. There is an orchestra playing on the stage in the town square, excuse me, the *zócalo*. (To sound extra-pretentious, one must pepper one's conversation with choice foreign words and phrases.) Cafés surround the square on three sides. On the fourth, there is a federal building with what looks like a small rally going on in front of it. (A speech is being broadcast over a loudspeaker. I have no idea what's being said, but it sounds very earnest.)

The trees in the *zócalo* look centuries old, as if the square was built around them. Their huge trunks, ten, twelve feet around, have been painted white, I think to fool the insects. These bleached trees watch over the square like a herd of white elephants, all massive and dusty. (I've never actually seen a white elephant, mind you, but I've enjoyed the sales.) Every so often, a dark-skinned man in a sweat-stained cowboy hat passes through pulling a wide wheeled barrel, sweeping the promenade with a broom as wide as he is tall, fashioned from sinewy branches. I notice that locals tend to stay within the core of the *zócalo*, while us tourists congregate on the periphery.

Other locals have set up shop on the grassy parts of the square—long cloths on the ground mounded with stacks of shirts and vests and *rebozos* (another new word) and belts and jewelry. One man stands next to a gaudy row of intertwined inflatable knockoffs of American icons: faux Mickey Mouses, pseudo–Lion Kings, and quasi-Batmans, wedged together with donkeys, clowns, baby bottles, and bumblebees. Women pose silently beneath teetering columns of white and pink cotton candy, crouch in the floaty shadows of tethered clusters of helium-filled Mylar balloons Magic Markered with crude hearts and skulls.

On the other side of the square, on the street nearer the *mercado* (according to my map), are makeshift tortilla stands—tables covered with bright-flowered oilcloth (great designs like old dishtowels from the Forties), behind which Oaxacan women cook tortillas on wide white disks seated over small wood fires. Gathered around the stands, sitting on plastic chairs, Mexican men drink beer and devour fat tacos. Farther down the street, there are wagons stacked with golden round loaves of bread blazoned with crusty bones, what Theresa calls *pan de muerto*.

I can't believe how picturesque everything is. (What I really can't believe is that I just used the word "picturesque." Is this what travel does to you? Will I be using the phrase "land of contrasts" next?)

It is early afternoon and warm, quite warm for fall, compared to Michigan. Theresa and I are sitting in one of the cafés on the *zócalo*, sipping drinks and eating peanuts drenched with the sweetest lime juice I have ever tasted. As we walked from our hotel (separate rooms—we are, after all, here as pals), we heard someone calling out, *"Calaveras, calaveras."* Theresa immediately turned around. A man down the street was selling spring-limbed painted clay skeletons hanging from wire, droll little marionettes of death. Theresa, of course, had to buy three. Now they dangle from the front of our café table—one dancing, one playing the fiddle, one devil—and it somehow makes me feel more a part of things. Around our table, I hear Spanish being spoken, and French, and Danish, and German. This is obviously where all the tourists sit. But I don't mind being a tourist. It's exciting hearing all these languages. In front of us, residents of Oaxaca scurry past, mostly oblivious to the invading hordes, determinedly off to their destinations—home, market, and graveyards, I would imagine. I see men dragging long stalks of sugarcane through the square, women carrying bags of food and drink. They are all headed somewhere.

Except for us. Me, I am ridiculously happy just sitting here with Theresa, to watch her watching all this. I must say, though, it is a bit scary to fulfill someone's dream. It's much more power than a guy like me is used to. As one would expect, there was a certain amount of reluctance on her part initially. Three days ago, tickets purchased, reservations confirmed, we were still going over it:

THERESA: No, J. Absolutely not. I cannot have someone do something like this for me. It is out of the question.

ME: Why is that?

THERESA: It would be like I owe you or something.

ME: You do owe me. I saved your life, remember?

THERESA: Not relevant, J. Not relevant.

And so on.

I persevered. What eventually did it was that I told her I was

going to go whether she went or not. Which was true. I had been
doing research on Los Dias de Muertos and decided that it was
somewhere I needed to go, for a few of my own reasons. I suppose
she needed to think that I wasn't just doing it for her. She may
have also realized there might not be another chance for a long
time. So, the night before I was scheduled to leave, she made up
her mind—grabbed what money she had, shoved various toi-
letries, articles of cat-scented clothing, and anything else she'd
need into a pink Salvation Army suitcase. In the morning, when
I picked her up, she had another small suitcase, covered with old
hotel stickers, but wouldn't tell me what was in it.

By the time we were at Metro Airport, she was excited—strike
that—thrilled, rapturous, peeing her pants with glee, about the
trip. I knew she would be, but I was ready to give her cab fare
from the airport anyway, just in case she should change her mind.
She didn't. (I really was ready to go by myself. Terrified, but
ready.)

I watch Theresa take a long swig of her Coca-Cola *con lima* and
she catches me looking at her.

"Hey," she says.

"Hey."

"Something wrong?"

"No," I say. "Just enjoying myself. I sort of forgot what it was
like."

"Yeah."

I decide that I would like another beer. I am self-conscious
about my pathetic high-school Spanish, but I finally manage to
flag down *la camarera* and bumble through *"Mas cerveza, por favor?"*
I see her stifling a smile. That's fine.

Today it's Halloween in Oaxaca. And from our café seat, we

watch the whole strange parade rush past. Halloween is just catching on in Mexico and the children are embracing it whole-heartedly. Waves of costumed children pass us, weave through the tables, begging for pesos. We give one to all of them. I think it feels strange for both of us—playing the gringo tourists dispensing largesse to the masses—but at this moment, I just don't care. We're having fun. They're having fun. What is so great is that these kids are dressed in the more traditional Halloween garb—no pre-molded plastic Saturday-morning-cartoon-tie-in costumes yet, just tiny homemade ghosts, skeletons, vampires, and witches. It reminds me of Halloween when I was a kid, except some of them have quite a refined taste for the macabre. It's a little unsettling at first—tiny, bloody apparitions toddling between tables. We are surrounded by murder and accident victims, kids with axes sticking from their backs and open head wounds.

"Check it out," I say to Theresa, pointing at a decapitation victim headed for our table. His right hand out, his left cradling his head.

Theresa starts to laugh. "Yo, Ichabod," she yells. She hands him a peso. He snatches it, then runs away.

"This is getting expensive," says Theresa. "I'll be right back." She gets up and runs into a small store a few doors down from the café called Supermercado La Lonja de Oaxaca. Three minutes later, she returns with a large bag of hard candy. Soon the children are swarming around our table, some scowling at me, most of them smiling at Theresa, a couple of them even squeaking out *gracias*. She seems so comfortable here it amazes me. I feel like thanking her myself. I know that I would have been lost here without her.

The Offerings

For the rest of the afternoon, we walk the streets of Oaxaca. Theresa wants to go everywhere. First, we go downtown to the markets, then uptown into every cramped shop or restaurant or store that has an altar. They are incredible, these *ofrendas*—white-sheathed tables crowded with fruit and mole, flowers and mescal, cigarettes and saints. Theresa steps as close as she can get to each one and stands reverently before it, studying it. We keep walking. Finally, we find ourselves in the shadow of a giant church. I hear Theresa gasp as she glimpses down a courtyard.

"J, look," she says.

I don't have to be told. I see them, too. Rows and rows of altars—a skyline of taut green stalks of sugarcane arced and rising, clouds of shimmering orange marigolds and purple-crimson coxcomb, air thick with incense smoke, sweet and acrid, smoldering in tin cans. Together, we walk briskly over to them. Once in the middle of it, we see that the altars are all tended by children, junior-high-school-age, dressed in navy and plaid Catholic school uniforms. I look at Theresa, who does not return my glance because she is absolutely enthralled. For a moment, I feel like we shouldn't be there, like we have walked into the middle of a big class project where we are not welcome, but the kids show no sign of caring. They scurry past us, around us, as though we are the giant white trees of the *zócalo*, nothing to worry about, just something you don't want to run into face first.

"This is so incredible," Theresa says.

The children are having a blast. The girls run from altar to altar, chattering away, peeking over at the boys. And though I can't understand a word, I don't need to. There are a few adults walking about as well, stopping at each of the altars. It looks as though the kids are being graded. We keep moving, passing each altar, catching glimpses of ancient tinted pictures of grandparents, war heroes; black-and-white photographs of aunts and uncles that these kids seem too young ever to have met. But there are newer images as well, color photos of people in clothes from recent years, people my age and younger, including one of a boy in his high school football uniform. I notice that there is no laughing or running near this altar. One girl sits quietly nearby, eyes squeezed shut.

Magic Bus

Nine-thirty P.M. We are on a bus with a lot of other people. Theresa and I are both tired after a day of walking around Oaxaca. Our fellow *touristas* are jabbering away except the two of us. They are in a surprisingly jovial mood considering we're on our way to a cemetery. Outside, scooters howl past, dusty VW Beetles (they're everywhere here) cut off the bus as we skitter through the outskirts of Oaxaca. Smells invade the bus—dust, chocolate, butchered meat, but mostly exhaust. We pass strange discount stores with huge signs advertising *Coca-Cola*, auto repair and tire shops, bakeries with long windows painted with dancing skeletons. At one point, a dog, black-and-white with patches of bare skin, limps in front of the bus. The driver slams on his brakes, curses in Spanish. The dog, oblivious, makes it to the side of the road, then sits a moment to scratch an open sore. Theresa turns her head away. Out of town, the road gets narrower and darker, the businesses sparser—crude stands of wood and tin, selling *refrescos* or cigarettes, cinder-block *taquerias*. The bus grows louder.

A man in his fifties, with coal-black hair, dressed in a nylon windbreaker and khaki pants, stands up at the front of the bus near the driver. He turns on his portable microphone and calls for our attention, *por favor*.

"*Bienvenidos*. Welcome. What you are about to see is an important ritual of the Mexican people. We are welcoming our dead back from the spirit world. Tonight, we prepare the graves. We clean and paint and decorate with many flowers and candles. You will find it very beautiful at the cemetery."

Theresa squeezes my forearm. She puts the tip of her finger in her mouth, sucks at it for a moment, then closes it in her fist and drops her hand to her lap.

"Tomorrow, it is the *angelitos* that will come, the dead children. Then the next day, the others, the faithful dead, will arrive. We light candles and burn copal to guide them here from the land of the dead. We leave food and drink out for the spirits to enjoy, then afterward we enjoy as well. We are going to the cemetery in a small town near Oaxaca. It is called Xoxocatlán. We call it Xoxo. Ho-ho. Like Santa Claus."

The tourists in the bus laugh. I stifle a snicker myself, until I look over at Theresa, who is in your basic trance. She's all right, I know she has taken her medicine, she is all right, she is just very serious about these things.

"Although many of the people in Xoxo are poor, there is great expense to make the graves very beautiful. This is a fiesta, so people may spend too much money, but that is all right. *Somos muy fiesteros*—we Mexicans enjoy a good celebration. It is a chance to make a show of abundance and to attract more. To squander is not always bad, we know. We believe waste gives back untold returns of wealth. In the words of our great poet Octavio Paz, "When life is thrown away, it increases.'"

This time, Theresa looks over at me.

The guide then bends down to pick up a box. It is filled with candles and small bundles of flowers. He walks up the aisle, handing one of each to everyone on the bus.

"These are not to keep. At the cemetery, when you see an undecorated grave, one that has been forgotten, please put your flowers on it or place a candle on it," he says. "This way, all the graves will be beautiful."

"I'm glad we're being put to work," I say to Theresa. "Makes me feel like less of a tourist."

"I know. I'm starting to feel a little weird about crashing the party."

About ten minutes later, the bus enters the ramshackle city limits of Xoxocatlán. Soon we are in its own, considerably less picturesque, *zócalo*.

"We are going now to the cemetery," says our guide.

The bus is parked behind a few other buses, and we are herded down a street, then a long dark alleyway lit only by one or two streetlights. After ten minutes of walking, we approach an area strung with colored lights, and open-air bars, even a small restaurant. I start to understand the circuitous back-door route. We have been routed past a few businesses, so we will stop for drinks and food. There are also makeshift stands that sell flowers and candles and glowing plaster skulls. The group of us stop at a stand where a man is pouring mescal from a red gallon jug into small plastic cups.

"Mescal first makes things more magical," says our guide as he bellies up to the counter, hands out cups to people in our group.

I find this hard to believe, but I accept a cup anyway.

"You may walk anywhere, just please be respectful," says the guide. "*Gracias*. Thank you." He raises his plastic cup to us and drinks.

I down my cup and gasp. It is orange-flavored fire that cuts a flesh swath on its way down my throat. Theresa laughs at the look on my face, then sniffs of the cup and squeezes her eyes shut.

"Whoo," she says.

We move on, hand in hand, now part of a phalanx through the colored lights and grill smoke and noise and crowd. Someone far ahead seems to know where we're going. We round a corner and catch our first sight of the Xoxocatlán cemetery. Theresa squeezes my hand so hard it hurts. I sense this is the moment she has waited for. I should be enjoying it through her, but I am too caught up in my own astonishment. Our little group collectively pauses. We stand there momentarily transfixed, not caring about the others jostling us. The light of the candles mesmerizes us, a deep warm glow, as if we've stumbled onto a place lit by embers instead of sun and moon.

Ahead of us, the iron gates of the cemetery, mottled gold, arc across the blue-black sky, and I wonder what it is we're about to enter. Beyond the gates, shimmering sweet plumes of incense smoke rise from the graves, flickering candles dot the hilly terrain like pinholes that reveal another world beneath, a world of light and spirit, where we are not allowed, not yet. Broken lines of people weave in and around graves painted turquoise and yellow and pink, bright with marigolds and coxcomb and gladioli, bright with candles lit for the souls of the departed. I don't believe I've ever seen anything so beautiful. I am not a religious guy, but somehow this sight makes me think there might be something to the whole thing. I feel the presence of something here. I look over at Theresa, her face shining with candlelight and tears.

"You okay?" I say.

She nods.

"Come on," I say, leading her through the gate, up a path of flicker and smoke into the dusty hillocked heart of the cemetery. We keep our heads down as much as we can out of respect, trying not to gawk at the beauty of what is going on, but it's no use. Around us, families are gathered near the headstones—apparently most of the cleaning has already taken place, which has given way to vigil and gossip and subdued merriment. One woman is even watching a small television. (Is she just passing time or did she and her loved one always watch TV together when he was a part of the living world?) The graves are parts of the families, it seems, people sit on and around them as comfortably as on a davenport. Space is limited only because of us tourists.

One grave is mounded with flowers—so many you can barely see the plot for all the purple and white and orange. The grave next to it is blanketed with lit candles laid in intricate patterns of circles and grids and crosses. It is as bright as afternoon, yet a young girl wrapped in a *rebozo* sleeps peacefully next to it. (I worry she is too close to the flames. *Rebozos* look highly flammable.) A few down, another plot has been meticulously airbrushed—a mural of a kind of groovy Jesus in front of a tall rainbow. The style looks familiar, and when I spot the flowers arranged in old Bondo cans, I am certain the person who did this also paints murals on vans. "*Descansa en paz,*" it says, painted in jaunty two-tone letters. Rest in peace.

A few Mexicans seem fascinated by us, some mildly disgusted. One ancient woman, sitting on a Fifties tubular kitchen chair with cracked yellow vinyl, scowls right at me. But mostly, people just look straight through us as if we are the useless spirits that accompany the welcome ones. I don't blame them. Though we are bringing money into their town, we are not part of their ceremony, we are observers, intruders, watchers of the deathwatch. It makes me feel better lugging around the flowers and candle, as though there is reason for me to be here, that I am of some small utility. When Theresa puts her flowers down and lights her candle over an empty, forgotten grave, I feel a twinge of guilt because I don't want to let go of mine. Then I do.

"Let's stop walking for a minute," says Theresa. "I just want to stand here." So we pause at the now glowing grave, and it makes me wonder something. Since we decorated it, are we allowed to fill it with whomever we want? Just for tonight?

Theresa turns to me. "Thank you, J. For helping me to see this."

We Come Only to Sleep, Only to Dream

That night when we get back to the hotel, Theresa asks if I will sleep in her room, in her bed. Nothing else, just sleep.

"That would be nice," I say. "Are you sure?"

"I asked you, didn't I?"

"Yes."

"Then shut up and let's go to sleep."

Even though I know Theresa probably just doesn't want to be

in a strange place alone, I don't really care. I no longer expect anything of anybody, including myself. So I grab a few things from my
room (shaving kit, something to sleep in) and come back to
Theresa's.

I don't know if it's because of the day of travel, all the walking, the exhilaration of our experience at the graveyard, or the tiny
glass of lethal mescal, but when we crawl into bed together (me
in tropical Fifties swim trunks, Theresa in a large T-shirt that
reads *Livonia Jaycees Softball*) and curl into a pair of mismatched
spoons, for the fifty-five seconds that I am conscious, I have a
hard time believing there is any man, woman, or spirit in Mexico
more content.

Awakening in Mexico

In the morning, when I open my eyes, Theresa is gone. Next to
the bed, my Elgin reads ten twenty-five. I didn't mean to sleep
so late. Probably Theresa just didn't want to wake me up. I turn
over and doze for another half hour. When I finally get up, it's
past eleven. I start to be a bit concerned about Theresa out on
her own. I decide that this is just some manly need to worry about
a woman, because I am quite sure that she is much better
equipped to survive in Mexico than me. Case in point: I could
get dressed and go out for breakfast or something, but I'm a little afraid to face the foreignness of it all alone. I decide to read
some of Theresa's books in bed and wait for her to return.

At twelve-fifteen, when I still haven't heard from her, I officially start to worry. I search around the room for clues. It looks

like she has taken her medication. I search for her wallet and passport, but can't find them. I can't tell what clothes she has taken from her suitcase, but what she wore yesterday is still slung over a chair. Is this good or bad? I throw on jeans and my shirt, walk down to the lobby, thinking that perhaps she's having lunch or something. I try the clerk at the little check-in desk.

"Señorita Zulinski? *Donde está?*"

He shrugs his shoulders like, "How the fuck should I know?" I hang around in the lobby, trying to stave off panic. I manage until one-thirty, then I panic. I can't decide whether she is walking around Oaxaca horribly lost, or has been abducted by the bandits that roam the deserted highways (about which I was warned by every fearful gringo to whom I mentioned central Mexico), or whether she has decided to try to hurt herself again.

At two, I head back up to the room, thinking maybe she somehow managed to sneak past me at some unguarded moment. On the way, it occurs to me (fool that I am) that I haven't even checked my room. If nothing else, I can at least get something new to read, having gone through all of Theresa's Day of the Dead books.

On my doorknob, there is a *No Molestar* sign that I did not put there. Quickly, I fumble for my key. When I finally unlock the door, I'm afraid to open it. But I do, and I'm not ready for what I see ahead—brilliant smear of color and light and sweet smoke from what was once my simple Mexican hotel room. Past the brief corridor into the room proper, up against the wall, stands a broad arch of sugarcane stalks, densely threaded with radiant orange marigolds and deep purple-red coxcomb, green garlands punctuated with delicate puffs of white baby's breath. As I squeeze past, I notice something: Tied between welts of flowers, there are crosses which look strange to me at first, then I realize that they are made from nylon dog bones.

Beneath the arch, on the floor, on the Indian blanket that I watched Theresa buy yesterday from a vendor on the *zócalo*, there are offerings—open boxes of Milk-Bones and Snausages, yellow tennis balls, flipchips, a new Frisbee, all of which she must have brought from home. Also: plates of stringy dark meat from the stands at the Benito Juárez market, open cans of Pedigree and Cacharro dog food from the *supermercado*, moss-green pottery bowls filled with water. Two long white candles, sunk in old tin cans, like the ones from the cemetery, flicker at the corners of the altar, with smaller candles placed here and there. (Though the labels on the squat candles are in Spanish, even I understand what *Lux Perpetua* means.) And just as we saw paths of marigold petals in front of the altars here, there is kibble sprinkled in front of this one, so to lead the spirits here from the Land of the Dead. There is a pillow on the floor, for those who want to rest after their journey. And in the back, near one of the stalks of sugarcane, is a small red plastic fire hydrant.

I step closer and kneel to examine the photographs taped and tucked among the flowers, on the walls, carefully positioned and spaced on the blanket—pictures of dogs of various breeds and infirmities: a terrier with mange, a German shepherd with a crudely bobbed tail, a burned Chihuahua, a one-eyed Bouvier, a three-legged collie. There are others even more gruesome. She must have gotten them from cruelty investigations—bleached, unfocused photos of puppies frozen inside tires, stumped and infected canine limbs, disemboweled dogs, a Dumpster filled with rotted, unrecognizable animal corpses. I feel as though I am getting a glimpse of Theresa's nightmares.

Then I hear her voice, her murmuring, and I remember who I came looking for. I step across the wide room to find Theresa lying on the tile floor in a fetal position down next to the bed. In front of her is a second altar, candles flickering, incense simmering away. Cursing myself for getting distracted, I grab her shoulders to rouse her, but quickly see that she's okay. Her breathing is not labored, there is no pool of vomit to be inhaled. She is fine, softly snoring to beat the band.

Just then, she pulls her head up slightly from the tile and smiles at me, the squinty grin of the somnolent. It is a beatific smile, a purified smile. "Hi honey," she says, then goes right back to sleep.

Theresa has never called me "honey" before, and I don't know why it makes me so happy to hear. It's the sort of thing we're likely to make fun of—honey, dear, snookums, sweetie—but for the first time I understand the idea behind disgusting pet names. Her voice just sounded so comfortable, so easy, so familiar. Once in a while (hardly ever, really) I detect that same feeling in the voices of couples I encounter in the store. I bend down to smooth a tuft of hair sticking from her head. Soon I find myself sitting, stroking her before the altar. She does not stir.

Theresa mumbles something that I, for the life of me, cannot understand. It sounds like she's talking to me, but I think it is simply the fatigued burbling of someone who has not slept well in a long, long time. I grab a pillow from the bed and tuck it beneath her head, smooth her hair once more before I stand to examine the other altar. I don't know when she found the time to do all this. She must have gotten up way early in the morning and headed straight for the markets.

This second altar has been built around the only window in the room. Sugarcane stalks embrace the framework, strung not only with marigolds and coxcomb, but with catnip mice, dried fish strung into tight crosses, long tendrils of red and yellow and green yarn. Pushed against the windowsill (a wonderful view) is a small table, and on it, more offerings: hard rubber balls with bells inside of them, rusty piles of Kit n' Kaboodle, bright-labeled open cans of 9 Lives and Contento (face of happy Mexican cat), a dish of salty ham, smooth black pottery bowl of milk. Under the table is a cardboard box filled with a shallow layer of sand. The rest of the floor is bare, so the cats may stretch out and cool their spirit fur on the tile. Tacked along the edge of the table is a red paper banner that she must have bought in town. Cut with great precision into the tissue is an eerily cheerful design depicting a dog, a chicken, a donkey, a cat, and a snake, all skeletons, in some sort of crazy conga line, paws to wings to shoulders to skin, dancing, one would assume, home from the animal afterworld.

Again, many photographs: whole litters, old fat cats with eyes clouded by cataracts, one-eared, three-footed, scarred, hairless cats. All the shelter animals Theresa has talked about—crazy street-wild, groomed pure-bred, scabby with mange, feral, piddled on the rug so we don't want her anymore, steel traps clamped to their legs, poisoned by a bowl of antifreeze the neighbors left out, in a home for five years then out because he didn't go with the furniture, acid-burned, thrown out of car windows on the freeway, genitals stumped off with pocket knives, we just got tired of her—all the unwanted, unneeded, beautiful, fucked-up, blessed animals.

"Do you like them?" I hear from across the room. The voice is drowsy, but rested.

"They're beautiful."

Theresa gets up from the floor. "Ow. My arm's asleep." She groans relievedly as she rubs it.

"J, are you all right?"

"I'm fine."

Theresa walks up behind me, lays her head between my shoulder blades. "They came, J."

"Who?" I try to turn around to face her, but she holds me so I can't.

"The animals," she whispers to me. "All the animals that I've killed. They filed past me and just looked at me. It was like I was dead and they were walking past my body. And they didn't even look familiar. I always thought I would never forget any of them, but I have. No, I take it back. Their eyes looked familiar. That last flash of life before the pentobarbital hits, before they go empty."

Theresa squeezes me from behind, hands crossed over my chest, over what I guess would be my heart.

"There were so many, J."

"I know."

"Something else happened."

"What?"

"It's kind of weird."

"What?"

"They were all starting to, well, devour me when I woke up."

This time, I pull away and actually turn around to face her. "Are you kidding?"

"No. It wasn't that bad. It was all right. Really."

"You dream about getting ripped apart and eaten by animals and it isn't that bad?"

Theresa laughs, puts her arms around me again. "I know, it

sounds bad, but it wasn't. It just wasn't. I felt forgiven. Or punished. Or rewarded. Or something."

I look at her. I have nothing to say.

"J, I don't think I'm going back to work. I mean, not because of the dream, just because."

"It's all right."

"I know."

Nuestra Dia de los Muertos

For the rest of the day, Theresa and I don't leave the room. We stay by the altars, try to keep the flies away, burn incense, nibble on Milk-Bones, hold each other. We do not talk much. I have added two small items from my wallet to Theresa's altars. A photograph of my mother on one, a photograph of my father on the other. I figure when they were alive they fought like cats and dogs, so why not? As for the two of them coming back to visit, I can't really say that I feel their presence here, but when I see my father's photograph with all the cat pictures, I do get an idea. I decide that I want people to see my father's photographs. And I, as a small business owner, have the venue in which to display them. (If not my store, then the empty one next door.) In my mind, I am already picking out the shots I will use for my first junk shop gallery exhibition. I think my customers will dig something like this. *Noir* Detroit of the Fifties and Sixties. It's perfect for the store. I can call up a couple of the local weekly entertainment rags to come out and write a story, throw some posters up around town, do a mailing. It could be great. I hope this will give my mother some rest as well, since I think she always felt bad about being the sensible one, the one that had to say *Someone has to support our family*. Sorry all the more for knowing that she had married him because he wasn't the sensible one.

I have also decided that when we get back I will clean my room. I will go through my parents' things. I will keep what I want, but I will not sell any of it. I will give those objects new life by sending them back into the system. I will give them to the people who I know will enjoy them—Theresa, Fred, friends, even a few regular customers that I'd like to reward for coming in once a week just to see what I have or just to talk. I may even award a piece or two to that pesky sister of mine.

I get so excited by my idea that I want to tell Theresa, but she is napping again and I don't want to wake her. I stand to look out the window. It is late afternoon and there are people making noise over in the *zócalo*—firecrackers, penny whistles, lots of music. It sounds like they're just having fun, but I know that what they are doing is important. They are the mummers—dancing, sending back the *angelitos*, sweetly shooing their spirits to the afterworld. Here in Mexico, it is common knowledge that the dead cannot stay long. I'm sorry we didn't realize it sooner.

Next to me on a palm-leaf mat, pillow beneath her head, Theresa opens her eyes. She has an almost fearful look on her face.

"Another dream?" I say.

Theresa shakes her head, then smiles at me, a smile I recognize. "Come here," she says, holding out her arms.

There on the floor, we chase the spirits away.

Something of Value

The next day, we get up early. Since it's our last full day in Mexico, Theresa wants to get out of the room. That's fine with me, since I am jonesing, in desperate need of a thrift store fix. We walk the streets of Oaxaca in search of junk shops, secondhand stores, flea markets, anything. My junking instincts are a little off, because so much of Mexico is like a flea market. Things are a bit quieter since it is the second day of the fiesta, but not much. A lot of stores are open and tourists are still out on the streets.

Walking around with Theresa feels different today. She is relaxed, calmer, freer than I have seen her in quite some time, more of the way she was when I first met her. She strolls along beside me, swinging her arms. She has on a white T-shirt rolled at the sleeves, a pair of long cutoffs, and an old canvas fishing cap pulled far down over her eyes. We keep walking and walking, far from the tourist areas, down one dusty street after another, until even I, keeper of the map, have no idea where we are.

"Let's go in there," Theresa says, about a place she sees down an alley that I completely missed. In front of the place there are a few old pots and pans, some dishes, an electric motor, and a broken chair that, I'm guessing, would usually seat the proprietor. It reminds me of a junk shop at home, something you'd see in a bad area, where they have to lure you in by putting the treasures out on the sidewalk.

"Come on," says Theresa, pulling me down the alley. "I have a feeling about this place. There's something here."

"Well, we can't walk away from that kind of intuition."

"I felt that the first time I noticed your store."

I snort. "Theresa, you've never even bought anything from my store."

Theresa flips up the visor of her hat à la Huntz Hall, and peers at me.

"Oh."

The place is truly a junk store. Not "junk" by my very liberal interpretation of the word, that includes cool stuff that people have discarded. No, this is real junk. There's a lot of things that I can't even identify. In fact, one whole side of the store is all mechanical parts of a mysterious nature or the mystery tools with which to fix or append them. Completely different items on another wall—sandals, some old heavily laundered linens, a few articles of clothing, a straw hat, a guitar. I feel as though I am looking at someone's personal effects. Still, there are a few vaguely interesting items that I gather—key fob from a Mexican service station, pocket mirror, tiny wallet with pictures of saints inside—small tokens to be purchased just to keep the curse off me.

Yet after a moment, I put them down. I decide that I just want to go. I look around to find Theresa so we can leave, but she has disappeared. A dark old Mexican guy enters from the back room. He is unshaven, a lit cigarette hanging from his mouth. In his hand, he holds the pack, the Delicados I have seen sold around town.

"*Buenas dias,*" he says to me, grumpily.

I nod to him and say *adios*.

Outside, I find Theresa in the vacant lot next to the store. I walk fast toward her. She is kneeling on the gravel and broken glass in this narrow space, looking at something. I can't tell what it is until I'm directly behind her. She is petting a small brown-

and-black mongrel, lying on its side. The dog is in bad shape.
Her belly, covered with teats and sores, is sunken, her eyes slitted and runny (but focused on Theresa), nose crusted, coat
cracked and bare in many places. The dog is panting rapidly. I
can hear a tiny wheeze with every strained breath.

"Is she—"

Theresa says nothing to me. She is stroking the dog, sores and
all, cooing to it, speaking Spanish to it in a gentle low voice. I
can only make out a word or two, here and there, "little one" and
"sweet." The wheezing stops. The owner of the store walks over
to us, glances down at Theresa and the dog.

"*Muerto?*"

Theresa looks up at him and nods. Then she turns to me. Her
face is wet. She grabs my hand. "Let's get out of here. I don't
think I want to know what he's going to do with the body."

We run down the street and keep running. At first, it is just to
get as far from the store as possible, but then the running just
becomes running for its own sake. We run until we reach the
zócalo. We collapse onto one of the benches near the bandstand.
For a few minutes we sit closely, just trying to catch our breath. I
look over at Theresa and she is still panting, face toward the sky,
eyes closed, like she is fighting something off.

"There's nothing you could have done," I say.

"I know," Theresa says, swallowing. Her breathing is quieter
now, almost back to normal. "It's just that I've never watched an
animal die that I didn't kill. It was strange not feeling responsible.
Just being there to comfort."

I lean forward to touch Theresa's shoulder, but I stop myself.

"That's all I ever wanted to do, J. Was to help them."

"You did help them."

"It's hard to believe." She opens her eyes and looks at me.

"I know."

"You all right?" I say.

"Yes. I suppose I am." Theresa takes my hand in hers, lifts it to her lips, holds it there.

One Final Crackpot Theory

I want to say something else here, something profound, but for the life of me, I can't think of anything. It's probably better that way. Because despite what has just happened with the dog, I feel happy to be here at this time, with this woman, in this place. So I'll just say this:

In the junk business, we collect the ugly with the beautiful, the bizarre with the elegant, the valuable with the worthless, sometimes forgetting which is which, or intentionally inverting them. We do it because, well, we can. We have the power. Junkers know that all of us have the authority to assign value, that we don't have to want the things we're told to want, that it's good to love that which seems to have no worth.

This is what has happened with me and Theresa. I suddenly am worth more than before and am glad she has deemed me so. (Though now I realize that there are a few fundamental differences between junk and me.) What I know, all I know, is that this is one of my moments, and that our lives are lived in these moments, certain seconds here and there, snapshots only we can see and remember, in the way only we can remember them. They are what we carry with us, what rubs off from our fingertips, what is absorbed by the people and things we touch. They are what we take to our deaths, the real objects of our lives, our remains, our junk.

Michael Zadoorian was born and raised in Detroit, Michigan. He is a graduate of Wayne State University. His short fiction has appeared in *The Literary Review, Beloit Fiction Journal, Ararat American Short Fiction, The North American Review*, and several international journals. He lives with his wife in a bungalow filled with many strange old objects and a death-row cat. *Second Hand* is his first novel.